HERE BE

BOOKS EDITED BY BILL FAWCETT

Masters of Fantasy
War Masters
The Fleet (6 volume series)
Battlestation (2 volume series)
Bolo (6 anthologies from series)
The Crafters
Crisis of Empire (3 volumes)
Gods of War
Liftport
It Seemed Like a Good Idea
You Did What?
You Said What?
How to Lose a Battle
Hunters and Shooters
The Teams

HERE BE DRAGONS:
TALES OF DRAGONCON

Edited by Bill Fawcett

HERE BE DRAGONS:
TALES OF DRAGONCON

TABLE OF CONTENTS

CON JOB, *Robert Asprin*..7

THEY STALK AMONG US, *Janny Wurts*.......................... 18

BEST IN SHOW, *Mike Resnick*... 25

TRIAL RUN, *Chelsea Quinn Yarbro*................................. 36

THE FAN AND THE FURY, *Michelle Poche*................... 67

RULES OF ENGAGEMENT, *Susan Sizemore*................. 90

THE SIMULATOR, *Karen DeWinter*................................106

DRAGONCON: TRIALS AND TRIBULATIONS

      Todd McCaffrey..122

ARTIFACT, *Teresa Patterson* 132

LOST IN THE CROWD, *Selina Rosen*.............................160

HERO MATERIAL, *Jean Marie Ward*..............................172

SIBLING RIVALRY, *Bradley H. Sinor*.............................196

PAT THE MAGIC DRAGON, *Jody Lynn Nye*................211

Con Job

Robert Asprin

The hotel room was American generic. Perhaps a bit larger and better decorated than most, but after all, this was the Hyatt in downtown Atlanta. Not so much better, though, as to justify the inflated room, room service, and drink prices the hotel charged. Especially at times like now when they were hosting a large convention.

Max spent most of his time on the road, and often wondered exactly why it was that his fellow travelers, businessmen and vacationers, would be willing to pay such high prices for impersonal rooms, short pour drinks, and mediocre food. The only answer he had come up with was that the situation was pretty much the same all across the country, so people became blind to how much they were paying for how little. Either that or they were willing to pay premium prices just to get away from wherever it was they called home.

Max knew exactly why he was willing to eat the expense. He was planning to make it all back, and then some, by the end of the long Labor Day weekend. He wasn't a businessman or a vacationer. Max was a professional thief and scam artist.

To be more exact, he was part of a team that toured the country, following the crowds and the money they brought to sports events, conventions, and festivals. While they had never worked a science fiction/fantasy media convention before, how different could it be? A crowd was a crowd, and the people that make up a crowd are notoriously careless with their money when away from home.

This DragonCon was supposed to draw somewhere between thirty and thirty-five thousand people. While they had worked bigger events before, they should be able to turn a tidy profit here.

He started to reach for the phone, then changed his mind. It would be better to get in the habit of using the cell phones. While today's computerized switchboards made it harder to listen in on conversations, there was no sense in getting careless. Reminding himself to keep his unit recharged, he flipped open his cell phone and cued up a number from his memory file.

"HELLO?" came the shouted response.

"Yeah, Doc. It's me, Max. Pass the word around the team that I've got Briar Patch established. It'll be room 912."

"WHAT ROOM?"

"Nine twelve."

"FIVE TWELVE?"

"Negative. That's NINE twelve."

"NINE TWELVE. GOT IT."

"Where are you, anyway? It sounds noisy at your end."

"I'M IN THE PARASOL. THAT'S THE LOBBY BAR AT THE HYATT. IT'S KIND OF A MADHOUSE DOWN HERE."

"What are you doing there?"

"JUST THOUGHT I'D SCOUT THE LAY OF THE LAND A LITTLE. YOU SHOULD SEE IT DOWN HERE."

"I thought the convention didn't start until tomorrow."

"IT DOESN'T. A LOT OF THE ATTENDEES HAVE ROLLED IN EARLY. WHY DON'T YOU COME DOWN AND I'LL BUY YOU A DRINK."

"No thanks. I think I'll turn in early so I'm rested tomorrow. Besides, I thought we agreed we shouldn't be seen together too much."

"BELIEVE ME, MAX, NO ONE WOULD NOTICE."

"Yeah, well, don't forget to get some sleep yourself. Oh, and while you're down there, see if you can pick up a program schedule for me. Top priority."

Max stared at the phone for several moments after ending the call.

Doc had sounded a bit strange, even for Doc. Of course, Doc had been the one to question this job when it was first proposed.

"DragonCon?" he had said. "That's one of the biggest multimedia cons in the country, if not *the* biggest."

"What? You've been to it before?" someone had asked.

"No, but I've heard of it. It's big."

"C'mon, Doc. We've worked Superbowls before. Weekend-long partying crowds are our bread and butter."

Doc had shaken his head.

"Yeah, but these are fans," he said.

"Overaged Trekkies in home-made costumes. So what? They can't be any worse than sports jocks."

"If you say so." Doc had shrugged, and they had moved on with their plans.

Maybe Doc was more familiar with these events than he had let on. Maybe that's why he seemed to be "going native." They'd just have to keep an eye on him and remind him to stay focused.

Check in *had* taken a bit longer than normal, but Max had shrugged it off as being the regular early rush at a big convention. In some ways, he had been lucky to even get a room at one of the main hotels. That's why they were resorting to the "briar patch" system.

One of the crew's usual tactics was to hire someone locally to infiltrate the hotel staff a few weeks before the event, preferably in reservations or on front desk. That would get them a master key to the rooms and access to room bookings.

This time, however, it turned out that all the rooms had been booked solid months in advance. Fortunately, with their man in place, they had managed to highjack a cancellation and put it in Max's name. Or, at least, the name he was using this weekend. Unfortunately, they could only manage one room, so they would be using this as their base of operations, their "briar patch" for the weekend.

The rest of the crew would be using it to change outfits and to stash various things it would be wisest not to carry with them constantly—like large amounts of cash or identifiable items that fell into their possession during the course of the job.

That also meant that someone would have to be in the room at all times, both to let people in and out, and to keep housekeeping from coming in and finding the very things they wanted to keep quiet. Max had been elected as room sitter and coordinator for the crew, though he expected to be relieved from time to time.

It was a system that had worked for them in the past, and there was no reason not to expect it to work now.

The next day, Max was roused by a knock on his door. It was Doc bearing, among other things, a Styrofoam takeout food box and a cardboard beverage cup.

"Morning, Max," he said gaily. "Wanted to drop off that program schedule you wanted and swung through the food court on the way to pick you up some breakfast. Wasn't sure if they had in-room coffee makers here, so I brought you some wake-up juice as well."

" 'Preciate it, Doc," Max said, seizing the coffee. "What does the event schedule look like?"

"Big," Doc said, with a shrug. "It's like I told you coming into this thing. What do you want a schedule for, anyway?"

Max frowned at him.

"I thought we went over this in the planning sessions," he said. "If we're going to hit some of the guest rooms, we need to know when they'll be out. The professional guests are most likely to be traveling with extra money and valuables, and the schedule tells us when they're slated for appearances, so we know they won't be in their rooms. All we need to do now is pass a list of their names to our plant at the front desk, and he can tell us what rooms they're in."

"Well, you'd better start on that fast, then," Doc said, shaking his head. "Registration is up to their eyebrows with check-ins, and someone is bound to notice if he tries to take an hour off to look up specific room bookings. He'll have to work it in a bit at a time."

"You think it will take him an hour?" Max frowned.

"Easy," Doc said. "There are something like eight hundred professional guests at this thing. You'll see when you try to sort out the schedule. There are fourteen or fifteen separate lines of programming running hourly starting at nine in the morning and going on until midnight or later. I don't envy you the job of sorting out who's going to be where and when."

Max rubbed a hand across his mouth and scowled.

"Maybe we'd be better off focusing on the attendees," he said. "I'm sure there are some major events that most of them will be attending. That might be a good time to hit the rooms."

"I don't know," Doc said. "The costume competition is probably the best attended, but not everyone goes to that. I heard they cover it with closed-circuit television, so people can watch it in their rooms or in the bar."

"This just gets better and better," Max said, shaking his head.

"Well, here's another little goodie to try planning around," Doc said. "After today, maybe even as soon as tonight, security will only let people into the various main hotels if they have convention member-ship badges."

"What? They can't do that!" Max said. "What about someone like me who's a paid, registered guest of the hotel but not registered for the convention?"

"You'll probably have to work something with hotel security," Doc said. "Of course, that will draw attention to yourself as someone who's wandering through the hotel who isn't a member of the conven-tion . . . "

" . . . and we don't want that," Max finished for him. "We'll just have to get convention badges for everyone."

"I was afraid you were going to say that." Doc sighed.

"What's wrong?"

"Well, there's about a three hour wait in line to register for the convention," Doc said, "plus it costs something like a hundred dollars apiece. That'll run our overhead for this job right through the ceiling."

Max stared at him.

"Doc, we're thieves," he said carefully. "I didn't say 'buy us all memberships'. *Steal* us some badges. Got it?"

"Got it," Doc said with a nod,

"I can't believe how tight a lid they're trying to keep on this thing," Max grumbled. "Who are they expecting, anyway? The Pope?"

"No. He was a guest two years ago," Doc said.

Max stared at him.

"I told you it was a big convention." Doc shrugged.

"You're kidding. Right?" Max said at last.

"As a matter of fact, I am." Doc grinned. "But it's still a big convention."

Max heaved a sigh.

"Okay. You got me, that time."

"Sure," Doc said. "If you bothered to check their website, you'd know the Pope canceled two months ago."

"Website?" Max said. "This thing has a website?"

Doc gave him a hard look.

"Max, my nephew has his own website. You might try living in this decade sometime."

"Yeah, well, they teach kids all kinds of stuff in college these days." Max grimaced.

"That's true enough," Doc said. "But my nephew's still in junior high. Well, I'd better start working on getting us those badges."

He headed for the door.

"The Pope canceled two months ago?" Max said, the comment finally sinking in. But Doc was already gone.

But Max's day was just beginning.

The next ones to check in at Briar Patch were Allen and Alexis, the brother/sister team of pickpockets. They both seemed a bit down at the mouth, which was surprising—particularly for Alexis. She was petite and curvaceous and always seemed to glow with sunny innocence. It was part of what made her the perfect distracter and let her brother do his work unnoticed.

"What's the trouble?" Max said. "You two look as if they just made petty theft a capital crime."

"It's this job," Allen said. "I'll tell you, Max, I'm about ready to throw in the towel. Pack it in and write the whole thing off as a bad caper."

"Is it the badges?" Max said. "They can't be *that* hard to liberate."

"No. In fact, that was easy. Here, we even got an extra for you in case you decide to wander around a little," Allen said, handing over a laminated rectangle on a lanyard. "We didn't even have to steal them. Doc figured out an angle. You see, if someone loses their badge, they go back to registration and report it, show some identification, and are issued a new badge for a token penalty fee. All we had to do is buy some badges from attendees for twenty bucks over the penalty fee. We get badges and they get replacement badges and a profit."

"Isn't that kind of crooked?" Max said.

"Well, duh. We are supposed to be thieves, aren't we?"

"I meant for the attendees."

"So?" Allen shrugged. "It's not like we have an exclusive on being crooked."

"Then what *is* the problem?" Max pressed. "I think that with crowds like this, the two of you would make out like bandits, if you'll excuse the expression."

"You haven't seen the crowds," Allen said. "There are a lot of costumes out there—and I mean a *lot*. It's hard to pick a pocket when all they're wearing is a spangled G-string and some glitter. If nothing else, it kills Little Sister's bit as a distraction. With so much flesh parading around, she barely rates a glance."

Max suddenly realized why Alexis seemed depressed.

"And that's not the worst of it," Allen continued. "Right along with the costumes everywhere, there are the photographers."

"Photographers?" Max said.

"So many of them that sometimes it's hard to move across the lobby," Allen confirmed. "They're mostly focusing on the costumers, but they're bound to get some of the crowd in the pictures as well. All we need is to have some sharp-eyed bunko expert spot us in a bunch of pictures and the balloon will go up big time."

"Well, if you two haven't been working, then what's all this?" Max said, waving a hand at the shopping bags the two had brought in with them.

"Alexis decided we should hit the Dealers' Room," Allen said.

"Dealers' Room?"

"It's kind of like a huge flea market," Allen explained. "There are three ballroom-sized rooms full of tables and booths selling just about anything. They've got T-shirts, DVDs, swords, capes, jewelry, posters, games, and masks. It's really quite impressive."

"If you can't beat 'em, join 'em," Alexis put in. "I'm not going to let a bunch of bimbos in wings and bondage rigs make me look like a wallflower. I picked up a few items that will put them in their place and put me back in position as the team's distracter."

"A few items?" Max said, eyeing the bags and trying not to picture Alexis in a spangled G-string. "Say, wait a minute. How many of those dealers are taking plastic and how many are only accepting cash?"

"I haven't the foggiest," Allen said. "To be honest, I wasn't paying attention. Why?"

"I just thought of a new angle for getting some money out of this job." Max smiled. "Hang on a second."

He grabbed his cell phone and called Doc.

"Hey, Doc," he said when the other answered, "I've got an assignment for you."

"Can it wait a half hour to an hour?" Doc said. "I'm in the autograph line right now."

"Autograph line?" Max said.

"Yeah. They've got a whole Hall of Fame here full of actors and actresses from the movies and television series'," Doc explained. "Some of my favorite Scream Queens from the B-films are here signing pictures of themselves and I want to meet them and pick up a couple souvenirs."

Max rubbed his forehead between his eyes.

"Well, when you get done there, I want you to scout the Dealers' Room," he said. "Watch to see which one's are only taking cash, and try to get their names. If we can find out what rooms they're in, it might be a better score than trying to go after the professional guests. Okay?"

There was only silence.

"Doc?"

"Yeah, I'm here, Max," came the reply. "I just got distracted for a moment. There's a Klingon and an Imperial Storm Trooper squaring off for duel."

"Did you hear what I said?"

"Sure. Dealers' Room. Look for cash only. Get names," Doc recited. "I'm on it."

"Check in with me when you're done," Max said, and broke the connection.

Staring at the phone, he shook his head.

"Autograph line," he muttered under his breath.

The day didn't get any better.

Several members of the team never checked in and weren't answering their phones. Max wasn't sure if that was because they had been picked up by the authorities, quit the job in disgust, or had been lured off by the various attractions of the convention.

The members that did check in were mostly discouraged by their lack of success, though nearly all admitted to being distracted by the convention attendees.

It was nearly eight o'clock when Doc knocked on the door again. Max was not smiling as he let him in.

"It's been over six hours," he said coldly.

"Yeah, well, it's worth your life to catch an elevator," Doc said, putting down his bags and packages.

"Elevators," Max said flatly.

"It's a mob scene what with everyone trying to get somewhere else," Doc said. "It must have taken me half an hour to get up here. Anyway, I brought you some dinner."

"That's half an hour," Max said, accepting the bag of food. "I want to hear about the other five and a half hours."

"Well, it took me another two hours to finish up in the Hall of Fame," Doc said, flopping down in a chair. "Then I hit the Dealers' Room like you told me. Man, that Dealers' Room is really something."

"I notice you made a few purchases," Max said, gesturing at the collection of stuff piled on the floor.

"Okay, I'll admit. I got sucked in a little," Doc said. "But really, you should see the stuff they have down there. I figure I'm all set for Christmas. I picked up some T-shirts and a couple Anime DVDs for my nephew. I even scored the complete run of some of the old television shows my Mom and Dad like. I don't know who I'll give the jewelry to, but it's nice enough to keep until the right person or occasion comes along."

"Of course, none of this is for you," Max said drily.

"Some of it is, sure," Doc said. "They've got stuff down there that I haven't seen for sale anywhere else."

"Did you manage to get any of the information I sent you after?" Max said.

"Sure I did," Doc said, acting slightly injured. "I'm not sure how much good it will do you, though. First of all, a lot of them go by nicknames like Big Buddha or the Dark Prince, which probably aren't the names they're registered under. I thought of trying to follow them back to their rooms, but with the crowds and the elevator situation, tailing them won't be all that easy."

"Did you even try?"

"I tried a couple times, but both times they headed for the bar and not their rooms," Doc said. "What's more, from what I overheard of their conversations, most of them have a pack of people staying in their rooms to run down extra inventory as needed, so I'm not sure that we'd ever find a time when the rooms were empty that we could crack them."

"Okay. That's it," Max said, getting to his feet. "I want you to man the Patch for me for a while."

"Where are you going?" Doc said.

"I'm going to check out this convention myself," Max said, gathering up the badge that Allen and Alexis had given him.

"But I think the Dealers' Room is closed now," Doc protested.

"I'm not thinking about the Dealers' Room," Max said. "I want to take a cruise through the whole convention and see exactly what's going on. I still think there's a way to make money of this damn event, and I'm going to try to figure out what it is."

It was early afternoon the next day before Max let himself back in the Briar Patch.

Dropping a couple bags of purchases on the floor, he flopped down on the bed and heaved a deep sigh.

"That," he said, "is one hell of a convention going on out there."

"You'll notice I'm not giving you the 'Where have you been' greeting that I got," Doc said, looking up from the book he was reading.

"Yeah, well, a couple of those bimbos Alexis was complaining about invited me to a room party," Max said. "One thing led to another, and it took a while."

"I see you found the Dealers' Room," Doc said, glancing at the bags.

"Yes, and you were right. They have some incredible things down there," Max said. "Some of it is flat-out irresistible."

"Well, for your information, while you were out the team had a little pow-wow," Doc said, putting his book aside. "The consensus seems to be that we should call it quits. There's no real score here worth our time, and we seem to be spending more than we're making. We'll write it off to experience and know not to come back next year."

Max sat up on the bed and gave him a grin.

"I wouldn't be too sure of that if I were you," he said.

"Why not?"

"I told you I'd find an angle, and I did," Max said.

"What've you got?" Doc said.

"Well, at that room party I mentioned, I got to chatting with a couple of the convention organizers," Max said, lying back down. "We'll be back next year, all right, but working for the convention as Security Consultants. That gets us free memberships and rooms as well as a hefty fee. It'll be a different kind of con job for us, but it gives us an excuse to come back."

Editor's note: There is a sad aspect to this amusing story. The day after Bob emailed it he died unexpectedly. He was a regular guest for many years and will all miss him greatly.

THEY STALK AMONG US

Janny Wurts

Been to DragonCon, dude? Then you know how it happens. You're suited up in your costume, having finished the masquerade. That night, I was strapped into the battle armor of a futuristic assault grunt, and bearing a mean-looking trumped-up beam weapon, designed as if it could take on a planet. The heat and the press had me sweating bullets, with my head a tad buzzed on cheap cola. As always, with the party hotel, the lobby was jammed past capacity with bodies and noise. The scenery also held its usual extraordinary: hot chicks wearing goth black and spikes and tattoos, or else elf ears, fluttery wisps of gauze leaves and fake wings over—well, you know—for each of the timid in leotards and wreaths, there'll be a bold one who's wearing paint and next to nothing. I was feeling the frisky spike of wishful sex, caught along with the rest of the pack trying to catch an overstuffed elevator up the tower to check out the night life.

No need to keep notes on the times and locations of the various parties and gatherings. I've always preferred the lazier habit of tagging the flow of the crowd. Tall enough not to crane my shaved head, I spotted a guy with spiked blue hair and three green antennae shoving a push cart loaded with beer. When the right hand side elevator dinged and flashed an "up" light, people jostled in readiness to move as soon as the steel doors swept open. The anxious surge to pile inside the elevator opened a space just in front of me. A rank opportunist, I stepped close behind a guy in a silvery alien suit. He appeared to be friends with the antenna-man, steering the kegs and the stash of stacked six-packs. I saw Killian's Red and some bottles of stout on his pile. No question which party I would crash, first. I'd follow wherever the lager went.

If everyone else had the same bright idea, I was big enough not to be jostled. When the beer cart plowed through the next open door, joined by an array of still more bizarre costumers, I crammed in too, crowding the tail of the alien-dressed dweeb, and squeezing my mean-looking fake weapon inside as the door closed.

Of course, the folks squished inside wished I hadn't. A few blatted, annoyed at my pushiness. But they knew, as I did, that nobody leaves an inch of free space on an elevator.

Packed closer than lovers, though not even friends, we were uncomfortable breathing each other's air. With nobody eager to start conversation, we had nothing to do except stare. Every random batch on a ride's a strange lot. You know the scene if you've attended a con. Jammed tight until you think you could suffocate, there's no living way to keep your hands to yourself, or your elbows from gouging your neighbor. I've inhaled tips of feathers from exotic headdresses, had my eyes tear up from perfume or B. O., even worn patches of rubbed off spangles from some corseted cat lady's mushrooming boobs. On the other hand, I'll tell you straight off, no ride to the top floor ever became as crazy-making as this one.

The guy with the beer cart was decked out in slime! It was green, and it oozed. In fact, greasy gobs of the stuff splashed and left steaming pocks on the hotel's floor tiles. The woods nymph beside him wore contacts that mimicked compound eyes like a bug. She had twiggy hands with eight moving fingers that I swear to Jesus were covered with bark. Living beetles and what looked like animate fungus squirmed in and out of the burlap she had on for clothes. No babe I ever saw, either, had duck feet, stuck on the end of scaly stilt legs that were built like a wading shore bird's.

I edged sidewards, uneasy, and accidentally stepped on my neighbor's toe. He—or she?—was suited up in gadgetry space gear and responded with an offended electronic bleep. As I said, "Sorry," I noticed their badge holder had holograms and blinking lights. Really cool tech, actually, that buzzed and flickered purple with genuine static electricity. I admired the effect, 'til I brushed up against the flash suit, which delivered a real electrical shock.

"Hey!" I said. "Nerd. Your gear's got a short. I just got zapped by your genius costume."

The twerp bleeped back a robotic-sounding obscenity, then pushed the elevator button to stop us at the third floor. When the car paused, and the door rumbled open, he went on the muscle and shoved to evict me like he was a bouncer.

Well, I said I was large. No way, in my fatigues and black battle gear, I was going to stand still for a twerp in a moon-walker's get-up to push me around. Our tussle was causing a bit of a fracas. The twig lady glared with her beetle eyes, while a stalk-headed pair to the side turned their necks, stuck together down to their flipper feet like otherworldly Siamese twins. The wet sleeve that fused them appeared to be made out of scales cut from mother-of-pearl. They honked, I swear, and flapped purple gills in a fish-brained fit of disapproval.

Me, I used my gun barrel and gave the jerk in the suit a warning jab in the groin. I suppose he wore a PVC codpiece, beneath. Or was frigid and female, since the hit didn't faze him. Rather than sympathize with my unfair plight, the whole lot in the elevator ganged up and pushed back, joining the plot to toss me out on my backside.

Now, if alien costumes give me the creeps, and ones that leak slime are just over the top, nothing, and I do mean nothing and nobody was gonna separate me from my mission to stick with the beer. There was stout on that cart, imported from Ireland. Before I'd settle for chugging down Schlitz, I was going to hang out with the brew and discover the room where that party was!

Slime guy thought otherwise. "Get out!" he demanded in a mechanical voice that raised my eyebrows to gawking amazement.

"Cool FX," I said, honest in admiration. "No need to get ticked. I was only trying to inform your geek friend, his costume has a malfunction."

More electronic bleeps emerged from the suit dude. I returned what I thought was a peacemaker's grin, and dammit, he gave me the finger! Oh, not the bird, but a prod with his glove that delivered a zing like a cattle prod!

"What's with the stunner?" I snapped, downright pissed. "I've a mind to report your rude game to the Klingon security. They confiscate badges. Toss cretins out of the con on their ass, who mess with weapons and threaten the public!"

Next thing I know, the guy leaking green slime tried to eject me head first through the elevator door. I latched my fist on the beer cart, snaked my arm between bodies, and jammed my thumb down on the 'close' button. Then I jabbed an armored elbow to fend the interfering fool off my backside. The move accidentally brushed across the blinking lights surrounding the suit person's badge.

At that point, you may decide I went nuts. But I swear as truth, the entire scene went crazy at the same moment.

The elevator banged shut. The car didn't go up, but instead, impossibly, lurched sideways. A force that upended my stomach also made my ears pop as though set under pressure. If I didn't shave my head like a soldier, I promise my hair would have stood up on end. Next, I was dazzled by a blinding flash. Before I could blink, the moving floor stopped with a teeth-rattling lurch that for certain shook up the six packs.

Then the door opened up with a whoosh. I stared out, amazed. First I thought I'd landed amidst the craziest costumer's hall party I'd ever seen at a convention. There were packs of guys dripping sticky green slime. More of those elongated females with the queer stick fingers and compound eyes. I saw other beings that looked like moving rocks, and at least a dozen of the Siamese-style fishies, striped and spotted in fluorescent colors. The weirdo in the shiny space suit was greeted by more of his cousins. As I yelled in surprise, every head stalk, tentacle, and bug eye in the place swiveled my way, inscrutably staring.

This wasn't the hotel I remembered, no way. The carpeting glowed, and it slurped as it swallowed the dripped slime that oozed from the skin of the creatures with the antennae. More lights shone overhead, haloed in violet, and a huge picture window offered a view of a cityscape that looked like a cross between a matte shot for a movie, and the random, splashed paint of an abstract.

I shoved into reverse. No way was I planning to mingle with a bunch of real freaks, or abandon my spot on the elevator.

But as I stepped back, I understood the elevator had changed also. Now, it had silver metal walls, rounded corners, and a silvered surface that reflected a distorted view of my frightened features. The beings who crowded to get out behind me were grousing, annoyed as my bulk held them up.

"We're forbidden to bring back earth specimens!" the guy with the flash badge-holder accused in his mechanical monotone. Throughout, the gizmo I'd mistaken for a pin to hold his convention badge winked and flashed and sizzled with electronic lightnings. I realized, shocked, the thing must be converting his speech to English from some lingo in Alien. Translators actually existed in this place! As that improbability raced my pulse to a gallop, I heard him conclude, "Now you know our secret! Since we can't risk exposure or let you go, you'll remain here as our living experiment."

Well, I freaked! Nobody in a tin foil suit, whose friends dripped repulsive green slime or had gills, was gonna jab their rude needles and probes into me! "I won't be your caged lab rat, or sit still while some bug-eyed sadist pokes an electrode up my butt!"

While the guys twitched their triple antennae, and the ones with stalks popped their eyes in revulsion, other ones jostled toward me with what seemed too much like lip-smacking eagerness. Something with hot breath and tentacles groped my arm with intent to yank me where I refused to go. The only way to prevent my abduction was to get into their alien faces. So I yanked my fake zapper gun from the holster strapped over my armored shoulder.

"Look here!" I yelled. "You have no idea who you're dealing with! The bigwigs who run the Galactic League have rules and regs for the taking of prisoners, and last I heard, trespassing's not on the rap sheet! I am not what I seem, and you've got trouble coming if you think you'll arrest me without any warrant! I've got friends in high places, and armed buddies who like bug hunts, and if you don't return me to the place where we came from, I'll vaporize this party, and take out every innocent bystander!"

The guy in the suit blatted back in monotone surprise. "You are not an earthling?"

I smirked, and tried not to let anyone see, that under my sweaty camouflage, my knee caps were shaking. "I did a nice job blending in, don't you think?"

"Could be faking," objected the slime-dripping geek.

"You gonna take that chance?" I waved my futuristic assault weapon in what I hoped was a menacing gesture, then kicked on the switch that made it whine as if it was charging its firing pack. "You have twenty seconds to send me back before I rake you with a plasma charge!" Then I added, for effect, "Don't think I won't be missed! You'll have an interstellar war on your hands, uglier than you ever bargained for."

Although no one seemed impressed with my threats, well, no hero rushed to take action. I figured I had nothing to lose. While the hesitation lasted, I waved my costume weapon, shouted, and barged backwards into the suited man with force enough to crush him against the beer cart. Before anybody found the aplomb to react, I grabbed hold of the flashing frame on his badge, jerked until I snapped the lanyard, and shouldered past before he recovered his staggered balance. Then I yelled like a madman, brandished my fake zapper, and jerked my thumb to indicate the suited guy had best take a quick hike and restrain his fellows.

"Mess with me," I told him, "and my people will make sure that you and every other crawling thing in your star system gets crisped to toast!"

One of the fishy thingies fainted at the thought. While its friends bent in attempt to revive it, and all the eyes and eye stalks within view swiveled to catch the drama sprawled on the carpet, I upped the ante and created mayhem.

Did I say before, I'm big? I can throw an impressive tantrum, and beer bottles make wicked ammo. Though it hurt my soul to lay good stout to waste, I chucked several bottles into the ranks of the enemy. Brown glass exploded into fragments and the foamy gush made the fluid-sucking carpet gag and gargle. The suited guy back-pedaled fast as he could, abandoning me inside with the beer truck. Jammed while rushing the door, his xeno pals began to fume, shriek and whistle in a clamoring frenzy. Me, I'm not an idiot. I used the suit man's fancy badge-holder. Punched its blinking buttons like a lunatic, all the while swearing under my breath. I kept that up until finally the transport unit shut its doors and flipped through its flash and shimmy sequence in reverse.

Next thing I know, I'm back in the real hotel elevator, all alone with a loaded cart of kegs and the best bottled brew. Figured, with that stash, I'd become the hero of whatever party I chose to crash. But a more important thing had to come first. I dropped the suit man's badge. Stomped the alien bit of tech beneath my heel until the static frame and flashing lights were crushed into smoking powder. No way was that thing going to send another person sideways across the galaxy, or hijack anymore of earth's beer who-knows-where, for some group of whackos whooping it up in the next dimension.

As I punched the up button and the elevator resumed its interrupted course to the fun waiting on the top floor, I reholstered my fake assault weapon and curled my lip at the reek of the other-worldly slime left splotched on the floor tiles.

Plenty of folks may claim I'm drunk. Tell you honestly, I don't give a flip. You bet I'll give warning that we've been invaded to anyone who'll listen. I'll repeat what happened to me, throughout the entire convention. They walk among us, dressed up as others. If you don't want to risk getting slobbered or abducted, you'd best keep a sharp eye out on the costumers who strut their stuff in the hallways. Take my advice, don't barge your way into crowded elevators at night without first making sure the company inside is really from earth, and bona fide human!

BEST IN SHOW

Mike Resnick

You expect a lot of things at DragonCon: great panels, a phenomenal dealers' room, enjoyable parties, gorgeous girls in skimpy costumes, elevators that never work. But the one thing you never really expect to see is a dragon. Admit it.

The first twenty people who saw it in line at Registration thought it was a costume. A very *big* costume. The twenty-first was Eric Flint, whose keen science fiction writer's mind knew instantly that it was a real dragon. Eric spent the next ten minutes trying to convert it to socialism.

Finally the dragon was first in line.

"Name?" said the bored female fan behind the desk, not looking up.

"Yes."

"What *is* it?"

"Bellwether."

"Well, maybe," she replied. "I think it may rain, though."

"No," said the dragon. "My *name* is Bellwether."

"Are you pre-registered?"

"Certainly."

She looked through the list that was laid out before her.

"I don't find you listed here."

"I sent in my entry fee months ago," said Bellwether.

"Entry fee?" she repeated. "Don't you mean your dues?"

"Certainly not. I am entered in the Light Green Fire-Breathing Adolescent Class, limit twelve tons."

The girl finally looked up from her paperwork. "You're the best dragon I've seen all year," she said admiringly. "Anne McCaffrey would be proud." She handed Bellwether a badge. "Here. Even if you're not registered, I couldn't keep a costume like this out of the masquerade."

"I am not wearing a costume!" snapped Bellwether, twin streams of smoke rushing out of its nostrils.

"Too bad," she said. "You'd have won the masquerade hands down. If you had any hands, that is."

Bellwether stared at her for a moment. "Are you suggesting that this *isn't* the 386th Annual Pan-Galactic Dragon Show?"

"Yeah, I think you could say that."

"But I've been training for months!" whined Bellwhether. "I even lost three thousand pounds getting in shape! I haven't eaten a knight in three weeks! I've even declared peace on any judges named St. George!"

"I'm not up to coping with this," said the fan. "You want to talk to a science fiction writer. They deal with this foolishness all the time."

"Where would I find one?" asked Bellwhether plaintively.

"Oh, they're all over. There's one walking by right now—the one in the kilt."

"Will he be able to help?"

She shook her head. "That's John Ringo. He eats dragons for breakfast. You don't want to mess with him." She paused thoughtfully. "I'd direct you to Mike Resnick, but he's always surrounded by so many gorgeous groupies that you'll never be able force your way through them." Suddenly she pointed. "There's Eric Flint. He's an international bestseller as well as an editor."

"I spoke to him before. He wants me to run for President."

"As a third party candidate?"

"An eighth party. He says the first seven are corrupt capitalist swine."

"Maybe you should just walk around and see if you can find any writers or editors to help you. Or possibly Don Maitz will put you on the cover of a book."

"It sounds painful," said Bellwether.

"He just uses paint," she said reassuringly.

"With lead in it?" asked Bellwether nervously.

"Look, I'd love to sit here all day and talk to you, but the line behind you is getting restless, and you never know what restless fans will do, except that it's bound to be diverting, loud, and possibly illegal. Run along, and good luck to you."

Bellwether thanked her, and started looking around. "When I find the travel agent who sent me here," it muttered, "he's toast. *Burnt* toast."

A pudgy fan (though no more than four hundred pounds—like Bellwether he'd been dieting) approached the dragon.

"Let me guess," said the fan. "You're from Pern."

"Actually, I'm from Beta Leporis IV," answered Bellwether.

"What do you call your costume?"

"I'm not wearing a costume!"

"That's the *real* you?"

"Yes."

"If that's not a costume, why aren't you wearing any pants?"

Bellwether hated questions like that, especially when the only answer was an embarrassed "I forgot," so it wandered off, down an escalator, through a long tunnel, and into another hotel.

"Dealers' room is on the second floor," said a guard.

"Why do I want a dealers' room?" asked Bellwether.

"They're sticking you out front to draw a crowd, aren't they?" The guard studied Bellwether for a moment. "Doesn't it get hot under there?"

"Under where?"

"Never mind. I know you method actors—you always stay in character."

"I don't suppose you know where the ring is," asked Bellwether.

"Probably in the jewelry shop."

"I mean the show ring."

"Beats the hell out of me," admitted the guard. "They tell us that a bunch of crazies are gonna overrun the place, and then they never give us specifics. I'd complain to the union, if we had one."

Bellwether left him Eric Flint's card, and then went off to find the dealers' room. As he slowed down to approach the staircase to the second floor—when you have twelve legs you have to be very careful on staircases—he was aware that a small feminine hand was rubbing his shoulder. He swung his long neck around until he was face-to-face with a woman who seemed to belong to the hand.

"Yes?" he said, remembering his manners.

"I didn't ask you anything," said Josepha Sherman.

"I thought you were trying to get my attention."

"No," she said. "I just love petting horses."

"Have you had your glasses checked lately?" he asked.

"You're the most horselike thing in the building," she said. "Well, except for Bill Fawcett, who bears an uncanny facial resemblance to Rex the Wonder Horse, but he only has two legs."

"I am not a horse."

"This is DragonCon," said Josepha. "You can't always choose. It's not your fault that you're not Secretariat."

"Big deal," Bellwether shot back. "You're not Margaret Meade, either."

"And you're not Big Brown!" snapped Josepha.

"And you're not Catherine Zeta-Jones!" snarled Bellwether.

"And you're not Man o' War!" yelled Josepha.

"Did someone mention war?" asked David Weber, emerging from the dealers' room.

"Only in passing," said Bellwether.

David turned to Josepha. "Is this dragon bothering you?"

"I haven't decided," she replied.

"Well, I'm not one to brag," bragged David, "but I know sixty-three sure-fire attacks and ninety-four unstoppable counters that are guaranteed to bring any dragon to its knees." He stared at Bellwether. "Which is a lot of knees, when you consider it."

Josepha thanked him, explained that it wasn't Bellwether's fault that it wasn't Seattle Slew, and went off to find Mike Resnick and worshipfully ask for his autograph.

"So," said David, "if you're not here to conquer us, what *are* you here for?"

"I guess you'd call it a kind of beauty contest."

"You're a judge, right?"

"You have two more guesses," said Bellwether in annoyed tones.

"Why don't you forget all this anyway?" suggested David. "Shouldn't you be out chasing lady dragons?"

"I'm only 168 years old," said Bellwether mournfully. "They won't give the time of day to a kid like me. Besides," it added, "I haven't decided whether to be a male or a female."

"You mean it's not arbitrary?" asked David, surprised.

"Look at that bearded giant over there," said Bellwether, pointing to Harry Turtledove. "Was having hair all over his face arbitrary?"

"No, but being 7 feet 3 inches was," noted David. "So was being a man instead of a woman."

"What's *wrong* with being a woman?" demanded a voice from behind them, and they both turned to find themselves confronting Toni Weisskopf. It took a moment to identify her, as she wasn't wearing the formal ermine robe and jewel-studded platinum crown that went with being the Publisher of Baen Books, though of course she wore the 34-carat diamond ring signifying her role as Editor-in-Chief, if only so supplicants bearing manuscripts would know what to kiss once they finished with her feet.

"Nothing's wrong with being a woman," said Bellwether nervously. "Some of my best friends are girls."

"*All* of my best friends are women," added David devoutly.

Toni stared at Bellwether. "Aren't you supposed to be getting ready for the masquerade?"

"I'm here for the show."

"The show?" repeated Toni. "That's in the next hotel down the row. "I think they're playing *The Vampire Strikes Back* right now."

"The *Dragon* show," Bellwether clarified.

"You must mean the Pern exhibit," said Toni. "It's down on the lower level somewhere."

"I'm not interested in dirty books," said the dragon.

"*Pern*," repeated Toni.

"Damned Southerners," muttered Bellwether. It was turning to descend the stairs when it noticed a huge line in the dealers' room, and decided anyone that popular with science fiction fans, who were clearly far above average in intelligence and sophistication, would be able to answer all its questions (well, those not concerning certain fantasies it had about lady dragons), or at least be able to point the direction to the dragon ring.

An hour and a half later Bellwether made it to the head of the line and found itself facing Kevin Anderson.

"Where's your book?" asked Kevin.

"I don't have one."

"Well, what *do* you want me to autograph? I'll sign anything except ladies' unmentionables; that's Resnick's department."

"I just want to ask you some questions," said Bellwether.

"Sure," said Kevin. "Anything you want to know about *Dune*, I'm your man."

"It isn't about *Dune*."

"Okay, the Seven Suns, then?"

"No."

"L. Ron Hubbard?"

"It has nothing to do with books."

"Oh, my movie producer status," said Kevin knowingly. "I can tell you for the record that Paris Hilton and I are just good friends, and I don't know how those photos of Pam Anderson and me got on the web."

"Where's the ring?" demanded Bellwether.

"I told you," said Kevin. "We're just good friends."

"The *show* ring!"

"Show ring, show ring," repeated Kevin, lowering his head and frowning. Suddenly he looked up. "You mean that cheap imitation diamond I bought for Lindsay Lohan? Well, what do you expect? I'm a producer now. I can't give real rings to every gorgeous starlet who throws herself at me, so some of them are going to get show rings."

"Stop understanding me so fast," said Bellwether. "I am here to compete in the Annual Pan-Galactic Dragon Show."

"Good luck," said Kevin. "If they film it, maybe we'll run it in the trailer to *Wiggleworms of Dune*."

Bellwether realized it wasn't going to get the answer it sought, and left the dealers' room, heading to the staircase.

"Still giving you a hard time, are they?" asked a familiar voice.

The dragon turned and found itself facing Eric Flint.

"It's very frustrating," admitted Bellwether.

"It certainly is," agreed Eric. "Us dragons have got to organize."

Bellwether cast him what it imagined was a withering glare, but which in fact merely looked myopic, and proceeded down the stairs to the lower level. When he turned left, a number of fans barred his way.

"You want to go to the right," explained one of them.

"How do you know?" asked Bellwether.

"You're entered in the competition, aren't you?"

"So I *am* on the right world!" exclaimed Bellwether happily. "Where do I go?"

"See that big double door?" said the fan. "Go right through it. And good luck."

"Thanks," said the dragon.

"And watch out for Conan and Barbarella," added the fan. "They're your main competition."

"How old is Conan?"

"I dunno. Maybe twenty-two."

"Twenty-two?" laughed Bellwether. "Why, he's still wet from the yolk!"

"You're yolking, right?" said the fan, guffawing at his own pun.

"How about this Barbarella?" persisted Bellwether.

"How about her?"

"How are her scales?"

"I suppose she can hit E above high C with the best of 'em," said the fan.

"I'm not making myself pellucid," said the dragon.

"Don't," said the fan.

"Don't be pellucid?"

"Right. There was a great Mahars of Pellucidar group last year, and then came in third."

"Well, thank you for all the advice," said Bellwether, hoping it had time to sort it out before it was due in the ring.

"Happy to help," said the fan. "And give my best to Annie Mac."

"Annie Mac?"

"Anne McCaffrey. She's one of the judges. I figured you knew. Otherwise, why come as a dragon?"

"I couldn't come as anything else," said Bellwether.

"Just passionate about those Pern books, eh? Damn! If I'd known there'd be something like you here, I'd have brought my Dragonrider costume and we'd go as a team. How could we lose at a DragonCon?"

"Hey, fella," said another fan, "you're blocking the way. Are you going to the competition or not?"

"I'm on my way," said Bellwether, heading off toward the double doors. It reached them, passed through them, and found itself surrounded by perhaps a hundred fans. Most wore elaborate costumes, and a handful of pretty girls *almost* wore them.

"Oh, hell!" said one of the girls. "It's not enough that there's a great Conan and a gorgeous Barbarella. Now we have to beat a ten-ton dragon!"

"11.237 tons," Bellwether corrected her.

"Well, it's just not fair!" said another girl.

"Yeah," said a third. "How do we compete against *that*?"

"Right," said Eric Flint, who had wandered into the room. "We naked girls have to unionize."

Bellwether looked around the room for the other dragons, but couldn't find any. It disliked the thought of inter-species competition; after all, it was still five feet and six tons short of its full adult size, and that could be a real handicap up against a purebred Gorgon, especially the short-coated Southern variety. And judges tended to favor lamias, partly because they were so rare, and partly because they had the breasts of a human female and most of the judges were males. (It didn't matter that they weren't human males; a fondness for ladies' breasts is a universal constant. If you think not, just pick up a copy of Mike Resnick's *The Outpost*.)

"Get ready," said a fan, whose badge boasted eight ribbons of varying colors, which seemed to give him some authority as well as a self-righteous swagger. "You're next."

"But where are the other dragons?" asked Bellwether.

"If you didn't bring 'em along, tough," said the fan. "You're on, with or without your group. You got a name for what you're wearing?"

"Skin?" asked Bellwether, feeling very disoriented.

"Whatever," said the fan with a shrug. He scribbled something down and handed it to David Drake, who was standing behind a microphone, one of the few places he was safe from impassioned groupies.

"Costume number 73," announced David, "is"—he stared at the card, frowning—"Skin."

"Get out there!" said the officious fan, giving Bellwether a shove.

The previous costume, a tall pudgy man dressed as Iron Man, hadn't quite left the stage yet. As he passed the row of judges, he paused to threaten Anne McCaffrey with exaggerated gestures. Bellwether, certain that Anne was under attack, rushed to her rescue. He bounded—well, thudded—across the stage, and with the swipe of a mighty forepaw (or perhaps it was a mighty twelvepaw; who knows?) he promptly separated Iron Man's head from his body.

"That's terrible!" cried Anne.

"It's not *that* terrible," said a few fans seated behind her. "After all, he was an editor."

"I hope the dragon's not going to eat him right in front of us," said another judge.

"He's not going to eat him at all," said David Drake with absolute certainty.

"Why not?" asked another fan.

"He was an editor," explained David. "Did you ever try to clean one of those things?"

The entire audience agreed that this was a telling point, and relaxed.

Bellwether struck a show pose, everyone thought it was bowing, and it was given a standing ovation. As it was leaving the stage, the Conan everyone had been discussing came on, brandishing his fearsome longsword. He swung it a little too close to Anne, and Bellwether simply exhaled a sheet of flame and melted it.

"Damn!" said Conan. "Do you know what that cost me in the dealers' room?"

"You shouldn't threaten the judges with it," said Bellwether.

"I was only *pretending* to threaten them."

"I was only pretending to correct you," said Bellwether with a shrug that knocked four stage assistants into the sixth row of the audience.

Conan turned toward the judges. "Can I get a ruling on what just happened, please? I would like for Skin to be disqualified."

"For what?" asked Anne.

"For melting my sword and ruining my presentation."

"Let me see if I've got this straight," said Anne. "You're standing there in nothing but a loincloth and a melted sword, and you want us to disqualify a ten-ton fire-breathing dragon that's standing forty feet away. Is that correct?"

"11.237 tons," interjected Bellwether gently.

"Well, it made a lot of sense before you summarized it," said Conan petulantly. He turned to Bellwether. "And that's a dumb costume, and an ever dumber name!"

Another flame shot out of the dragon's mouth, incinerating Conan's loincloth and exposing his . . . ah . . . shortcomings for the entire audience to see. He ran off, stage left, down the stairs, and totally out of this story, though I'm told he's due to make a comeback in Eric Flint's *Foundation and Stays*, yet another saga in the Foundation series.

The competition got back on track, with three Tarzans (100, 350, and 400 pounds), two Red Sonjas (83 and 382 pounds), the Hulk (4 feet 11 inches) and other equally captivating costumes. Finally it was over, and the judges withdrew to deliberate.

It didn't take long. In less than five minutes they had returned, and handed their decision to David Drake, who read it, looked at them like they had finally lost their wits, shrugged, and announced that the prizes for Most Authentic, Most Legs, Most Green, Most Combustable, and Best in Show were all awarded to Bellwether.

"The prizes include free passage to next year's DragonCon," David announced, "as well as a complimentary suite with asbestos wallpaper. Have you anything to say, Skin?"

Bellwether got out the words "I would like to thank my—" when an orchestra started playing and they cut to commercial. (It was a demonstration about why crosses had no power against vampires in Jewish neighborhoods, and was sponsored by a manufacturer of Stars of David.)

Finally the masquerade was over, and Bellwether hung around backstage, graciously accepting a victory kiss from Anne.

David Weber came up to congratulate the dragon. "By the way, have you decided what sex to be yet?"

"No, I'm still basking in the glow of winning, even if it's not the Pan-Galactic Dragon Show," said Bellwether. "But I'm sure I'll decide before I come back next year. After all, there are only seven sexes to choose from."

"Seven?" said David, his eyes widening with interest. "Where *is* this planet of yours?"

"Don't tell him," cautioned Eric Flint. "We seven-sexed dragons have to organize first."

TRIAL RUN

——

Chelsea Quinn Yarbro

"But in a year I'll be away at college," Dylan Rhys-Kayes reminded his mother over the breakfast table. He was doing his best to sound sensible, not whiney, not too much like a disappointed kid. "I'll have to figure out how to handle myself then, won't I? So why not let me give this a try?"

"Atlanta is a long way from Toronto, Dylan, to be off on your own," said his mother, Arian, her Welsh accent still strong after fifteen years in Canada. "If anything should happen . . ."

"Then I'll just have to make sure it doesn't," he said, wishing he could ease the worry from her eyes. "Look, Ma, they *invited* me. They want to showcase my videos, and have me participate on two panels, and that could mean some contacts that will help me out in the future. I could end up paying more of my way to college than we expected, *and* have a really good job at the end of it." He took his mug of black coffee and drank it down, painfully aware of the broken nails on his left hand—nails he could not remember breaking. "I'll be careful. I've got every reason to be."

"Well enough," she said, without a trace of conviction. "But in the middle of an exciting convention, don't you think it would be easy to forget about the risks?"

"If things get touchy, I'll head off for the night, somewhere away from the convention." He leaned forward, looking straight into her worried eyes. "I'm staying at a b&b, single room. I've got my prescriptions. But just in case, there's open country around Atlanta. I've checked. If I have to, I can find some isolation and walk off my stress."

His mother picked at the last of her French toast. "I just wish one of your friends were going with you. Seventeen and all alone in Georgia."

"Next year, I'll be eighteen and all alone in Los Angeles," he pointed out. He stood up and took his mug to the sink. Tall and lanky, he often looked as if he had forgotten to take the hanger out of his jacket before he put it on; his hair was a kind of light-brown that shone like pewter, his face was angular, his hands and feet were long, and he had the slightly unfinished appearance of many teen-agers. "You're gonna be late to work, Ma," he said as he put the dishes in the sink to soak.

"You, too, Dylan," Arian said, pushing her chair back from the table.

"Everything'll be fine, Ma," he said, still hoping to assuage her worry. "With thirty thousand attending, who's gonna notice me? Even if I fall asleep over dinner, who'll pay any attention in such a mob?"

Arian was not so sanguine as her son. "That's thirty thousand witnesses."

"To a special effect; that's what they're going to think in a place like that, assuming it happens at all; I'm going to make sure it doesn't," he said, running the water and adding a little detergent.

"You hope," she said.

"Dad held down a job for two decades and no one ever suspected he had a problem," Dylan reminded her.

"Not no one, but he was very careful, which is what you need to be," she corrected him. "Tell you what, Dylan," she went on as she brought her breakfast dishes to him, "I'll think about it today and let you know this evening what I've decided."

"It won't cost you anything. My job'll give me enough for the trip." For most of the school year, the job was part-time, but now, during Easter vacation, it was as full-time as hers, and would be so throughout the summer. "I won't do anything extravagant."

"That money is for college," she reminded him, twitching her russet, wool-blend duster to hang smoothly over her orchid turtle-neck and tan slacks. "I don't want you blowing it all on a weekend in Georgia."

"Of course I wouldn't take *all* my savings," he assured her. "But I don't expect *you* to pay for it, either. Or Uncle Perry."

There was a trace of disappointment in her tired features. "I realize that, Dylan. It's not the money—or not only the money—that concerns me, and you know it." She took hold of his sleeve so he would face her. "This is a major step. You need to think about what you're doing."

"I know, Ma. But I gotta make a try at being out on my own eventually, and better to have a little experience before I go to college."

Her face lost some of its grimness. "Oh, honey, I'm sorry to be on your case like this, but I'm worried about you. I don't want you risking your whole future for a single long weekend."

Dylan shook his head. "Yeah, Ma, I know."

"Will there be a full moon while you're in Atlanta?" A frown puckered her brows.

"New one." He tried to smile without strain. "They have a parade."

"Oh, mercy upon us." She stepped back. "A parade!"

"Somebody messed up the *Spartan Warrior 4* disk," said Theo Westin as Dylan came through the employees entrance into the electronic services store on Queen Street where he worked. Theo was the assistant manager, a thirty-ish geek with keen hazel eyes and hair so furiously ringletted that he appeared to have just stuck his finger in a light-socket.

"I'll get on it. Probably trying to change something they didn't like, or add something they liked better. Amateurs." He removed his raincoat and hung it on a hook near the door. "Who else is coming in this morning?"

"Just you and me holding the fort until lunch; Pat's out front with the walk-ins and phones," said Theo. "Casey's installing a new system for Professor Hazeltine since Easter break means an empty office, Annamarie's out at Sunlight Power doing their upgrade. Terry's at the dentist. Walter won't be in until two; he's picking his parents up at the airport—more Easter. And Jenna's on vacation. Poor girl's suffering in Bermuda." He pointed to the alcove where coffee brewers, a refrigerator, and a microwave waited on a counter next to a small, round table with three chairs. "You want some caffeine to jump-start the morning?"

"Already had some; don't want to stunt my growth," said Dylan, making for his work-station after taking the *Spartan Warrior 4* from Theo. His east-facing window filled his cubicle with light.

"Speaking of vacation, you already got things straightened out with your mom about Atlanta? Or is she still worried about you being out on your own? Hey, it's only b'cause she loves you." He had sat down in his work-station, but gave little attention to the screen in front of him, his curiosity getting the better of him. "I really hope you get to go."

"We're working it out," he said a bit distantly, listening to the hum of his machine.

"She's gonna say yes, isn't she?" Theo persisted a couple seconds later. "It's a big chance."

"I sure hope so; I've already told DragonCon that I'm going to be there," Dylan answered, and adjusted the angle of his screen to eliminate the window-glare from its surface.

"Think it would help if I talked to her? Explained about your project? Maybe Annamarie could talk to her, too, you know: woman to woman. I'm part of your video—maybe I could make her see what an opportunity this is, for all of us," he offered. "I know how well you take care of yourself. It's not as if you're gonna die there. You're gonna open a lot of doors."

"I don't know; if you put it to her that way, she may refuse completely. But I'll keep you in mind; and I'll show you the next segment once I get the script in order," Dylan assured him as he concentrated on *Spartan Warrior 4*.

Uncle Perry was softer and rounder than Dylan's dad had been, and perhaps three inches shorter, but there was a strong family resemblance: a suggestion of a lantern-jaw, straight brows, long nose, and the same prominent shoulders that Dylan had inherited. At fifty-one, Perry Rhys-Kayes was a successful forensic geneticist with clients all over Canada and the upper Midwest. He sipped at his single-malt whiskey and studied his nephew. "Tell me how you plan to handle the narcolepsy again."

Dylan sighed. "I'll be careful to take my meds. If there is trouble, I'll get out of the city, away from anything that could add to the problem. I'll keep stress down as much as I can, I'll stay away from high sugar in my diet, and I'll try not to get really tired."

Perry nodded. "A good plan. But you don't want to have to run off at the last minute if you feel an episode coming on. That could lead to real problems for you. Confusion and crowds can mean difficulties. You don't want to collapse in public."

"I know that," said Dylan, getting up from his chair and pacing the length of Perry's wood-paneled study.

"How do you plan to take care of yourself when you recover?" Perry was calm but his eyes were keen; he focused all his attention on his nephew.

"You mean if I have an episode and have to recover, don't you?" Dylan challenged.

"I guess I do," Perry said. "You're right. You may not have an episode, after all. And it's not as if you don't know how to deal with the aftermath."

"You mean that I shouldn't go running around all hyper, come morning? Or have an episode in the morning and spend half the time scarping about, then crash for the afternoon and evening? Assuming I go out for the night and don't return to normal until the next day, the way I usually do? I'll have to do my best to improvise, if it comes to that. I know when my presentation is—2:00 to 2:30 p.m.—and I'll make sure to get a nap before it's scheduled; a real nap, with my meds, not an episode. One panel is at 10:00 a.m., the other at 3:30 in the afternoon. All good times, when I'll be fed and rested and ready." He put his glass of light beer on the nearest bookshelf and made a gesture of exasperation.

"That's exactly what I mean," Perry said to his nephew. "Look what happened to your father, Dylan. I wouldn't want anything of the sort to happen to you."

40

Dylan shuddered in spite of himself. "Neither do I."

"And Atlanta! The CDC would find you *fascinating.*"

"They've seen narcolepsy before," Dylan observed.

"Not like yours, they haven't. Your kind—with somnambulism and amnesia accompanying the narcolepsy—is extremely rare: fewer than ten percent of narcoleptics have it. Ambien has nothing on it. Rarity is a good part of the CDC's stock in trade. They'd like it better if you had something contagious, but your kind of neurological glitch would set them slavering. I've worked with some of those fellows before, and you wouldn't like to fall into their hands, believe me."

"Oh, I do," said Dylan, trying not to think of his late father, a prisoner in all but name in the hands of the Europeans for six years before he died. "At least I won't be in transit during the full moon. Think what could happen with airport security if I had an episode." He intended to be funny, but saw in his uncle's face the very alarm he was seeking to quell.

"You believe you'd be at increased risk of an episode," said Perry.

"And that's the least of it." He took a little sip of beer. "If the moon were going to be full, I might share Ma's worries. But a new moon is a piece of cake. Unless I get fatigued, or stressed—I know, I know."

"This whole full moon thing may be the result of your expectations, not anything specifically associated with the moon itself, or your condition. Arian may subscribe to the idea, but the statistics don't support the mythology." He said it as if he had little interest in the matter, but the angle of his brows gave him away.

"Look, Uncle Perry, I know the full moon makes a difference. I can feel it. It has since all this started. Psychosomatic or not, full moons up the chance of an episode. Dad told me about the full moon—it affected him, too." He continued to wander around the study. "You know I'll keep my mouth shut—I won't tell everyone 'Hey, I sometimes just fall asleep for no reason and I sometimes do weird things while I'm asleep, like run around with all my clothes off'—and I won't expose myself to anything too risky that might trigger an episode. I'd be really stupid to do that. But, Uncle Perry, I need to get out there, to learn how to handle myself during public presentations, to make sure I can take care of myself in the real world without you and Ma for backup. I want to be ready for college next year."

"I understand that, and I sympathize," said Perry. "But you can't blame Arian and me for being concerned."

"Probably not," Dylan allowed.

"I told your Ma I'd get you a cell phone with extended range, so you can keep in touch."

"You mean report in, don't you?" Dylan asked.

"I don't. Your mother does," said Perry, giving Dylan a rueful chuckle. "Don't fash yourself about it, just think of it as another layer of protection. You can work out a schedule to call in to Arian. That would make her much less anxious."

"Unless I miss a call by five minutes," said Dylan.

Perry used his most rational tone. "Dylan, think about it from your mother's side: she doesn't want you to get into trouble. She's not being unreasonable. You aren't of legal age. You're traveling a signifi-cant distance alone for the first time. You'll be in a foreign country."

"All right," muttered Dylan, knowing he was secretly relieved to know he would have the cell phone if he needed it.

There was an uncomfortable silence for the better part of a minute, and then Perry looked up at Dylan. "Do you think you could show me your videos?"

"Uncle Perry—"

"I'd like to see what you've done."

Dylan shrugged. "If you'd like, but I don't think they're your cup of tea, Uncle Perry."

"Probably not," he concurred. "But I'd like to know what kind of work you're doing. Would you show me? Or at least tell me about the one that got you the invitation to DragonCon?"

This was too good an opportunity to turn down. "Well, it's half live-action and half computer animation," Dylan began, trying to figure out how to explain his videos to his uncle. "The story-line is kind of contemporary with a lot of fantasy elements. I guess you'd call it surrealistic."

"What's it about?"

Dylan dropped into the antique over-stuffed chair and stared up at the handsome ceiling. "Well, there's a guy—Brian McKay—who's being haunted by various figures from what might be the past or could be another dimension. Brian is an emergency medical tech, about twenty-five, who sometimes gets into dangerous situations, which is when the ghosts or other-dimensional beings kick in. Sometimes they help, sometimes they make things worse, but Brian can't ignore them. Once in a while he slips into the ghosts' worlds and then he really gets confused. It gets in the way of his life a lot, too. He's got a girl-friend—Amy Xi. She knows a little about the ghosts but she doesn't really believe in them, and that kind of messes up their relationship from time to time. She doesn't think he's a freak, but she does think he's kind of weird. I'm taking the first three adventures with me and I'm working on a couple more."

"An interesting concept," said Perry with genuine interest.

"Brian and Amy are the live-action part of the work—some of the settings I took around here, just went out and shot exteriors with my videocam. One of the guys I work with—Theo Westin—plays the live-action Brian, and Jenny Chin, who lives two doors down from Ma and me, plays the live-action Amy. We use the media lab at school for the most part to shoot the live-action. We have a green-screen and everything." He got up and fetched his beer. "They could be better. In time, they *will* be better."

"You told me you've posted them on the Internet," said Perry, encouraging Dylan to tell him more.

"Just the first one. I got some good feedback, and I sent a copy of the second one to DragonCon after they contacted me about the first." He returned to the chair and sank down into it. "That's when they said they wanted to have me on the program. I've got enough money for the ticket, and the b&b where I'm staying isn't as expensive as the convention hotels are."

"I can see why you'd want to go," said Perry.

"Could you explain it to Ma?" Dylan asked. "She says she gets it, but she doesn't, not really."

Perry didn't answer the question, and instead asked one of his own.

"What kind of adventures does Brian McKay have? Tell me about the best one you did."

Dylan hesitated, but he couldn't keep from blurting out the whole thing. "It's kind of . . . Brian is called out to pick up some burn victims near a forest fire. He goes in a helicopter—there's a couple of news 'copters covering it—and they drop into a clearing where the burned guys are in big tents, and a bunch of fire-fighters and rescue workers are all over the place. The media lab has some pretty good stock footage of rescue units and forest fires. While Brian's working at loading some of the victims into the 'copter, Ivray, one of his ghosts, who's kind of like one of those northern barbarians who attacked Rome back in the Dark Ages, starts materializing and telling him there could be trouble because the wind is shifting. Brian doesn't pay much attention, but then there's a alarm, and everyone starts to panic. Ivray comes back and orders Brian to get the 'copter—which he calls a levitating machine—out of there or risk getting killed. Brian does what Ivray tells him, and as he starts to climb into the 'copter, he's almost brained by Yash Quoatl, who's kind of like a Mayan priest, and who thinks the 'copter is dangerous to Brian and seems to think that he can save him. Brian gets dragged into a fight with the priest as the fire comes nearer and nearer, and then *pop!* he's in Yash Quoatl's world, where only Yash Quoatl can see him. It's a really whacked place, with some creatures that don't exist, and a bunch of strange-looking people. Oh, and a green sky. Then the priest does something, and Brian's back at the 'copter, being pulled into it as it starts to rise. They get out as the flames get to the edge of the clearing—Mister Guardini, my communications teacher, says that the montage-work I did was really good—and the 'copter reaches the hospital and Brian knocks off for the day. While he's getting a beer at his favorite bar, Amy arrives, annoyed at him for having put himself in danger again. She works for a TV station, and saw footage of the fire, and got to see Brian almost fall out of the 'copter. She tries to make him promise not to do anything so dangerous again. About then, Valtor, a magician who always materializes out of a whirlwind, shows up and gives Brian a stern warning that there's more trouble ahead, and he better get back to work because there's a forty-car pileup on the freeway, and lots of people are hurt. Amy gets upset when Brian says he has to go. To calm her down, he suggests that there's going to be a big story breaking any minute. She asks him how he knows, and just then the bar TV shows the first raw pictures of the mess. She and Brian leave the bar together, going their separate ways." He stopped and hitched his shoulders up. "And that's the end of the best video."

"Sounds exciting," said Perry. "How long does it run?"

"Just under eighteen minutes."

"How's that for video length?" Perry appeared to be eager to learn.

Dylan shrugged. "The next ones will be better."

"That's to be expected," Perry said as if he hadn't noticed that Dylan had failed to answer his question. "The ones you do after you go to DragonCon ought to be better still."

"Yeah. I hope so." He sounded miles away, and Perry scowled in worry.

"Are you all right, Dylan?"

Dylan sat, fidgeting, finished his beer, then said distantly, "I sometimes wonder if my condition is what people had back when everyone believed in werewolves."

"There are no such things as werewolves," said Perry sharply, and in a way that suggested he had said it before.

"No, but there may have been something *like* werewolves. People who acted like wolves, or went crazy and howled at the moon. Think about it, Uncle Perry. I fall asleep without warning, I sometimes act out while I'm asleep, and I can't remember it afterward." He thought about the episode he'd had the week before; he still could only recall flashes, mainly of him running in the park, and someone screaming.

"Werewolves sometimes remember what they do, according to the legends," said Perry. "Your condition is neurological, not folkloric."

Dylan remained still a short while, then suddenly got to his feet. "Well, I should get on home. Ma's probably nervous."

"Don't blame her for that," Perry said.

"Yeah. First my Dad and then me: genetics, right? I'd probably be edgy, too." He took a turn about Perry's study. "Do you find all these books are really worthwhile?"

"Yes, I do. Reading relaxes me."

"Huh." Dylan considered his uncle's answer. "Must be a generational thing."

Perry's smile was mordant. "Must be," he agreed.

The images on his computer screen enthralled Dylan. This was his last project before summer vacation began, and he had until the end of May to turn it in; just another week. He wanted to show Mister Guardini how much he had improved, so he threw himself into his vision. It was late on Friday night, and he was working on his new video, grinning. His eyes had a glazed look; he was dressed in jeans and a tee-shirt, though his room was chilly enough for a sweatshirt, for though the days were getting warm, the nights were still cool. He waved one hand at the manipulated images of a very old city street. The point of view was that of a man running, so the screen's vision rocked with each virtual step, and the sound of panting accompanied the movement. It wasn't yet clear if the man were pursuing or being pursued. The video stopped abruptly and Dylan clicked onto his files of stock footage. He scrolled through the files, selecting one called *By the River*, and began to search through it for the section with the arched wooden bridge, adapting his interface with the previous, more complete video, so that it soon appeared that the point-of-view runner had turned away from the street and was now moving beside the river toward the arched bridge. It took Dylan longer than he had anticipated to finesse the two sections of video into a believable whole, and when he was finally done, he felt a little giddy, and that was not a good sign. He wanted to ignore it, to go on working, but it was already past midnight and he was very tired.

"Sorry, Brian," he said to the figure on the screen, and put his computer on hibernate. He got up and stretched, looking toward the door of his computer room, and decided to get a bite to eat in the kitchen before he took his meds.

He woke up shortly after dawn on the floor of the mud-room at the back of the house. His clothes were a mess, stained and torn, and his head ached along with many other assorted pains from all parts of his body. As he touched his forehead, he felt an oblong, painful lump over his left eye. Without doubt he would be sporting a black eye for several days. He made an inspection of his face moving his fingers gingerly, discovering scratches and some sore regions that he suspected were bruises. He managed to get to his feet and stumble in the direction of the bathroom where he gathered up his courage and stared in the mirror in the dim light from the window, appalled at what he saw.

"What the fu—?" he asked his reflection. Where had he gone? What could he have done to make him look like he had been in a fight and then thrown into a thorn-bush? Trying not to panic, he skinned out of his clothes, finding more scrapes and bruises on his legs and arms, and one spectacular livid mark the size of a sheet of paper on the side of his hip. His knuckles were skinned, and when he stepped into the shower, a host of small and large hurts revealed themselves as the water struck them. He washed himself thoroughly and carefully, thinking as he did that he would have to come up with some explanation for his appearance, since there was no way to pass it off as a minor fall or a fight with their bad-tempered Pekinese, Ming the Merciless. If he admitted to a serious episode, Arian might change her mind about letting him go to Atlanta, and maybe even about college in LA. Whatever story he came up with, it would have to be the most convincing one of his whole life.

Once he had toweled himself off, he searched the medicine chest for some antibiotic ointment and daubed it on any cut or scrape he could see. He opened the sink-cabinet drawer and took out the green vial of his medication and gulped down two tablets with a handful of water. Then he gathered up his ruined clothes, tightened the towel around himself and headed off to his bedroom as quietly as he could. He'd put the ruined clothes in a plastic bag and planned to stuff it in the trash-bin at school. Carefully he selected his clothes for the day, making sure the long sleeves of his shirt covered up most of the damage on his arms; his hands would have to be bandaged. By the time he was ready for breakfast, he had the beginnings of an explanation forming in his mind. In an hour or so he would flesh it out, the same way he worked out the story lines for his videos.

"What the devil happened to you?" Dylan's mother asked him when she caught sight of him in the kitchen; she was more frightened than angry, and it came out in the unusually high pitch of her voice. "Don't tell me you were out on Friday night, Dylan. I thought we agreed you'd stay in on Friday and Saturday nights, as a precaution."

"I had a fall." He reached for the coffee pot and a mug, which he filled. "I went out last night to shoot some new video near the river." He held up his hand to keep his Ma from protesting. "I stayed away from the busy places, and I didn't plan to be gone long. The trouble is, I wasn't paying attention to where I was walking and I fell into the bushes—you know the ones that line the bank to help control erosion?—I almost slid into the river. I had to grab hold of some of the bushes to keep from getting wet." He came toward the table in the breakfast nook to put his cup down, then went back to the kitchen. "I dropped my videocam. It took me almost an hour to find it." It sounded so sensible he almost believed it himself.

Arian looked skeptical. "But you're okay?" There were layers of meaning in her question.

"I'm okay. No episode. Nothing like that." He hated lying, but he knew he had to, or he would have to stay home. "It was a pretty bad fall and I'm feeling a little rocky. Nothing important is damaged, except maybe my ego. I've already taken my meds, so I'll call Theo and tell him I'm coming in at noon, just as a safeguard, in case I fall asleep. My hands are stiff, and that'll slow down my work, anyway. If I rest up, I'll work better. I'm going to soak them in Epsom salts. Saturday mornings tend to be a little slow. He won't ask many questions when he sees me if I tell him what happened on the phone."

She got up from her seat and came to give him a close inspection, her face showing more than worry. "You slid through the bushes at the edge of the river?"

"I hadn't planned on it, it happened. It was a dumb thing to do, Ma.

I know it. I wasn't paying enough attention." He opened the cupboard and took out a box of what he thought of as health-nut cereal, then retrieved a bowl from the drying rack next to the sink and measured out his breakfast into it. Going to the refrigerator, he removed the milk carton and went back to the table.

"Dumb is right. What if you'd fallen into the river? What then?" She returned to her place at the table.

Dylan paused in pouring milk onto the cereal. "I know, Ma. It wouldn't have been good."

"You told me you would always have a second person with you when you go after background video, to scout for you. What happened this time?" She frowned at her plate of thin pancakes with butter and blueberry syrup on them and three bites missing as if they had turned to oozey mud topped with purple slime. "You shouldn't have gone alone."

"I know," he said again with heavy emphasis. "But I figured it would only take me about twenty minutes, and it being so late . . . "

She sighed. "Couldn't you find background footage on the Internet?"

"I had a certain look in mind: the arched bridge. It's part of the last four minutes of my class project." He set the milk down, took a spoon from the container of utensils in the center of the table, and began eating.

"How long were you out?"

He looked up abruptly, then realized she meant not how long had he been in his narcoleptic state, but how long had he been gone from the house. "A little under an hour, I think. Maybe a little over an hour."

"That's a long time for the middle of the night, and not just because of the risk of an episode." She shook her head, every line of her face showing worry and disappointment. "Do I need to reconsider your trip to DragonCon? I have to know you're not going to do anything irresponsible while you're away from Toronto. I have to be able to trust your judgment. It's too important, Dylan. You could end up blowing everything. You could hurt yourself."

"I didn't want to fall, Ma," he said, knowing he would be more convincing if he had been telling the truth. "It was an accident, is all. The kind of thing someone like me would be a real idiot to—"

"How can I be sure?" Now she looked troubled. "If you were sleep-walking, you might have wandered into a busy street."

"I wasn't sleepwalking, Ma," he said, doing his best to conceal his mendacity with a glare of impatience.

"I trust not."

"Hey, I don't want to go through anything like that again, especially while I'm in Atlanta. I mean, look at my face. Do you think I'd want to make a public presentation all banged up like this? I did something impulsive and I paid for it. I get it. I won't do it again." Dylan found it an effort to be indignant because he was being decep-tive, and he strove to appear affronted by her question.

"I would hope that's all it was," she replied dubiously, pushing her plate away, her appetite gone and her stomach queasy.

"You know I wouldn't take a chance like that." That statement was true enough.

"I know you wouldn't if you were awake," she said pointedly.

"It wasn't like that, Ma," he said, a flush coming over his face, because it was just like that.

Arian got up from the table and went to open the porch door in order to let Ming the Merciless into the house; the little dog bounded in, his claws scrabbling noisily on the floor, his tongue lolling. "Who's the good dog, eh? Who's the good dog?"

Ming obliged by standing on his hind legs, one paw on her shin, panting in anticipation of affection and breakfast. He gave a pair of friendly yaps, then suddenly he stopped his enthusiastic display and turned toward Dylan, growling protectively, moving in front of Arian. The growl grew louder and ended in three loud, challenging barks.

"Ming! Mind your manners!"

"It's okay, Ma," said Dylan, trying not to feel too disconcerted; he almost supposed that Ming was aware of his prevarications and was upbraiding him for them. *What else could that ferocious little dog picking up on*? he asked himself.

"No, it's not," she said. "Down, Ming! Down! You know you aren't supposed to growl at people."

Reluctantly, the Pekinese put all four paws on the floor and toddled over to Dylan's Ma and sat at her feet, head cocked as if trying to explain himself. Arian reached down and scratched the dog's ears, making an apology for her sharp words. "Good Ming. Lie down."

"He probably smells the ointment I put on the scrapes. You know how he doesn't like medicinal odors," said Dylan, tasting his coffee and finding it too hot—he drank it anyway while Ming glowered at him.

"I want you to see Doctor Hastings as soon as possible. I'll call his office and leave a message to set you an appointment this coming week. Tell him about your fall, and that episode you had three weeks ago." When Arian spoke so decisively, Dylan knew it was useless to refuse. "You need to have a physical, anyway. We can kill two birds with one appointment."

"Do you think it's necessary?" he asked.

"You may need some adjustment in your meds." Arian looked at Dylan intently. "It's a good idea to tend to that now, so you'll have adapted to the difference by the time you head off to Atlanta."

He almost choked on his coffee. He was still going to DragonCon! He hadn't wrecked his chance! Beaming, he looked around at his Ma. "Thanks. Really, Ma, thanks." He reached out and put his hand on her shoulder, ignoring the hint of a growl from Ming.

"You should tell Doctor Hastings about your travels, too, so he'll know that you may need a little more flexibility in your prescriptions." She pressed her lips together, then said, "I know how much you want to go, and I know it can mean many things to you, more of them good than bad. I just want to be certain you're prepared."

"Okay. You're probably right about the meds," he said by way of concession, and resumed his breakfast.

August turned hot and sticky. All Toronto sweltered under the relentless heat; residents and tourists alike complained, and waited for a break in the weather.

"Your Ma tells me that the adjustment in your medication is working out quite well," said Uncle Perry as he sat with Arian and Dylan in a small, superior, air-conditioned restaurant tucked away in a tree-lined side-street near the university; the sky was aglow with the long twilight of Canadian summer.

"No episode at all in two months," said Dylan, a mixture of pride and diffidence coloring his words.

"That's encouraging. Isn't it, Arian?" Perry remarked, and signaled the waiter.

"A bottle of the number 78, the Australian Shiraz. Two glasses. And a chilled bottle of the Panna, three glasses, no ice."

"So far," said Arian as the waiter departed. "If everything continues this way, I'll be reassured when he leaves in six days. I'm planning on having the living room painted while he's gone."

Perry offered his nephew a satisfied smile. "That's all good news. Are you packed yet?" He winked to show his question was in good fun.

"I haven't done my laundry, but I got my duffle out of the closet, and I'm starting to choose what to take," said Dylan. He had been busy making copies of his videos to offer dealers at DragonCon; he had bought a special carrying case for them, and had secured the forms for customs. That seemed a lot more important than clothes, but he didn't want to make a poor appearance, so he was now turning his attention to clothes. "Ma'll make sure I'm all ready the day before I leave."

"I'm going to get him a set of new clothes for his presentation," said Arian. "Something a little more formal than jeans, but comfortable in the heat. A good linen sports jacket and a couple of lightweight shirts, and a pair of khaki slacks. We're going shopping day after tomorrow."

"And shoes, Ma; you said you'd get me new shoes," Dylan reminded her.

"Yes—and new shoes," she appended.

The waiter brought the wine and the glasses and went through a ritual of tasting and approving the bottle, then poured for Perry and Arian, promising to return with their water.

"To your Atlanta trip," said Perry, raising his glass toward Dylan.

"May it be successful in every way," said Arian, sounding especially Welsh as she joined in the toast.

Fighting a sudden welling of shyness, Dylan said, "Thanks. I'm hoping it goes well, too."

"I'm looking forward to hearing all about it," said Perry.

The waiter brought the water and poured it into the crystal goblets on the table. He then took their dinner orders and went off to the kitchen.

"Anything interesting happening at work, Uncle Perry?" Dylan asked, as much to be polite at to find out about the cases he might be working on.

"It's hardly dinner conversation," said Perry.

"You never know. I'm always looking for material for more videos," said Dylan. "This sounds really promising."

"You mean for your Brian McKay character to pursue?" Perry inquired.

"Yeah," said Dylan.

Perry paused, ruminating. "Well, I'm consulting on a case attempting to identify what appears to be a body that was torn apart by wild animals."

"Perry," Arian admonished him. "You're right—this isn't dinner conversation."

But Dylan looked interested. "Wild animals in Toronto?"

"On the outskirts," said Perry. "There isn't much left to go on. The victim has been dead for between two or three months." He saw the shock in Arian's face and used his napkin to wipe his lips. "Sorry, Arian. I'll tell you about it after DragonCon," he assured Dylan.

"Thanks, Uncle Perry. It sounds like a really good story. I'll get a great video out of it, I bet." He toasted his uncle with his glass of water.

Arian shook her head. "Toasting with water is supposed to be bad luck."

"It would be if he were old enough to drink legally," said Perry, and picked up his wineglass again. "To DragonCon."

Dylan touched the rim of his water goblet to Perry's wine-glass. "To solving your case."

Having cleared US customs at the Toronto airport, Dylan arrived in Atlanta ready to make his way to the convention, once he sorted out the shuttle to baggage claim, and then the ground transportation, Arian's admonitions ringing in his ears as he made his way toward the front of the airport. He had decided on the plane to take the convention center shuttle, pick up his membership materials and then taxi to his b&b and decide what to do about supper. The summer swelter had Atlanta in its grip and Dylan could feel his new shirt sticking to his back, a dull headache beginning behind his eyes. Toronto could be muggy in the summer, but this was ridiculous, he thought.

At Registration Dylan found the *Invited Guests—Video Presentations* line; the noise echoing through the broad hall was so huge that it became one voice, like the roar of the sea. Dylan told himself to keep his mind on his purpose as he fell in behind a guy about his own age with shoulder-length black hair who was carrying a backpack that said *Taos* in sand-and-turquoise letters over an olive-green t-shirt and black jeans; there were fifteen people ahead of them, many of them chatting, so summoning up his courage, Dylan asked, "You from there?"

"What?" The guy turned around, revealing pleasant features marked by a square jaw and aquiline nose. "Oh, this." He patted the straps of the back-pack. "Nope. I'm from Cerrillos; that's west of Albuquerque. In New Mexico. I go up to Taos to ski."

The line moved forward by one.

The guy from Cerrillos rubbed his hand on his t-shirt and held it out. "I'm Matt Alland."

Dylan took the hand and shook it. "Dylan Rhys-Kayes, from Toronto."

"Canada? Cool." He cocked his head. "This your first time at DragonCon? I don't remember seeing you around."

"Yeah. You?"

"My third, but my first as an invited guest. I've been interning at the new special effects studio in Albuquerque all summer and I've made a presentation for the con." He grinned. "I've got a video with a lot of Tewa legends—you know, talking animals, nature gods, like that—in it. I made my presentation video with the CG software they've got at the studio. My Mom's Tewa; teaches cultural anthropology at UNM."

"Tewa. That's Indian, right?" Dylan guessed, hoping he was.

"Yep. Dad's Irish and Mexican. A real southwestern family." He moved ahead another a step. "What kind of name is Rhys-Kayes?"

"Welsh, all the way back, both sides," said Dylan. "I was born there—in Wales."

"What was it like?"

"I don't remember much." He decided to explain. "We moved to Canada when I was about three."

"That's right; you already told me you're from Canada," said Matt, his face brightening. "Lots of Indians up there."

"Yeah," said Dylan, trying to decide what he thought of this guy from New Mexico. "You on any panels?"

"Other than my presentation? One. On developing legends and folklore to video forms: that's my long suit. There's this fascinating dude from Iceland who's on it with me and two others: he's talking about the Eddas—the Icelandic dude. Mom asked me to take notes."

"Sounds really cool," said Dylan, meaning it. "It's always good to get new material."

"That it is," said Matt. After they shuffled forward a few more paces, he asked, "Where are you staying?"

"The Peachtree Garden Bed and Breakfast," said Dylan. "You?"

"Catty-corner from here," Matt answered, gesturing in its general direction. "It's all taken up by the convention. Is the b&b nearby?"

"A mile and half from here, according to the map." He patted his duffle and stepped up another space. "I thought I'd get a cab over the first time, to learn the best way. But I'll probably walk it most of the time." As he listened to himself, he began to have doubts.

"In *this* humidity?" Matt chortled. "You'll be soggy toast by the time you get here."

"It should be cooler in the morning, and at night," said Dylan, doubting it even as he spoke.

"It might be, but don't count on it," said Matt. "Sometimes I think about the Civil War, and all those guys fighting in this heat, no air conditioning, and I wonder why they didn't all just collapse from it." He looked around the room. "Want to grab a bite after this? There's a good place about a block away—Cajun-style."

"Sure," said Dylan, pleasantly surprised at the offer.

"Okay. I'll see you out front at five-thirty."

"On the sidewalk?" Dylan asked, to be certain.

"Yeah. At the corner." He gestured again to establish the direction. "I'm meeting up with a couple of DragonCon friends then. You'll like them. They do videos, too. Three of them are making presentations."

"Sounds good," said Dylan.

They reached the front of the line; Matt gave his name, exchanging greetings with the young woman manning the table, agreeing to meet her later that evening.

"Dylan Rhys-Kayes," he said as Matt stepped aside.

"Spell the last name, please," the young woman asked, frowning at the list on her laptop screen.

"R-h-y-s hyphen K-a-y-e-s."

"Oh. Not R-e-e-c-e. Here it is," she said, turned around to a box to retrieve is package. "Your badge is inside." She patted the oversized envelope. "Please wear it for all DragonCon events. Your schedule is in this envelope. Please check the daily postings for any changes in programming. Be in the green room twenty minutes before your panels and your presentation." She smiled. "Welcome to DragonCon."

"Thanks." He moved away, wanting to look inside his envelope, but knowing it would be best to get out of all the confusion. After a few minutes passed, he sought out the nearest men's room, and after attending to his bladder, he sat down on the upholstered bench and took out his badge, hanging it around his neck as instructed. He then glanced over his schedule, noticing that his 3:30 panel had been moved back to 5:00 p.m. "Five tomorrow," he said, to set it in his thoughts.

He hefted his duffle and decided to check in at the b&b, then come back and meet Matt and his friends. He supposed he could do it all in two hours. He stuffed his envelope into the outer pocket of his duffle and went off to find a cab.

"Dylan Rhys-Kayes, meet Everard Mitchell," said the square-bodied guy next to Matt.

"From Eureka. Call me Mitch."

"Eureka? Like the TV show?" Dylan asked, chuckling a little. He had changed from his traveling shirt into a t-shirt, and felt much more in tune with Matt's four other companions. Around them, a swirl of conventioneers eddied like floodwater, leaving the six of them in a still center amid the busy flow of excited attendees. Traffic crawled in the streets while DragonCon-goers threaded their way through the cars that straggled into the intersection.

"It's in northern California, way north, on the coast." Mitch's tone said he had answered this question more times than he wanted to. "I've just done a summer internship at LucasFilm in San Francisco, and I'm starting my sophomore year at SF State." He was tawny-haired and his lightly-freckled skin was flushed from the heat.

"Awesome," said Dylan. "LucasFilm."

"It was," said Mitch.

"This is Kevin Bessabhi," Matt went on, indicating a small, wiry kid with the darkest eyes Dylan had ever seen.

"Nice to meet you." He shook hands awkwardly. "I like your Brian McKay; I saw it on the Internet." His voice was soft and fairly high, as if it hadn't finished dropping yet. He wore blue-and-white striped Bermuda shorts, a light-blue shirt and a baseball cap.

"Thanks," said Dylan.

"This is Nicole Swenson." The girl Matt introduced was about average height, angular of build, dressed in loose cargo-style pants and a plain camisole top, showing off her golden tan to advantage, one of the few concessions she made to femininity. Her hair, a mahogany-brown, was tied back with an orange scarf, and sunglasses obscured the color and shape of her eyes.

"From Charleston," she said, and volunteered nothing more.

"And this," Matt said, bowing slightly to the skinny, pale-skinned kid with the thatch of unruly red hair, "is Liam Haskins from Portland."

"Oregon?" Dylan asked, extending his hand.

"Maine." He shook Dylan's hand firmly but without trying to crush it. "Doing Computer Sciences at MIT."

"The restaurant's just this way," said Matt, already walking in its direction. "The food's good, not too pricey, and the staff's used to DragonCon. We won't get hassled."

"So you're here from Canada," Kevin said, falling in beside Dylan.

"Yeah. You?"

"Pretty much everywhere. My dad's in the Air Force. We move around a lot." It was impossible to tell from how he said it if he liked moving or not. "I was born in Nevada; we moved to Oklahoma when I was two, then to France, then to Florida, then to Turkey, then to Colorado. We're still in Colorado, but next year dad's going to the Philippines. I'll be in college."

Dylan looked at Kevin closely. "Aren't you . . . a little young?"

"I'm fifteen next month. I'm smart. Full scholarship. Cal Tech." The boast was not the obnoxious kind; Dylan was impressed.

"I have early acceptance to Cal Arts, outside LA, next year," Dylan said. "Nothing like going to Cal Tech on full scholarship, though, let alone at fifteen."

Kevin nodded, a slight frown settling between his brows. "Dad tells me it's a lot to live up to."

"Turn left," Matt ordered. Obediently, they followed him, doing their best to stick close together in the jumble of people on the sidewalk. Matt stopped and pointed to the sign overhead. "We're here: Bayou Bijou." He marched up to the door of the restaurant and opened it. The smell of frying oysters, garlic, and hot pepper sauce met them as they stepped into the air-conditioned interior.

They were told there would be a ten minute wait while they prepared a table for a party of six. "We're busy tonight," said the receptionist, pointing to the waiting area adjoining the bar.

Dylan sat down, wishing he had a glass of orange juice so he could take his meds. The walk back to the convention from the b&b had left him more enervated than he had thought he would be. The wear and tear of traveling was catching up with him, and he could feel his legs getting a bit unsteady, a sure sign of a nervous system overload. Not a good thing, he told himself. He needed to take his meds, and soon. As the others sat down, Dylan remained standing, then went to the receptionist. "Do you think I could order a glass of orange juice? I'm feeling a bit dehydrated."

"Atlanta's like that in the summer," the receptionist said, and signaled a waiter. "This young man needs orange juice. He's with his friends in the waiting area." She favored Dylan with a broad smile. "There you go, darlin'."

"Thank you," he said, and went to join the others, thinking as he went that keeping track of his medication schedule might prove to be trickier than he had assumed it would be. He removed the two pills from his pocket and palmed them. "I'm getting some orange juice," he announced.

Matt laughed. "After the walk from the b&b, I'm surprised you don't want a gallon of ice-water."

"It was wearing," Dylan admitted. He pulled a ten dollar bill out of his pocket and handed it to the waiter, who came toward him with a large glass of orange juice on a bar-tray. "Much appreciated."

"Do you want change?" the waiter asked.

"How much is it?" Dylan asked.

"Four dollars."

Dylan felt very awkward; he knew he was blushing, and that made it worse. "Give me four back, if you would." He could hear Uncle Perry admonishing him against over-tipping, but he didn't want to look like a cheapskate to his new friends.

The waiter gave him the four dollars and a knowing wink before he went off to the bar again.

"You should probably carry water with you all the time," Matt recommended. "We always have water at home when it's hot."

Dylan popped his pills and took a long drink of orange juice, feeling its chill spread down his torso. He hoped this was the worst time he would have while he was in Atlanta. "Sounds like a good idea. I'll pick up some bottles tomorrow morning."

"That'll help," Liam approved; until he spoke, Dylan was unaware that he was paying attention, for he had been staring at the murals on the opposite wall in a fine, abstracted air. "If you find yourself getting queasy, get to some place cool and eat a handful of trail mix."

"Okay," said Dylan.

"Hey, I'm a red-head. I have to be careful in the heat, and I sunburn in about five minutes flat, even with industrial-strength sunscreen." He gave a self-effacing grin. "I'm diabetic, too; that makes things worse. I always have a protein bar with me." He slapped his pocket as if to confirm this.

Matt snapped his fingers. "We'll keep an eye on you, until you get used to DragonCon and Atlanta weather. We keep an eye on Liam, as well. He needs to eat often."

"Thanks," said Dylan, trying not to sound annoyed. Why did everyone think he had to be taken care of? He glanced at Liam. "Sorry about the diabetes. It can't be easy."

"It takes some getting used to." Mitch admitted, then slapped Dylan on his shoulder. "Hey, look, Dylan, I'm staying at the Hilton. I'm having a critique session tomorrow night for some of my videos I'm not presenting here. Matt's got a new video that's not ready for public viewing yet; he wants to show it—he's asking for feedback. Why don't you come along? Bring anything you want to show, provided it isn't hours long."

"What time would that be?" Dylan asked, drinking more orange juice. "I have a panel at five."

"No problemo. Nine-ish. We'll call Room Service for sandwiches, if you like." The others nodded.

"I'd really like to," said Dylan, thinking he'd be able to sleep in the following morning if the evening went on too late. He would pace himself, not get too exhausted. "Yeah. Okay."

The receptionist appeared and told them their table was ready, and they made their way to a booth at the rear of the dining room.

For Dylan, Friday went by in a blur filled with presentations, panels, autograph lines, passes through the Dealers' Rooms, and spates of excited conversations with other convention-goers. His own panel on the mixing of computer graphics with live action went reasonably well, though Dylan said very little on it, preferring to listen to the other members of the panel. By the time it was over, he was hungry, and eager for a break; he took a couple minutes to linger in the empty panel room, to phone home, telling Arian he was fine, had met some really interesting people, and found out a lot. She asked him how he was feeling, he reiterated he was fine, promised to call the next day, sent greetings to Uncle Perry, and hung up.

"Good panel," said Mitch; he came up to Dylan as he left the room.

"Oh. Hey. I didn't notice you were in the audience," he said, feeling embarrassed for such an oversight.

"I was in the back," said Mitch. "I know how it goes at these things."

"I thought the guy from Disney was really interesting," said Dylan as they made their way along the wide corridor.

"Me, too. And it shows what you can do with a huge budget. Most of us don't have millions of dollars to spend on interfacing live action and CG, and hundreds of techies to work on it." Mitch pointed toward one of the side-doors. "Let's go this way. It's less crowded."

"Okay," said Dylan, and stepped out into the blaze of the late afternoon. "Where to?"

"There's a grill around the corner. You'll like it. You're looking a little pale around the gills." He laughed. "Don't poker up on me, dude. I'm not dissing you."

Dylan couldn't think of anything to say in response.

Mitch went on, "One of the things that brought the five of us together is that we all have something we have to deal with. Liam's got diabetes—you know that. Nicole's severely dyslexic. Kevin's small, young, and hyper-bright. Last year Matt had a bad asthma attack the first day of the con—from allergies, it turned out—and we started to watch him, make sure he had his inhaler; still do. Liam's the best at handling these things. You look a bit peaked. We see a lot of heat stress at this con. Something cool to drink and Parmigian-encrusted veggies would probably put you to rights."

"I get worn out in the heat," Dylan admitted. "It's been quite a day."

"And there's a busy day tomorrow. So let's get a couple of grill baskets and some ice-tea and relax." Mitch pointed out the grill. "Did I hear you tell Kevin yesterday that you're going to Cal Arts?"

"Next year, yeah. I got early acceptance."

"That's what Kevin told me," said Mitch, and tugged the door open. "So tell me about what you'll be showing tonight?"

"One thing more," Dylan said.

"What is it?"

"You said all five of you have something to—"

"—deal with. Uh-huh. I have lupus." As Dylan gave him a shocked stare, Mitch went on, "Don't worry; it's under control. But it's always there."

The five were draped over the two king-sized beds in Mitch's hotel room, facing the TV screen where the end of Dylan's most recent video was fading to sketchy credits. The noise from outside had abated a while ago, and the night seemed very still as the video ended.

"I don't know what music to use; nothing seems to fit, Brian running up that hill, away from the shadow-beasts," Dylan admitted, glancing at the clock, and astonished to see it was after 2:00 a.m. Five hours had gone by so quickly. "I thought maybe just the sound of Brian panting, but Theo, who plays him, says it won't work."

Nicole chuckled. "He's probably right."

Matt grinned. "It could be kind of sexy."

"That's what Theo said." Dylan scowled; much as he did not want to, he had to agree with them. "It isn't supposed to be sexy, it's supposed to be scary."

"They're not mutually exclusive," said Mitch. "Maybe you could, you know, blend them somehow."

"I guess I could," said Dylan, his mind already active. "Like something's going to happen that could be really good, or really horrible."

"Something like that," said Mitch. "You got a good couple in your actors. You might as well make the most of them."

"Yeah," said Dylan.

"That scene in the trees at night—was that green screen or real?" Nicole asked.

"A little of both; we got the live action in the park around ten at night, and I added in most of the shadows later," Dylan answered, rubbing his eyes. It would be three by the time he made it back to his b&b. He yawned and stretched. "Kevin, how long's your video?"

"Thirty minutes," said Kevin. He picked up his computer and held it out to Mitch to connect to the TV.

"You can sleep here, if you want to," Mitch offered. "No one will notice if you wear the same thing two days in a row. Or care."

Dylan had to admit he was tired. "You wouldn't mind?"

"Of course not," Mitch said, working on linking Kevin's computer to the TV.

"It's tempting," Dylan allowed. He had his meds with him; he could take his pills and go to sleep. He was pretty sure Arian would not approve, but he was here to learn how to handle himself alone. "Thanks. I will."

"Then the bed nearer the window is yours. When we're through here, you can konk."

"Thanks," said Dylan, feeling his fatigue well up within him; he stretched again and lay back.

"Holy shit!" Matt exclaimed as Dylan opened his eyes to see the five of them leaning over him.

"You awake?" Liam asked.

Dylan lay on the floor, his shoulder was sore, and the window was filled with the slanting rays of the rising sun. "Oh, God."

"What was that?" Mitch asked; he crouched down beside Dylan.

"I guess I had an episode, didn't I?" said Dylan, chagrin coming over him like a cold wind. "What did I do? How bad was it?" He braced himself for the repugnance he knew was coming.

"Do? Bad?" Kevin leaned over him, holding out a bottle of water. "You probably need this."

"I'm sorry," Dylan muttered as he reached for the water.

"Sorry?" Matt exclaimed, pushing himself off the bed. "Why be sorry? You were *great!*"

"Great?" Dylan repeated, certain he hadn't heard right.

"In*cred*ible!" Mitch seconded; he got to his feet.

"Better than the Incredible Hulk," Liam assured him. "What—?"

"You mean I didn't do anything . . . bad?" Dylan raised himself on his elbow and looked at his arms and hands, and found only one small bruise forming above his left elbow.

Liam was more curious than alarmed. "Don't you remember? Not any of it at all?"

"No. I don't." Dylan rubbed his face, trying to clear away the fuzziness of his thoughts. "I have narcolepsy," he said the word as if it tasted rotten, "and when I fall into that kind of sleep, I don't remember what I do."

"That sucks," said Nicole. "'Cause you were—amazing."

"What did I do?" Dylan asked again, more alarmed than before.

Matt came toward him, almost bouncing. "It was . . . it was like you changed shape. Mom's gonna *freak* when I tell her about this."

His grogginess was fading to be replaced by dismay; Dylan sat up, and felt in his pocket for his meds. "Don't. Please don't tell her."

"Why not, dude? You've got a *talent*! A big one." Matt clapped his hands, and the others murmured agreement. "You're a living special effect. You can . . . you can morph yourself."

"No, I can't," said Dylan, appalled.

"Sure, you can," said Mitch. "We just watched you do it." He watched while Dylan swallowed his pills. "Not big-green-monster morph, but your body changes a lot. How you move is entirely different. With a little CG sweetening, you could end up with a huge career, just doing the change."

"You're so flexible," Nicole declared.

"I am?" Dylan strained to remember, and wondered if that was why his shoulder was sore.

"You want to see?" Kevin asked. "I got part of it on my videocam."

"So did I," said Mitch.

"Man-oh-man, I could use you in my next video," Matt went on enthusiastically

"I want to do a story about a shape-shifter, but all the CG effects I've experimented with are whacked. But you! You could just do your—"

"No, I couldn't," said Dylan, very seriously. "I can't make it happen, and if I do fall into a narcoleptic state, most times I just sleep. I don't know what makes me sleepwalk. I can't begin to guess."

"What about staying off your meds?" Mitch suggested.

"Or using some kind of mental thing—maybe yoga or martial arts?" Liam remarked.

"What about hypnosis?" Nicole asked.

Mitch began to set up his videocam with the TV. "Have a look at what you did last night. I wish this room had a higher ceiling."

"Why?" Dylan felt a sinking sensation in his gut; he rose from the floor and looked toward the bathroom. "I'll be back in a minute," he said, and went to use the toilet and to restore a little order to his appearance. When he returned, an image of him in the process of vaulting to the top of the TV armoire was frozen on the screen. He stared at it as the image began to move. Astounded by what he saw, Dylan sat on the end of the nearer bed, all but mesmerized by the incredible gymnastics his narcoleptic self was performing.

"Pretty cool, hmm?" Matt said, grinning.

"Um," said Dylan, seeing himself extend his arms and torso beyond anything he thought would be possible, and then launch himself at the wall in a way that would do Jackie Chan proud, ending in a turning back-flip to land on his feet. Mitch once again froze the action.

"You see what we mean about shape-shifting?" Liam remarked.

"Yeah," said Dylan, "I do." Maybe, he thought, all the scrapes and bruises he had acquired in the past had come from similar athletic feats, and were not the result of violence and mayhem. Maybe Matt was right, and his rare form of narcolepsy was more a gift than a curse. As his image moved on the screen once more, a panoply of possibilities began to take form in his mind, and a future he would never have imagined a day ago opened to him.

"Do you think you can learn to control it—get so you can do it on demand?" Kevin asked, pointing to the complex series of actions displayed on the screen.

For the first time since he had thought about coming to DragonCon, Dylan felt free of any trace of anxiety. "I don't know," he said, trying to get used to seeing his condition as an asset, "but I'm damn well going to try."

THE FAN AND THE FURY

Michelle Poche

"Oh, God, help me!"

"Which one?" I said. "They're kind of loath to do anything if you can't get more specific than that."

She just stared at me with a curious mixture of terror and blankness.

I grinned and shrugged. "Geez, lighten up. I'm only here to kill you." She apparently was not comforted since she wordlessly darted off into the crowd of wizards, aliens, and elves. I heaved an unnecessarily heavy sigh and followed after her, grimacing as I jostled past a robed teenage boy with a fake scar in the shape of a lightning bolt that zigzagged across his pimply forehead and who probably had never been within two feet of a woman unrelated to him. My blonde hair, laced with hissing vipers, was generally sufficient to deter the boldest of men, but I was gone before the wannabe Harry Potter could do anything slimier than gawk.

I hadn't bothered to cloak myself here. Frankly, it was easier to blend in wearing a micro-mini Grecian gown, bleeding eyes, serpent hair, and scaly wings. If I wore my usual tee-shirt, jeans and notable absence of wings, I'd attract way too much attention. Still, I had to admit some of the participants creeped me out, and *I'm* supposed to be the monster. Not but ten minutes earlier I had bumped into a gargantuan man dressed in a loin cloth and sporting a single eye. I chuckled at an inside joke regarding the inaccuracies of the costume (after all, I had seen a real Cyclops), but was quickly smacked back to earth by the accuracy of the smell. Not pretty.

Wanda spun around to see if I was still nipping at her heels.

Surprise. I gave the condemned a small three finger wave. She opened her mouth in horror, working her jaw open and closed like she was gnawing on gristle. Finally, some words escaped those lips. "Your eyes . . . they're bleeding."

"Only sucks when I wear contacts."

"Cool FX," said a lycra-sheened alien who ogled my sporty bleeding eyes.

"Thanks." I turned back to the condemned. "Okay, sister, let's get a move on. I've got things to do and people to kill."

"I don't want to die!"

The alien dude swept his gaze between the two of us. His mouth trembled between a smile and grimace.

"And I don't want to have snakes coiling around in my hair, but do you hear me complain?" I winked at the alien. "This 'do gives new meaning to the term 'bad hair day,' don't you think?"

He smiled, relieved to think my little exchange with crazy girl was all an act. Did I mention how much I loved DragonCon?

"You're crazy!" Wanda's voice was loud and shrill, but no one paid her heed. As the alien returned to the river of pirates and other creatures, it was apparent that my little victim's rant was not going to elicit anything more than an arched eyebrow.

"No, but *you* will be in about . . . " even though I didn't wear a watch I lifted my wrist like I was gauging time, " . . . three minutes. Time to find a rooftop."

Wanda reached for a guy who made the mistake of passing too close to her. He was dressed as a Cyberman from Dr. Who. "Please help me; she's trying to kill me."

I grinned toothily at him and gave him a cheerful thumbs up. "She really gets into the role."

"Cool," he said behind his mask. I offered him a smile designed to cause much wailing and gnashing of teeth, but since he thought I was just role-playing creepy, he was good with it.

Wanda clutched her head and moaned. I sent her a montage of creepy crawlies. Sometimes I get such a kick out of making a mind snap. It actually has a harmonious quality to it. I kid you not.

"Nooo," Wanda keened. Her eyes did a loop-de-loop in their sockets. "Make it stop!"

"Not until you take your own life."

"I had to—my grandfather was evil."

She was right. The guy had been a bona fide sociopath. For a split second, I hesitated. But the feeling passed almost as quickly as it arrived. I wasn't the judge or the jury, just the executioner. "And that's supposed to make a difference to me how?" I pointed toward the stairwell and nodded my head toward it. "This is America. Land of the free and well-medicated. No excuse for homicide when you have access to the happy pill."

I turned to the stairs, confident that I had fragmented her rationality enough to take my suggestion, but when I glanced back, I saw her actually cant toward the elevators.

Hey, at least the girl was thinking *up*. It was a start.

The teeming masses parted for me. I'd like to think I had Moses-like qualities, burning bushes and parting the seas. But, really, wouldn't you get out of the way of a snake-headed chick with really bloody eyes?

The elevator dinged right as I nestled behind Wanda. When the doors swooshed open, an impossible number of people jostled their way out of the box. Arms, antennas and wings folded and unfolded in a flurry to exit. I resisted the urge to crawl into Wanda's thoughts so I could tool around with her sanity in private, but it wasn't often I could let my hair, or rather serpents, down and just be out there as a Fury.

"Are you the Grim Reaper?"

"I prefer to think of myself as a Happy Harvester," I said brightly.

Pretty much every species of weird occupied the interior. If we wedged ourselves in, we might have a sporting chance. I pushed her forward. "Could somebody please press the highest floor for me? Thank you!"

"You're sick," Wanda screeched, right as the doors closed.

"Sticks and stones."

The elevator door closed. Everyone got really quiet and I felt eyes staring at the girls. "Okay, everyone, chill. They're actually all quite tame."

"They can't be real. Those are poisonous," some chick with fake vampire teeth said.

I rolled my eyes. "Of course they're real. I mean, because it's both possible and intelligent to surgically connect snakes to my head. Or perhaps I was born this way?" Vampire-Teeth blushed, and one of my pets hissed and shook a rattle. A kid dressed as a princess yelped and clutched the hand of what must be her older sister. About ten seconds later, Vampire-Teeth had mustered up some kind of response.

"Are you dressed up as Medusa?" I suspect she wanted me to be impressed at her stunning intimacy with Greek mythology. I wasn't. I really, really hated Medusa. She got all the attention, and really she wasn't that important when it came down to it. Besides, she was ugly as sin to boot.

"No."

"Oh."

An uncomfortable silence settled on the elevator. When the door opened on the seventh floor, Vampire-Teeth slid out, though I had seen her press eleven. Nifty little trick on my part. A lot of other people departed as well. By some grace of Hades, no one else got on. There was myself, Wanda, and a pirate left on the elevator. Since I knew we had a few floors remaining before Captain Kidd left us, I figured I might as well have a bit of fun.

Wanda trembled in the corner, blathering about floods, yarn and something that sounded like chick peas, but could have been Rick Steves. I gave her a fetching smile, winked devilishly, and vanished—but only to her. She let out a wail and started sobbing with what sounded like relief. Captain Kidd glanced at her with furrowed eyebrows. I shrugged at him and he shrugged back. I reappeared and her screams took on a tortured tone. The pirate was not slow in getting off when the door next opened.

"Alone at last."

Wanda stood with eyes that saucered in terror. "I didn't want to—I had to kill him."

"Yeah, about that. See, I've heard that before. Many, many times. And wow, they all died anyway," I said. "So guess what?"

She didn't seem to be absorbing my simple lesson, so I decided to wax philosophical on her. I had a lot of time on my hands, sort of a job pre-req when you're immortal. "Look, you accepted the potential ramifications when you killed your grandfather. You knew the law might find you. Yes, it's true that you eluded justice—at least the justice of man. But some laws are enforced by those above mankind. Spilling the blood of your kin is a crime that can not and will not go unpunished."

The elevator opened, and Wanda backed out of it hesitatingly. I mentally directed her to the left. She proceeded this way for about a hundred feet. Her terrified eyes stared at me from her sallow face, framed by a mess of hair matted with sweat. I advanced towards her with retribution burning in my eyes. She took the seventh and sixth last steps of her life backing away from me.

"You're a Christian, right? How about this: 'The path of the righteous man is beset on all sides with the iniquities of the selfish and the tyranny of evil men. Blessed is he who in the name of charity and good will shepherds the weak through the valley of darkness, for he is truly his brother's keeper and the finder of lost children. And I will strike down upon those with great vengeance and with furious anger those who attempt to poison and destroy my brothers. And you will know that my name is the Lord when I lay my vengeance upon thee.' "

"That isn't even from the Bible. That's a quote from *Pulp Fiction*." Her voice was surprisingly lucid. I almost smiled. "Almost" being the key word.

"Ooohh. Girl knows her trivia." I advanced further—and she took her fifth, fourth, third and second last steps. "The point is this: your 'God' cannot help you now, not that he would if he could, something about free-will and all that."

She tried to lift her leg to lever herself over the railing, but since it was so high I had to send a wave of energy to help with the process. She sat on the side of the thick metal rail, trembling. I wasn't going to push. She had to make the decision to jump herself. I continued my analysis of her God, "I prefer to think He's just an absentee landlord."

Her lips quivered. "What do you want from me?"

"Your life. Now jump."

She did. They always do.

The name's Megaera. I am one of the few people in this world that it is truly unpleasant to meet for just about everyone. This could have something to do with the fact that the people I meet generally die within a few days, or even hours. It could also have something to do with the fact that their deaths generally involve me (insert innocent looking smile here). But I like to think that if I wasn't here to kill you, I would be a blast to hang out with.

There's a very high probability that whatever god you believe in doesn't exist, unless you happen to belong to the ever-shrinking minority of people who believe in Zeus, Poseidon and company—or, I suppose, their inherited Roman counterparts. I am living, breathing testament to the fallacy of your religion—I am a Fury. I live in Hades, and I bring justice to criminals who slay their kin.

That's about all you need to know about me—I have two sisters, and we are the Erinyes in Greek Mythology, the Furies in Roman Mythology, and just really scary bitches in everything else. You probably haven't heard of us, but perhaps you've heard of Oedipus Rex—big shot hero, married his mom, killed his dad, and gouged his eyes out? Yeah. That was us.

What we do is bring justice to those who have avoided it. While we don't actually *kill* these people, we compel them to do that themselves, and we are very good at what we do. My sister Tisiphone is off in Miami tailing some football player who killed his wife in the nineties—I forget his name. My other sister, Alecto, is off stalking some fellow in Amsterdam. And I'm here, in Atlanta—at DragonCon. It's a coveted job—we all are keen on letting our wings unfold in public every once in a while.

Anyway, I was here to take care of a few jobs. You wouldn't believe how many fratricidal psychopaths get a kick out of dressing up as robots and playing *Magic: The Gathering*. Then again, maybe you would.

At any rate, Wanda was my first job at DragonCon. It had taken me about seven hours to break her, beginning this morning when I appeared behind her for an instant while she was washing her face in front of the mirror. I'm a sucker for that cheesy movie crap, I really am. The Technology Age really made people fear the strangest things. Next time, I'm crawling out of really staticky TV in nothing more than a white night dress and super greasy hair, but I get ahead of myself. Anyway, I'm not complaining—it's just fun to contrast the differences in tormenting Orestes and tormenting the polygamist Warren Jeffs.

Not that I have yet, but he's on my to-do list.

Okay, that's neither here nor there. What I meant to say is that I'm halfway done with my trip to DragonCon, which is upsetting because I really do enjoy walking among living, breathing, normal (kind of) human beings. Cerberus isn't the best company, you see, and I like humans. They can be a rotten bunch, but fun to toy with. Occasionally they can even carry on a conversation. But let me be the first to say that humans really, really freak out about death. Even the most stalwart role players would break ranks when death reared its ugly head—and that's precisely what was happening in the Hyatt atrium.

The truth is I couldn't have planned Wanda's death in a more picturesque fashion. I know that sounds sadistic, but it's kind of my job. Wanda was really helpful in dramatizing her death—her scream was among the shrillest, most genuine screams I'd ever heard. Trust me when I tell you I've heard a fair amount of screams in my day. Nearly every eye in the atrium was drawn to the careening woman, and nearly every mouth was agape in horror. The ever-considerate masses scattered as people tried to get out of Wanda's way. That or they didn't want blood to jack up their costumes. By the time she hit the ground, right smack dab in the bar area, she'd toppled several tall stools. Making kindling of one in particular.

In keeping with her trend of dying well, Wanda's body made

a delightful, bone-crunching *thud* as she hit the floor. I winced at approximately the same time a young woman (dressed as Xena the Warrior Princess, in case you were wondering) vomited across the floor. Considering the price of food at this con, it was the real tragedy of the day.

I quickly became disinterested in the body. All the fun goes out of it, and I mean that in the most literal sense. As usual, I was the lone possessor of that opinion since everyone swarmed around the corpse like snatching candy from a burst piñata. I took one last look at Wanda's body, and felt a bit like a young child who had broken a favorite doll. I never understood the fascination humans have with the dead. They kept their distance, of course, but not a single eye left Wanda or the broadening pool of blood she lay in.

A man with a katana was crouched over her, feeling her pulse as if there was any chance she had survived the fall. Obviously not, but people still grimaced when he ceremoniously stood up and shook his head dourly as if he was the harbinger of some shocking news. By the time the first eyes turned upwards to where Wanda had jumped, I had already made myself invisible and swooped down to the fifth floor, where my room and a pot of coffee waited.

And so I spent the next hour staring into a mug of java as if it could somehow liberate me from the pervasive sullenness that had settled over me. I really shouldn't drink this stuff—it tastes like shit. If it actually tasted half as good as it smelled, I would have to forgive all humans for their sins, both past and present, just because of that fact. I took a sip and grimaced.

And as the coffee chilled, my thoughts did as well. Okay, maybe Wanda wasn't the most deserving of her death, but why did I care? I was just doing my job. Still, it felt wrong. Big time. I shook my head to rid myself of the blasphemous thoughts. Maybe I was having a crisis of conscience, which was a nifty trick since I wasn't supposed to have one. I stood and stretched, trying to shake the memory of Wanda's tear-streaked face as she tipped over the edge. The sadness in those eyes spoke volumes.

I assured myself that Wanda was the worst of humanity, a kin-slayer; and I felt marginally better. By the time I left my room, my mind was on my next target.

His name was Brian Fawcett, and about two years ago he became the last person in his bloodline by poisoning his brother. The crime had been well-executed and, while the suspicions of the authorities had been aroused, there had never been enough proof for the law to find him guilty. The law of man was certainly not infallible, and guys like Brian escaped justice every day. Therein lay the problem: every criminal thought they could outsmart the justice system, and a fair few were right. Brian was smart, and that meant he would be harder to break than the mediocre Wanda.

But I had never failed.

I went to the railing and looked down at the atrium floor. The cops had situated themselves near Wanda's now-vacated landing spot. Scanning the floors that opened to the atrium below, I saw a veritable plague of blue uniforms on each one. Business had resumed to something that resembled normal, but there was no denying that a dark tone had settled over the con. A pair of officers huddled outside a door about fifteen yards away from me. They appeared to take interest in my presence. I considered cloaking myself, but instead decided to try and sidle past.

A balding man of about forty grabbed my elbow. It wasn't an unkind grasp but it was certainly firm. The movers and shakers in the Underworld wouldn't be overjoyed if I broke an innocent's wrist just because he wanted to ask a question. So I glowered at him but stopped walking.

"Miss, do you mind if we ask you a few questions?" His tone was meek, too meek to represent the iron hand of the law or the talon grip on my elbow. I removed my arm from his grasp.

"Not at all." But my mind hissed, *touch me again and I'll simmer your liver in that coffee pot back in my room*. Instead, I offered my most winning smile, but I sensed the writhing snakes and hemorrhaging eyes ruined the effect. The girls didn't get out in public much and they were partying down.

"Those real?"

I rolled my eyes up to the girls. "Yes, but I have a patent pending, so can't chit-chat about it." I made a zipping gesture across my lips.

"Bunch of smart asses around here." Baldy took out a notebook, licked his finger, and turned the pages until he got to a blank one. "Your name?"

"Do you mean my character's name, or my name?" I knew I didn't really have time to waste with these idiots, but I couldn't resist being cheeky.

Baldy just stared at me.

"Meghan." It was the name I always used when I had to give a human name, for the obvious reason that it sounded like Megaera but did not sound like it came from the second century.

Baldy stared expectantly at me, and his friend, an Italian guy who probably fancied the notion that he was a tough cop, gave me a withering look. I grinned and added, "Peterson. My name is Meghan Peterson."

"Date of birth? The year as well, please." My lip curled scornfully at his attempt at sarcasm. I vaguely considered telling him my true birth date, but he would probably have regarded my honesty (I was born in a time that now has "Before Common Era" after every year) as flippancy.

"A woman never tells her age. You should know that."

He rolled his eyes and jotted something down.

"What do you know about Wanda Vincent?"

"Not a damn thing."

"Oh, really?" Baldy glanced at his friend as he interjected. I stared passively at the Italian as he stepped close to me. I was tall for a woman, and a bit of the intimidation factor melted away when he stepped on his tip-toes to make our eyes level. "We have two sources that saw you with Vincent minutes before her death."

"I don't know who Wanda is, and I don't know what sources you're referring to. You'll need something more substantial than that." I wasn't going to yield an inch because I knew that admitting that I had been anywhere near Wanda at any point today would only mean further questions. And while it would not be hard to escape from that,

I always preferred to not forever scar people by vanishing suddenly, if they were not deserving of it.

I figured if I just played dumb for a while even the Italian would get bored—it looked like his enthusiasm had faded some when I had remained unfazed by his belligerence, and Baldy already looked like he wished he were anywhere else.

"Bullshit. Your exact description was given to us. Not a lot of people walking around with—" he gestured at the girls, "those things in their hair."

"There's a patent-pending, so I should hope not," I winked at Baldy.

"The witnesses . . ." The Italian thumbed through his notebook, " . . . Donald Smith and Jerry Anderson."

"Who? I'm sorry, those names mean very little to me."

"A robot and a pirate."

I grinned. "Well, there you have it! Who are you going to believe, a robot and a pirate, or the girl with a bleeding heart . . . okay, technically my eyes are bleeding, but you get the idea." I realized that such an argument held more water when I didn't have an eight foot wing-span, and though it took a few moments for the Italian to pick up on this obvious contradiction, he eventually did.

"And what are you supposed to be, Medusa?" He sneered, and elbowed Baldy as if he had said the funniest thing ever. My eyes narrowed.

Son of a bitch.

If there was one way to piss me off, it was to call me Medusa. No joke, I lost it there. Five seconds later the Italian was sitting on his ass with a broken nose, and Baldy lost his remaining hair. *No more comb-overs for you, Mister.*

I ducked around a corner, made myself invisible, and leapt into the atrium as if *I* was Wanda—a major difference being my ability to fly. I glided down to a secluded corner and scolded myself. I would not be able to truly reveal myself to anyone but my prey now, which is a huge downer since I'd be wasting a perfectly good DragonCon. I supposed I could find another disguise. I reminded myself that this was secondary to finding and eliminating my target, but what was the big rush? I didn't have anything to do but kill Brian today.

While I could change my image in ten seconds flat to make myself a troll or samurai or fox-woman, I couldn't settle on which one. I rarely dressed up for anything, really, and that's a real drag since I'd been around for a few eons.

Next thing I knew, I was squeezing myself between Aragorn and Boromir in an attempt to get through the crowd. I had transformed to fox-woman, complete with twitching whiskers and a sporting fluffy tail. The girls weren't too happy with their banishment, but hey, they had their fun. Time to find my target.

I thrust my arms out and released the energy into the Hyatt. It cascaded, emanating across the crowd in ever-expanding concentric circles. And then I felt him, like a fish tugging at its line. I followed the vibes. When I'm hunting all sound recedes. An eerie silence devours everything; the lips of con participants open and close in conversations that I can't hear.

And then I heard a pop, almost like a cork had been disengaged from a large bottle. Each individual noise punched through the soundless barrier. The clatter of costumes collided with the hum of conversations. My gaze swept the space settling on my target: Brian Fawcett.

He had straight silver hair of moderate length and a rather pale complexion. His eyes were a piercing blue color that I noticed from across the room, but what distinguished him from anyone else in the room was the fact that he was not dressed up like he was born a thousand years in the past or future: he wore khaki pants and a blue polo shirt. He certainly didn't look like a murderer—but I'd found over the years that such a thing wasn't uncommon.

The only reason I knew it was him was because I have an eye for such things—two eyes, actually. My vision is as good as any creature alive, but what truly distinguishes it from a normal being is that it can see beyond the material world. I can see the worst in people—for instance, the Italian cop had once essentially tortured an innocent man in a sadistic attempt to assert his dominance (that fact made my punch all the easier—but it was secondary to the Medusa remark) and Captain Kidd, the dude from the elevator earlier, once ran over a Yorkie-poo and never so much as stopped.

So much evil in the world, so little time.

The point is, the moment my eyes passed over Brian, I could see that he had killed his brother. The strange thing was that I found my attention drawn to him before it even registered that he was a murderer. When my gaze fell over him, I found that he was staring unwaveringly at me. He didn't even try and avert his gaze when I noticed it. If anything, those piercing blue eyes seemed to scope every part of me. He wasn't checking me out because I looked hot, either; he was evaluating me, judging me. Okay, this just doesn't happen. Ever.

I shuddered. His eyes seemed inhuman, though I knew that there was nothing visibly strange about his gaze. I wondered if I was getting sick. It happened once during the Plague. I'd rather not remember, thank you very much.

Anyway, driving a person to insanity is not an easy thing to do. It helps to become familiar with the workings of his or her mind. For Wanda, there were many phobias I could exploit—knowing that she had a fear of spiders, for instance, had allowed me to really freak her out by penetrating her mind and making her believe she was in a veritable river of tarantulas, black widows, and daddy longlegs (daddy longlegs totally give me the creeps . . . strange, I know, since I flit about with pet snakes in my hair).

I generally spend about an hour or so scoping the mind of a person before ever revealing myself to them, but I got the strangest sense that Brian was not only aware of my presence, but privy to something I wasn't.

Either that or I was hallucinating from bad coffee.

Whatever the reasons, I found myself terrified of the task before me. Still, I picked my way through the crowd in his direction trying to appear nonchalant. The crowd parted around him like a boulder in a stream. Though I deliberately watched the glass elevators sweep up and down, chock full of strange creatures, I could feel his unnatural stare boring into me.

The closer I got, the louder my heart echoed in my ears. Soon I was only a few feet away from him. I forced myself to look at him. He stared back at me unblinkingly. I felt as if we were engaging in some juvenile game of "Don't Blink." I mustered up my toughest Fury stare while he sat unperturbed by a look that had sent many a king over the edge. I didn't know whether I should run screaming in the night, or beat the shit out of him.

I decided to dazzle him with the power of my intellect instead. "What are you looking at?" Brilliant. I know.

He stared at me wordlessly. I'd like to think I humbled him with my withering cross examination, but I was the one more creeped out by him. It made no sense—I regularly had afternoon tea with the desperate housewives of Hades (a really scary bunch, I might add). Yet this guy, who looked about as threatening as a mayonnaise sandwich, set my teeth on edge and strummed every nerve in my body. I decided to ratchet up my verbal assault on the man. "Well? Cat got your tongue?"

"Not really."

Well, at least he said something. But it didn't exactly shed light on the situation. Was he being sarcastic? I found myself to be a curious blend of pissed-off and fearful. I scolded myself for letting my emotions get the better of me—it's not like I didn't serve up my victims with a side dish of smart ass. I mean, come on, I called myself a Happy Harvester just hours earlier. Wouldn't you want to smack me around if given the chance?

Okay, so friendly chit-chat was not going to work with Brian here. I decided to expedite the process by entering his mind and toying with it a bit. I closed my eyes and soon my vision was his: I could feel every fluctuation of his emotions as if they were my own; I could feel the snugness of his too-small loafers; I could taste the spaghetti he had eaten last night and could feel the nagging hunger that accompanied his lack of eating today. And as I began to settle myself smugly in the corner of his mind and familiarize myself with his darkest fears, I was suddenly and brutally evicted from his thoughts. I surged back into my own body and staggered backwards into a passing werewolf that grunted indignantly.

I was naturally surprised—that had never happened before—and I knew my eyes were as wide as saucers as I gaped at him. He actually looked a bit shocked himself, though I could not tell if his surprise was an indication that he was aware of my intrusion or surprised at the flailing about that I did as I was expelled from his mind. I had looked about as graceful as an epileptic at a disco.

I gritted my teeth and tried to reenter his mind, only to find some sort of barrier preventing my entrance. I had absolutely no explanation for this. Even incredibly strong minds melted at my touch. And here I was, being bested by a mere human, a human of no great importance.

Could he be protected by some divine right? Athena had protected Orestes from our wrath—but only when Orestes had prayed to Apollo, who had ordered Orestes to murder his mother. Every now and then, Hades granted clemency, but no one in the last few hundred years had been protected or had bested us. I had difficulty with the idea that a man of such unassuming demeanor could shatter my hot streak.

Couldn't he at least be dressed as a Pirate?

"What are you?" My voice was not particularly loud amidst the roar of the crowd, but he somehow heard me.

"My name is—"

"I know what your name is. You are Brian Fawcett, and you killed your brother. You were born on November seventh, nineteen fifty seven. You used to have two siblings, but your younger sister drowned when you were six. Your alcoholic father died in a car accident when you were seventeen. You and your older brother moved to Indianapolis. The two of you enrolled in a community college and worked in various janitorial positions until you graduated. Near the end of college, you fell in love with a woman named Diane, who you dated for some time. She left you when you were twenty-six. You killed your brother when you were twenty-seven. I don't know why. Did I miss anything?" I smirked, confident that I had shaken his psyche enough to elicit some surprised response. I had not been in his mind for long, but in that short term I had gleaned the general outline of his life.

The smirk fell from my face when he merely laughed brazenly and shook his head.

"Wrong, wrong, and did I mention wrong? Although bonus points for getting the killing my brother part right, which is the reason I got this job in the first place, but I digress. We were talking about why you were confusing me with someone else, Megaera."

I felt the blood drain from my face. I did not know how he knew my name, or what else about me he could possibly know. Icy trepidation gripped my heart. Not only had my principal weapons been ineffectual against him, the attempt at reading his thoughts backfired big time.

I said something that sounded like "gaaa," another sterling example of my loquaciousness. I just couldn't wrap my mind around what was happening, much less form a coherent sentence.

"So, Megaera, if you are here to kill me, you should perhaps pursue a different strategy. You'll find my thoughts aren't so easily fragmented as hers." He gestured vaguely in the direction where Wanda had lain.

Another chill shook me. He knew precisely what I was doing here and what had already been done here. What was I supposed to do with this guy if he had the power to block my primary attack? I wondered if he infiltrated my own thoughts, but I definitely would have been able to detect such an intrusion. Besides, I had wards set up to protect myself from an assault. One perk of working for an all-powerful deity like Hades is that his health insurance policy is pretty damn comprehensive.

"What are you?" At least I'd graduated from "gaaa." Making progress here.

"My name is not Brian Fawcett—he doesn't exist. As you've probably deduced, those who call me human are flexibly using the term. My name is Karian, and we work for the same person—Hades."

"Ha!" It sounded as loud and fake to my own ears, as it must have to his. I knew he spoke the truth despite the fact that I had never heard of "Karian." I said as much.

He smiled knowingly but joylessly. "No human and very few deities have heard of me. I work in the shadows. My task is to find the deities who try and run . . . "

I laughed that high nervous thing I had just developed. "Oh, so you're sort of a LoJack for the Gods? A GPS for deities on the run?" I tried to smile to show him how cool I was, but I'm pretty sure it looked like a grimace. Still, I pushed on. "Oops. Kinda messed up here, ol' Karian, I'm not lost or running. I'm just doing my job."

"Let me finish. I'm also here to dispatch those who displease Hades."

My heart literally crash-dived into my gut.

He continued, "I have killed men and gods. In some ways, I am like you, with different tactics and slightly different objectives. I don't often do things for Hades, since rarely does he care enough to kill someone without being able to do it himself. But he's busy, as you know—which is why he sent me here." His tone had become hard and icy, and fear ignited, hot and fast, in my chest.

I hadn't done a thing to incur Hades' wrath. I opened my mouth to object but, before I could, I felt a crushing blow in my gut. He hadn't so much as lifted a finger when I found myself lifted off my feet and barreling through the crowd. I landed on my back a few yards away. Gasping for breath, I lifted myself slowly to my feet. Well, that was fun!

Karian had not moved the entire time, but he now stepped forward so that he was about a yard away from me. The crowd peered at us curiously and, although many continued with their business, many more stopped to find out what was happening.

"You may be asking yourself, 'Oh Gods, why me?' I suppose I should grace you with an explanation, if only so your damned soul does not haunt me from the Underworld. You know as well as I do that Hades demands unequivocal, unwavering, unquestioning allegiance—which is why I am carrying out this task, though I must admit a small part of me is remorseful. We have observed your last few missions, and it has become clear to us that you are not committed to your objectives."

"Wait a minute, Hades is firing me because I don't have a 'go get 'em sport' attitude?"

"Putting it crudely, yes."

"So it's not enough to dispatch my target with brutal efficiency; instead he wants me to turn a few cartwheels and wave my pom-poms after I execute them? Am I hearing you correctly?"

Karian shook his head. "We know you wonder why you must fracture the sanity of a woman like Wanda; I know you wonder why what she did was so bad; I know you thought her grandfather, who raped her and killed a friend of hers, deserved death; I know you questioned why you were commanded to kill someone like Wanda when men like her grandfather eluded your wrath."

"Maybe Hades needs to think outside the box, been hanging out in Hades—oh wait, his namesake—a little too long. I ask you, Karian, who is more dangerous, a homicidal pedophile or a woman who killed her rapist relative?"

"You exist only to avenge the kindred souls who were murdered." His blue eyes were as steely as arctic ice. "Our Lord is all-knowing. He has concluded that it would not be long before you wavered from your task, from your ruthlessness—after all, you almost decided not to pursue Brian. Hades is not willing to tolerate such disloyalty, and though you have not yet faltered, you will."

"So I'm to be executed on a hunch?"

"Precisely."

"You know that's just swell. Really marvelous." I was stalling. My thoughts scatter-shot in a million directions. *Think*. It's not like I could plead with him when he had a contract with Hades for my life. I knew that the only way I would survive is by besting Karian in combat. That would be tricky since he had the blessing of Hades and I no longer did. I needed a plan yesterday. I thought about contacting my sisters, but tossed that idea out pretty quickly. All messages to them were channeled through the Underworld, and Hades would surely intercept them and manipulate them.

It also meant that my mind was no longer protected by Hades, and hence if it was within Karian's power he would know precisely every action I was to take and easily defeat me. He gave no indication that he was aware of my thoughts, however; and it occurred to me that his intimacy with my history had nothing to do with reading my thoughts but rather knowledge granted him by Hades. If I was wrong, I was doomed either way. If I was right, I had a chance of survival, however remote.

The crowd around us apparently thought this was some kind of act. While a few people had grown bored and moved on, far more had gathered to watch. A few even laughed at the vicious scowl I shot at Karian. I even heard a portly man in a shiny suit of armor murmur a remark to his horse-faced queen of a companion about what a talentless actress I was. I memorized his face so I could knock his teeth out at my leisure should I survive. I launched myself into the air and my fox-red hair fell away as my body contorted into its natural shape. Wings sprung out of my back and I flew into the center of the room. The crowd oohed and aahed at this stunning display of special effects.

Karian stared at me passively, shrugged, and mimicked my display, though perhaps even more impressively. His entire skin seemed to shed away as he leapt into the air, a dark being emerged from his body. He was the picture of dead: his eyes glowed a flashing red, and he looked unlike any creature I had ever seen. His skin was as black as coal and he unsheathed enormous, terrifying claws. His wings were broad and leathery, like a bat's, and his head was reptilian and slimy. He was more repulsive than any creature I'd seen at DragonCon, even nastier than that teenage boy who approached me earlier, and *that* was saying a lot.

He flew until he was level with me and snorted. His voice was now darker and deeper. It sent shivers down my spine.

"You think that you can possibly defeat me? I once bested Ares in a sparring match. You are only further violating the code you've sworn to—these mortals must now perish to obviate the damage you've done." His voice was calm, but it felt like he was snarling at me.

I wasn't one to balk at death. Matter of fact, I pick on the humans about their lack of composure when facing their own mortality. But maybe I'd been a little hard on them; now my ass was on the line. Score one for the humans.

Still, I wouldn't go down without a fight even though I was keenly aware of the power that reverberated from him. My primary weapon was to use a man against himself, to drive him to take his own life. I couldn't do that against a being of Karian's potency. I surveyed my surroundings to see if I could discern any way to use the terrain to my advantage. No brilliant strategy came to mind. Just great.

Shrugging, I peered through the crowd of police officers and role players. I sent out powerful mental messages to a policeman leaning against a wall gawking at me, as well as a man with a katana that I recognized as the one who felt Wanda's pulse. I worked quickly, distorting their reality and pleading with them to toss me their weapons.

The policeman hesitatingly removed his pistol from its holster and lobbed it at me, looking bewildered as he did it. The man with the katana was equally befuddled, but he threw the sword in my direction. I caught both and immediately began firing the gun at Karian, who seemed surprised at the sudden assault. Several bullets bored into his body and he snarled in pain, but to my horror the holes made by my attack quickly disappeared as his body regenerated itself. After discharging all my ammunition, Karian looked as if he had been unaffected by my strike. I let the gun fall from my hand into the now-entranced crowd of people, and braced myself as Karian launched himself at me.

I swung the katana at him as he came, but he only grabbed the blade and snapped it like a twig. I had no time to react, as he seized me and crashed me into a wall. The wind knocked from my body and my teeth snapped shut with such force that I saw stars. He sank his teeth into my shoulder. I moaned at the intense pain that wracked my body, and my vision became blurred as his claws sliced at my neck. Gritting my teeth, I pushed him with all my force, while slamming my knee into his groin. He screeched, but released me. I spun away and resumed flight, looking over my shoulder at Karian, who was slowly turning around.

My blood was running freely and dripped over the crowd as I soared above them. Everyone still seemed to believe this was some sort of show, albeit the best one they'd ever seen. I had now realized that in straight combat, there was absolutely no chance of my defeating Karian. He was extremely powerful, and it had taken all my strength just to defend against his onslaught. There was no glaring weakness in his combat style, nor was there any apparent vulnerability I could exploit. I began to experience a feeling I had only heard of in stories and in observing my prey: despair.

His mind was impervious to my manipulation, and I simply did not have access to the weaponry necessary to bring him down.

Or did I? No being was infallible. All had weaknesses: Achilles had his heel, Zeus his womanizing, Hades his jealousy of his powerful brother. As much as I hated to admit it, Karian was a stronger version of me. He himself had pointed out our similarities. I could only hope that he had the same weaknesses I did.

There's something that a lot of people don't know about a vampire's aversion to garlic and sunlight, or a werewolf's aversion to silver, or a fairy's aversion to iron: it's bullshit. The principle reason is that those creatures don't actually exist. Believe me, I would know if they did. But the lore actually had some truth in it. Find the weakness and exploit it.

Ouranos, from who I had been begotten, had such a vulnerability: silver. It's a fact unobserved by historians and dabblers in Greek mythology because such knowledge was dangerous—armed with such knowledge, humanity could have overcome divinity. I had inherited this vulnerability, as had all the creatures fathered by Ouranos—and surprise, surprise, so must have Karian.

The inherent difficulty was that I could not so much as handle silver without bringing excruciating pain to myself. But if I could penetrate Karian's heart with silver, he would surely die. And if he did not, then his power was unparalleled, and I was condemned. I obviously had nothing to lose, so I began to scan the crowd for a piece of silver large enough to kill Karian with.

By this time, Karian had flown up level with me, and I could tell he was watching me warily. He exuded confidence, but he was neither stupid nor arrogant, and he knew that I was not resigned to my fate. I could feel his crimson eyes weighing me, evaluating me, preparing to strike, and I knew I must act quickly.

My eyes settled on a beautiful woman in a flowing dress. Her name was Terry Patterson. She had flowing brown hair and an impossibly tiny waist that was cinched with a large, hammered silver belt. Her eyes locked with mine for a split second. I sent her a plea while swooping down toward her. The air around me vibrated as Karian moved to intercept me. I was about a foot away from Terry when Karian barreled into me, sending me skidding across the tile floor in a path made by the frantically parting crowd.

I careened into the wall and felt my right wing snap from the impact. I got up dizzily, wincing in pain, and through my blurred vision I could see the beast advancing on me. I shook my head to regain my dazzled senses, and leapt to the side as he slashed with his lethal claws. He ravaged through the delicate webbing on my other wing, and I stumbled away clumsily to escape his wrath.

I knew I could no longer fly—my wings were tattered and hung uselessly from my back. I groaned and found Terry again. Karian was rounding on me, preparing to finish me off. I knew I had little time and I sprinted to the woman. She'd received my message and unhooked the belt, tossing it while I was in mid-leap. My hand latched around the silver part as I caught it.

The pain was excruciating.

Smoke billowed from my palm, and I let out a shrill wail that made me reminisce of Wanda's spectacular death. I had never felt such pain, and flames danced from the spot where the silver burned my skin. I barely could retain my senses, but managed to seize the leather portion of the belt. The relief was instantaneous.

I spun around to meet Karian, who dashed towards me. He slammed into me with such force I didn't have time to react. He seized me as his powerful wings pumped to lift us in the air. I couldn't breath or move, but somehow I managed to press the belt against those talons. His grasp loosened just enough for me to wriggle my arms free. I arched my back while snapping the belt loose. It whipped around his backside and I seized both ends. I pushed the silver flat against his throat. His eyes bulged. Fire sizzled at the apex of his neck. I gritted my teeth. "See you in Hades, bastard."

He howled in pain, and his wings immediately stopped beating. We crashed into the floor. I pulled with all my strength as the creature writhed beneath my grip. The sound of agony was indescribable as it thundered through the hotel. Fire ignited and I watched as his face collapsed into the growing hole at his throat. When his body stopped thrashing, I released the belt and watched as the silver disappeared into the quick burning inferno that consumed him.

I rolled away from him, looking at the blackened palm of my hand. It smoked like a campfire that had just been doused, and I cradled it in my good arm. Tears sprang to my eyes and mingled with the blood on my face. I looked at Karian, whose body dissolved into ashes. He was gone. Completely. The only thing remaining was Terry's belt.

I got to my feet, picked up the belt, careful not to touch the silver and carried it back to the regal woman who stood waiting. I handed it to her. "Thank you."

I had never spoken those words to another being ever. Especially to a human.

"You're welcome."

I nodded and turned to face the silent crowd. Suddenly, they erupted into applause. I let a rare smile creep across my face as I realized that even humans such as this were not inclined to believe anything that might unravel the fabric of their reality. So I bowed, and turned, and left the hotel.

My name is Megaera. I was once the harbinger of justice, until I realized that it was not justice at all—I am now a renegade. It's been a few weeks since my excursion in DragonCon, and I do not yet know what I shall do. I may continue to fight evil, I may not. I may fight alongside my sisters, or against them. But I will not fight for that which is not just, and I will remain fervent in my opposition to my former mission. If that means fighting Hades himself, so be it.

He was always kind of a jerk anyway.

RULES OF ENGAGEMENT

Susan Sizemore

"I don't do dragons."

"I—see."

Sara didn't, but she duly tapped this information into the form on her laptop. She rather hoped, with all the noise echoing around the Hyatt lobby, that she hadn't heard correctly, but her client's next statement left her in no doubt.

"I mean, they are *so* arrogant. When you're with them they don't focus on *you*. Oh, no, a dragon is always smugly preening and looking around to make sure everyone's aware of how gorgeous they are. They used to hoard gold; now their greed's turned to feeding their egos."

"I—see."

Sara hated repeating herself, but what did one say to a maniac? Maybe "maniac" wasn't quite the right word. Maybe this client was just very deeply into role-playing. Many of the thousands of people gathered at this Atlanta convention were into that sort of thing. She wished she'd had more time to read Beth's notes before conducting her first interview of the day, but she'd been running late and was under-slept (how did anyone get any rest with the all-night noise that roared up from the lobby?) when she met "Lady Cassandra" for this consultation over breakfast.

Sara took a sip of coffee, trying to buy time to get her wits about her, and hoping a hit of caffeine would help make this seem more real. It didn't help when a dozen or so semi-naked men pretending to be Spartan warriors marched by. Many of them were quite buff in their little leather Speedos. They all carried bronze shields. Costumed con-goers were everywhere and the day was—Sara checked her watch—incredibly young.

Sara gestured toward the Spartans. "Perhaps one of them—?"

After all, Lady Cassandra was dressed in white, flowing robes that were perhaps intended to look like ancient Greek clothing.

Lady Cassandra gave a disdainful glance across the low wall that separated the restaurant from the open lobby, just as someone dressed in a purple dinosaur suit blundered by. "Mortals?" she scoffed. Her dark eyes sparked with fury. "Do you think I'm interested in mortals?"

"Um—well . . . " Sara was totally at sea. All she could do was quote company advertising copy. "Matchmaking is an art that Bethany Thorson and Associates have perfected to a science. We guarantee that our clients will find the right person, at the right time and in the right place to spark the right chemistry that forms everlasting love." She smiled wanly as she finished this treacle-coated crap.

Lady Cassandra sighed dramatically. "You don't believe a word I'm saying, do you? That's all right, I'm used to it."

"No, no," Sara hastened to say. Where was Beth? She was supposed to help her through her first couple of interviews. She had to soldier on without her boss. "No dragons. Yes, well. Why don't you tell me about the sort of person that does interest you?"

Lady Cassandra touched a blood red nail to her delicately pointed chin. "Space pirates are good for a fling, but I'm so over that part of my life. Demigods are not on the agenda, either. Been there, done that. I need stability. Someone who'll come home more often than a superhero is also required. I don't want any of those, 'Honey, I have to save the world, I'll see you whenever I get back' excuses. They know you can't argue with that, even if really takes ten seconds to push the asteroid out of earth's path and they spend the rest of the month high rolling in Vegas."

Lady Cassandra continued to speak, while Sara stared at her, completely helpless.

"I knew this was a bad idea," Beth muttered as she caught sight of Sara and the demigoddess. Sara looked thunderstruck. Cassandra looked like she was about to throw lightning. Beth wove through the crowd, hoping to salvage the situation.

Beth Thorson was the absolute best matchmaker in all the multiverse—she had an award back in her office in L.A. to attest to it—and this was her busiest time of year. And this year DragonCon was going to be more of a challenge than usual.

It would have helped if Linda hadn't been put on bed rest when the baby wasn't due for another four months. Sara was certainly an excellent matchmaker, and even though she'd never been to a con before, she was into the same sorts of books, movies, television series, games and other hobbies that interested the people who attended DragonCon. Beth knew that Sara was going to fit right in working with their mortal clientele. Beth's original plan was that she and Linda would take the supernatural appointments as they had in years before. But this year things hadn't worked out the way they were supposed to. Disaster was in the offing. Beth smiled. Immanent disaster was one of her favorite challenges.

She hurried up to the table and drew Sara aside.

When they were out of earshot of Cassandra, Sara said, "I think she really believes—"

"I know." Beth grasped Sara by the shoulders. She didn't think her young protégé was likely to bolt, but a firm grasp helped to make sure. Besides, it was meant to be comforting. She looked Sara in the eye and said slowly and firmly, "Her reality is every bit as real as your reality. There are many realities, and Atlanta, Georgia, over Labor Day weekend is one of those points in the multiverse where realities converge for a short time. It has to do with the belief in multiple possibilities that all these thousands of multi-media fandoms generate—like Dorothy's believing that *There's no place like home* could really get her back to Kansas. Though why she wanted to go back to Kansas doesn't really make a lot of sense. But then, I'm a California girl."

"Multiverse. Reality," Sara repeated. "Realities." Her gaze shifted away from Beth. She was focused on someone in a large white rabbit costume when she said, "I see."

"People come to DragonCon for many reasons," Beth went doggedly on. "They come to meet friends that share the same interests. They come to see the guests, to hear the music, to shop, to go to panels, to wear costumes, to go to parties, to game. Some come hoping to meet their ideal mate. That's why we're here."

"I knew all this coming in," Sara reminded her.

Beth found that she was reluctant to go any deeper into the truth at the moment. Maybe it was better to find out some things in one's own time—which meant the hard way. She had a backlog of clients to deal with anyway.

"I'll tell you what, Sara. I'll finish the interview with Cassandra. I'm supposed to be meeting with Prince Barahael in the Hilton lobby in ten minutes. Double booked is not good. I need you to go over there and bring him to the Hyatt. Be charming."

Sara looked dubious. "Ten minutes isn't much time to get from here to there and back again. How do I recognize him in this crowd? Aren't I always charming?"

"No, but you're polite and discreet and that's usually good enough. Barahael's a high elf lord. You'll recognize him when you see him. Go."

"High elf lord, my ass," Sara muttered as she hurried down the steps at the back entrance of the Hyatt. From there she had to cross the street and go through the Marriott and across another street to get to the Hilton, going downhill from one DragonCon venue to the next—much like the day, she suspected. She was alternately blasted by hot humid outside air and the frigid temperatures of hotel air conditioning. Sweat. Freeze. Sweat. Freeze. The physical discomfort didn't help her mood any. But the sights and sounds did make her smile. The energy generated by this eclectic crowd was invigorating. Sara just didn't like the notion that maybe a few of them were more than a little bit out of the mainstream. At least, she didn't like the notion of working with complete nutjobs—or suspecting that her boss was one of the nutjobs.

"Oh, rats," she complained once she finally reached the Hilton lobby. "Elf lords are thick on the ground over here."

Beth hadn't told her where she was supposed to meet this Barahael person. How did one pick one elf lord out of thousands of milling fans, some of them in sort of elf costumes? Not to mention the ones dressed like Sephiroth or elfy-looking anime characters. All Sara could do was wander around and hope for the best. Especially after she discovered that Beth wasn't answering her cell phone. Either her usual black one, or the large bright red one with too many numbers and odd symbols that was her *special* phone.

She said hello to several false Barahael's before she encountered the crowd outside one of the Dealers' Halls. There were people gathered ten deep around a shouting man, cameras and camera phones were being held up like lighters at a rock concert.

The shouting man paid no attention to the buzzing, flashing circle around him. He kept right on shouting questions at the short man in front of him. Not that it did him any good, because the person he'd chosen to speak to was dressed as Silent Bob, and he was not breaking character.

The Bob just looked on in a benign, bemused way, and occasionally gave a little shrug. People chuckled.

When Sara finally took a good look at the cause of all the commotion, she realized what Beth had meant by *You'll recognize him when you see him*. If that man wasn't an elf, he damned well ought to be. He sort of *shone*. And it wasn't just because he was dressed in silver and white and had platinum hair down to his ass. Whatever makeup he was wearing gave his skin a translucent sheen that seemed like an inner glow. Sara didn't recognize the language he was shouting, but he had the most beautiful voice she'd ever heard.

Sara worked her way to the front of the crowd and called, "Prince Barahael?"

The elf immediately turned his gaze on her. What color were those eyes, anyway? Silver? Aquamarine? Where did he get the specialty contact lenses? Could he actually see anything?

None of these questions mattered when he spoke to her. "Good morrow, beautiful lady. How may I serve you?"

He was not speaking English, but Sara somehow knew that as long as his attention was on her she was able to understand him. She hoped that he could understand her.

"I think I'm here to serve you," she responded. "That is, if you have an appointment with Beth Thorson."

His smile was bright enough to light up the world. More photos were snapped. He stepped closer to her. Sara fought the urge to let her knees buckle.

"Meeting with Lady Beth is indeed my mission," Prince Barahael said. "Please lead me to her. "And you are, dear maiden—?"

Sara fought the urge to tell him that she wasn't particularly dear, and certainly not a maiden, but that would have been neither polite nor discreet. Besides, it sounded cute coming from the elf prince. She guessed you could put up with a lot from guys with pointy ears— which possibly explained why her mother'd always had it so bad for Mr. Spock.

"Sara," she told him as he took her arm. And he was the one who actually did the leading, at her direction. Somehow he managed to slip them through the crowd with a speed and grace that boggled her mind. Maybe it helped that people tended to stop and stare at him as they passed—and these were people who were used to seeing brilliant costume work.

His current surroundings were totally alien, and Prince Barahael of the Silver Kingdom was completely wary though he walked with the appearance of utter confidence. He did not trust the treaty with the Golden Elves to hold. He was not sure if this strange meeting place crowded with mortals was meant as an insult or a trap. The treaty stipulated that no mortal was to be harmed, so he walked here without any weapon other than the natural magic of his kind. *He* came in peace. Whether his betrothed did so was yet to be seen. He kept a close eye on his mortal guide, determined with all his honor to keep the innocent woman safe if being at his side put her in danger.

Though they passed many a strange sight on the journey through the maze of buildings, none of them evoked any alarm in the young woman. When they reached her lady, the Lady of Thorson was with a centaur.

The centaur woman was under a glamour, but Barahael saw through the illusion of mortal shape and bowed deeply. "Ally of old, I welcome you."

The centaur snickered as she rose to her feet to return the bow. "Lord Prince, I pledge my bow to your service."

He gave her a gracious smile. "Then stand at my side at my wedding."

The centaur gasped. "So the rumor of an alliance with the Golden Ones is true?"

"It will be truth soon." He bowed to Lady Thorson. "Greetings, Facilitator Between the Worlds."

Beth liked the title, but she wasn't so sure she liked the conversation between her two clients. "What do you mean by alliance?" she asked the elf prince. "I've arranged for you to meet the heiress of the Golden Realm in my capacity as a matchmaker." She'd promised each of the elves to find them a mate, and that was all. "Diplomacy will cost you extra. You do know that, don't you? You signed a contract."

"I honor my pledged work," he told her. "Does the Golden Princess?"

This was a problematical question, but Beth was prepared to explain the delay. "The Golden Council has expressed some concern about security issues."

Which was, technically, true, but those concerns had been voiced several weeks before. The Princess was just late and Beth was covering for her. Beth did not pretend to herself that the princess was a spoiled rotten little bitch, but she said, "She is a shy, delicate lady, so she is hesitating to cross into a such a boisterous, loud assemblage as here in this meeting place. She is working up her courage—"

"I saw her courage at the Battle of Greyhound Fields," Asli the centaur spoke up.

Beth was about to tell the centaur that if she couldn't say anything helpful, then not to say anything at all.

But Asli went on. "That was where the Golden One and all her bodyguards turned and fled the field of battle."

Beth subtracted ten percent off the centaur's fee. "There, you see, Lord Barahael? She obviously doesn't like crowds." Battlefields were crowded, right? "I know that she's anxious to meet you, but is uncomfortable with the only neutral territory where your meeting is possible. I'm sure she'll be here soon."

Barahael nodded reluctantly. Beth could tell that he was trying hard to be convinced. And that he wasn't any more anxious to meet the elf girl than she was him. Hmmm . . . well, if they didn't want each other, she'd work out something else for each of them. There just better not be the peace of a couple of worlds at stake, because she would be the only one happy when the Elves of Silver and Gold received the bill.

"I will await her coming—for now," Barahael said. "Send word that I offer her my protection among all these strangers."

"I'll do that. I'm sure she'll appreciate your gallantry. I'll let you know as soon as she arrives. Why don't you enjoy the con while you wait?" She looked at her watch. "Look at the time! I'm meeting a troll at the Marriott in five minutes. I'll check in with both of you in a bit," she told her supernatural clients. She took Sara aside before leaving. "Here's your laptop. You know your schedule for this afternoon?"

"Thanks. Yes." She gave Barahael a dubious look.

"Don't worry, there's no one else like him on your schedule."

"I don't think there is anyone else like him," Sara answered. She sounded relieved, but Beth made a note of the hormonally stunned look in her assistant's eyes.

"Keep an eye on Barahael if you get the chance. Make sure he's doing all right. I think he could use some looking after."

She didn't wait for Sara's response before rushing off to her next appointment.

That man doesn't need looking after, Sara thought as Barahael went by with the mostly female posse he'd gathered over the last couple of days. *What that man needs is a security force to keep the straight women and gay guys off him.*

Then she noticed the trio bringing up the rear of Team Bara-hael. They were wearing Air Force uniforms sporting *Stargate* sleeve patches. She wasn't sure if it was legal for the costumers to appear so legitimately military, but they certainly looked like an armed honor guard. Those rifles weren't real, were they?

Keeping an eye on Barahael hadn't been difficult while she went about her duties, since he seemed to be everywhere. His startling good looks and amazing costumes certainly drew the eye, and attention, and lots of friends. The Cosplay kids had taken him as their hero. He was the hit of the convention, which certainly said a lot, considering the thousands of people who were here, including famous actors and authors.

Let him party, she thought grudgingly as she returned her attention to her client across the table.

"Did you see that elf?" the client asked. "Can you get me an introduction to him?"

Sara forced a smile. "I can certainly try. Now, Ms. Fuller—"

"Sara, fair maiden, you work too hard. Come, have a respite." Barahael was at her side, his hand lightly on her shoulder.

Sara looked up, and spoke over the sound of her client's loud sigh. "I—" Those eyes! "—I'll be with you in a moment." She wrote a name and room number down on a slip of paper. "Here," she said to Ms. Fuller. "Give him a call." She closed her laptop and got to her feet.

"What novelty would please your heart?" Barahael asked. "I am at your service to provide it."

His smile dazzled. His expression was utterly sincere. The man absolutely never broke character, but since his elf lord character was such a nice person, the chivalrous persona was utterly endearing.

"I know what I'd like to do," she answered. She glanced toward the crowds waiting in the elevator alcove. "But the timing is impossible."

"Nothing is impossible," he answered.

"You obviously aren't staying at the Hyatt." Not enough elevators for too many people. "My favorite writer's doing a book signing, but I left the book I want autographed in my room. There's no way I can get to my room and to the signing before she's finished."

Barahael solemnly contemplated her problem before he nodded. "I see. Come with me." He led her toward the elevators and the crowd parted like the sea before Moses. Not only that, the doors of an empty elevator opened just as they reached it. They stepped inside, and no one pushed in after them.

Sara stared at Barahael in gape-mouthed wonder. "You really are a magical being!"

His silver-aquamarine eyes twinkled. "It would appear so."

Sara put her keycard into the reader and rode beside Barahael in stunned silence up to the Concierge level. Once in her room she decided to get more into the spirit of the con and changed into the *"Have fun storming the castle"* tee-shirt she'd bought as a present for her sister.

Barahael waited patiently while she tucked her laptop in a drawer and grabbed the fantasy novel, but he stepped in front of the door when she turned to leave. He held up a hand. "One moment, please."

She thought *I'm alone in a bedroom with the most gorgeous man in the universe. Maybe . . . .*

"Has Lady Beth had any word of the Golden Princess?"

Right. He was a client waiting for a potential hook-up. How had she forgotten that? "I don't believe so," she answered.

He nodded gravely. "I fear that trouble may be brewing."

She didn't know what he meant, but she immediately took out her phone and called Beth. "Boss, do you have any—?"

"Do you know where Barahael is?" Beth cut her off.

"With me. In my room."

"Lucky girl. Get him down here."

"And *down here* is?"

"The dealer's area in the basement of the Hilton. I think all hell is about to break loose, and I do not mean that metaphorically." Beth hung up.

Sara looked at Barahael.

"I heard," he said. "For safety's sake perhaps you should—"

"When my boss tells me to get someone somewhere, I do as I'm told." Sara wasn't afraid of hell, but she was afraid of Beth Thorson's temper. "Let's go."

He took a moment to kiss her hand. "Your bravery warms my heart."

She tingled all over and wore a dazed smile all the way to the dealers' room.

Along the way people kept joining them, starting with Asli—who seemed to have acquired a bow and quiver of arrows without anyone working security noticing. Barahael didn't say or overtly do anything, but it was like he was selecting certain people out of the crowds to join his warband.

Warband? Sara shook her head, annoyed at letting her imagination get out of hand from hanging out with Cosplayers and costumers. She vowed to give up *World of Warcraft* for a while after she got home. Still, she couldn't help feeling a martial glow of comradeship as she marched forward at the elf lord's side.

Reality set back in when she saw Beth standing at the bottom of the escalator outside the shopping area. She'd never seen her volatile boss so steamed before.

"She's not happy," Sara murmured, wondering if she should hide behind Barahael's broad back, or make a break for it. But Barahael strode up to Beth with Sara's hand clasped in his and there was nothing she could do but accompany her digits.

"What news?" Barahael asked Beth.

"There are some Golden Elves here, but your princess isn't one of them." Beth pointed a finger at Barahael. "They're here to start trouble."

"I feared a trap."

"It's a trap all right, but for me, not for you. They intend to shut down the annual meeting of worlds."

"How?" Sara asked. Then realized she was going along with a lot of nonsense because of her faith in Beth's opinions. "I mean—"

"They're here to start a fight with you," Beth said to Barahael.

"Any disruption in neutral territory will get them banned from ever returning," he answered.

"I don't think they care. I think their point is to close off the meeting point altogether. Do you know how much business I'll lose if that happens?"

Beth's shrill anger grated on Sara's ears, and Barahael actually flinched. "Mortals could be harmed if it comes to a fight," he said. He glanced Sara's way. "Innocents must be protected."

"I'd relish a fight," Asli said.

"Didn't you tell me you wanted to settle down and have a few foals?" Beth asked her. "You're never going to get the chance to meet your match if arrows start flying."

"That is so," Barahael said. "We need a way to make the Golden Elves withdraw without any violence. I think I know a way." He turned to Sara. "Say nothing. And remember that your honor is dear to me." He put his arm through hers. "Come, fair maiden. There is something I wish to show you."

Sara was completely clueless, but she went along with Barahael. She had to admit that no matter what this game was or who he really was she still enjoyed being with the elf lord. Chivalry was sexy.

Asli and other members of his posse fanned out around them, inconspicuous among all the other shoppers. It didn't take Sara long to realize that there were other elves in the room.

Where Barahael was a vision in shades of silver, this new group was costumed in gold. Instead of platinum, their hair was blond, their skins creamy instead of pale. The gold elves converged around Barahael's group in a slow, subtle maneuver. Sara knew that Barahael was pretending not to notice and tried to look as unaware. But the newcomers creeped her out. She felt like some innocent herbivore being surrounded by a hungry wolf pack.

Finally, when her nerves were very close to breaking, and the game didn't feel like fun, but some dangerous adventure, Barahael brought her to a stop in front of one of the dealer booths.

"I will make you a gift, my love," he said, rather louder than necessary.

What does he mean by that? She wondered before she looked up and saw a wall of brocade and steel. "This is a corset shop."

"Indeed," Barahael said. He leered at her. The expression did not belong on his ethereal face. "I found out about these garments when I was drafted onto a costuming panel. I am told they make women look and feel sexy. Try one on."

Sara wondered if she should protest that she wasn't that sort of girl, but the corsets were gorgeous. She noticed several customers laced into the garments looking at themselves with cinched waist and swelling bosoms in the shop's mirrors. Not only did they look sexy in this S&M gear, but they looked like they felt sexy. Besides, Barahael had asked her to go along with him.

"Okay," she said as the dealer came up, holding up a red and gold dragon patterned corset. Recalling her first client, Sara said, "I'm not sure I should do dragons."

"Let me pick one for you, my love," Barahael said.

But one of the Golden Elves blocked his way before he could approach corset racks. "Love?" He sneered, and the unpleasant expression worked surprisingly well on his features. "How is it you call this mortal *love*? Are you not the Lord of the Silver kind?"

Barahael's arm came around her shoulders. He pulled her possessively closer. She discovered he was wearing real chain mail beneath his lavishly embroidered tunic.

"I am Barahael," he told the other elf. "Should I know you?"

His tone implied indulgence at rudeness on the other elf's part. The other elf conveyed outrage with the lift of a single gold brow. "Do you not recognize the captain of the Golden Lady's bodyguard?"

Barahael looked the bodyguard up and down. "Hmmm . . . perhaps if you were to show me your back you might seem more familiar."

Most of the nearby shoppers were watching this exchange. Laughter and applause sounded all around the elves. The elves had eyes only for each other.

"Is not the Golden Lady your love?" the bodyguard asked after a significant pause.

"Should she be?"

The gold elf gave a dangerous smile. His amber eyes gleamed. Boy, was this guy spoiling for a fight!

"Are you forsworn, then, Silver Lord?"

"Never!" Barahael answered.

"Then why do you call a mortal love when you are betrothed to—" he gestured at the other elves gathered around them, "—our lady?"

There was a general murmuring—of loyalty from the elves, interest from the audience and annoyance from the abandoned vendors

A brilliant smile lit Barahael's features "Has the lady arrived at last? When may we meet?"

His blatant eagerness annoyed Sara. It disconcerted the hell out the gold elf.

"Uh—no. The lady is not—"

"Is not what? "

"Here."

Barahael turned back to Sara. "Where were we, my love?"

"I was about to make an exhibition of myself," Sara said.

"Ah, yes."

They turned back toward the racks of stiffened brocade but the gold elf once more interrupted their shopping. "You are forsworn!"

"If I prove to you that I am not will you quit this world? Will you leave this festival in peace?"

"You are forsworn and I will you here and now for my lady's honor!" The gold elf's hand was on the pommel of a sheathed dagger. Sara gasped, knowing at last that no role playing was going on between these two.

"He wants to kill you!" she blurted at Barahael.

Barahael touched her cheek. "But my death would make you grieve, and bringing you sadness would be unkind of me."

Sara was not the only woman within hearing who sighed, but she was certain hers was more romantic than the others.

Barahael gestured at the spectators. "Lady Thorson, will you attend me?"

Sara hadn't noticed that her boss had joined Barahael's entourage, but there she stood between Asli and the lady who didn't do dragons. Beth's glare at Golden Boy was as dangerous as his dagger as she moved to stand beside Barahael.

"What has she to do with our quarrel?" Golden Boy demanded. "Will you use a mortal as a shield?"

"I would never use this lady as a shield," Barahael said. "Not when she makes a far better weapon."

Beth snorted. There was more applause from the audience. The gold elf came a menacing step closer. Sara wondered when Con security was going to show up.

"You have not yet agreed to my proposal," Barahael said.

"I agree to your rules of engagement," the other elf snarled.

"And all your men?"

"I command their agreement."

The Gold Elves shouted, "Aye, aye, aye!" It sounded very martial.

"We ought to get these guys together with the Spartans," somebody in the crowd said.

"You came here to deliberately provoke a quarrel that would deny all of us the use of this place. You came to rekindle our ancient war. You would have every right to exploit this incident your own lady has provoked if she and I were truly betrothed." Barahael turned to Beth. "Are the Golden Lady and I truly betrothed, Facilitator Between the Worlds?"

"You most certainly are not," Beth answered. She pulled a tiny laptop out of her huge purse and brought up a file. Sara got a look at the small screen, but she didn't recognize the language. Beth handed the computer to the gold elf. "Read this. It's the standard contract for my services at DragonCon. There is nothing in there that promises marriage. I put people together; chemistry and free will take over from there. Prince Barahael signed the contract. So did your lady. If anybody is in breach of the contract, she is. Barahael showed up, she didn't. If I can't introduce them, my job is to introduce Barahael to another suitable candidate." She glanced at Sara. "The contract is fulfilled, and your princess is out her fee and meeting a really nice guy."

"Thank you, Lady Thorson," Barahael said.

The gold elf handed back the computer. "This is an outrage!"

"And your loss, sucker," Asli said.

"The Golden Lady told us Barahael would forswear the betrothal!" one of the other gold elves said. "We came to defend her honor."

"But if there is no betrothal, we have no cause to fight," another said. He sounded incredibly disappointed.

"We must withdraw," a third elf spoke up.

Golden Boy did not look at all happy with his squad. He stood as stiff as a statue for a few moments, his hand still on his weapon. It was Beth who stared him down.

"Come back next year and I'll find you a nice girl," she told him.

He glared for form's sake, but Beth saw the hopeful gleam in his eye. She loved her job.

"We withdraw," the elf conceded.

Asli and her crew followed the Gold Elves to make sure they were really leaving. Beth turned back to her client, and smiled knowingly. Barahael and Sara had gone back to corset shopping. He said something in her ear, they both laughed. Maybe her speech to the gold elf had some truth in it.

"Chemistry and free will," she said. "Works every time."

THE SIMULATOR

Karen DeWinter

I had him in my crosshairs. This guy had eluded me for an hour to no avail, but now he was mine. If I made a mistake, the one-man fighter would return to the planet below, and I would miss my chance. There would be other ships. There were always others. Privateers were constantly on the lookout for new cargo. If I screwed this up, I could always take on another one. I just needed enough kills to—no, I wouldn't think of that. I worked hard to put this guy on the defensive, and now it was personal. I steadied my hand on the throttle. The sweat from my palms made it difficult to maneuver. A white glare beamed from the fighter as it grew larger in my scope. The ship was mostly triangular–shaped, with wings that swooped upward. I was so close, I could see into the exhaust. The right wing suddenly dropped. He rotated.

Oh, no, you don't.

That was exactly what he did last time. First the rotation to the right to throw me off guard, and then he would pull a hard left. I wasn't going to fall for that again. I moved the site off him, shifted it to the left and waited. Another second and I would blow him out of the sky. His left wing started to move into the site. *Almost there . . .* The ship was nearly on target. I began to count down in my head. *Three . . . two . . .*

A blaze of lights filled the scope as the ship exploded.

What happened? I looked down at my hand to see if I had inadvertently pushed the firing mechanism. *Nope.*

Then I heard Burt's unmistakable laughter. "I'm sorry, kiddo, I just couldn't resist."

I looked across the gaming table at him. "How could you? That would have been my highest frag count ever."

"Alright, I'm sorry. It's just—you looked so serious. I had to do something. Besides, you scored high enough to get into the finals. A little late though, I had that score an hour ago."

"Oh, shut up, will ya." I examined the room. I wondered which of the twenty participants had also made it to the finals. Well, it didn't matter. The important thing was that I made it and so did Burt. For the past four months, I ate, slept, and dreamt *Voo Dong Privateers*. And now it paid off. The excitement was overwhelming. The gaming company had gone all out this year. They'd run a four-month long contest promoting this new game. Twenty of the top players from around the nation would then compete in a semi-final round at DragonCon. The finalists would battle it out for the grand prize . . . a first class ticket to Germany and a position at Stocker-Heim Studios as a Quality Assurance Tester.

I couldn't believe I made it this far. It was like finding Wonka's Golden Ticket with a lifetime supply of chocolate. I imagined what it would be like living in Germany. I could just see myself sitting in one of those Gasthauses along the Rhine, sipping Riesling, conversing with all those gorgeous young men from the university—and best of all, I'd be getting paid to play video games.

"Kylie! Weren't you listening? We have to meet back here in five hours."

"Oh, I'm sorry, Burt. I don't know where my mind was."

"I do, across the Atlantic. You've been dreaming of this for a long time and now it looks like you're finally going to get what you want."

I took a strand of my chestnut-colored hair and twirled it around my index finger. I couldn't believe the officials were going to make us wait five hours. I was anxious. Never thought my entire future would hinge on my performance in a computer game.

"I still have to play the finals. And, I wasn't even the top player. You far outfragged me. Looks like if anyone is going, it will be you."

"You give up too easy, kiddo. Anyway, you think I'm going to give up a six-figure a year job just to play computer games? I told you—I'm just here for the beer."

Burt was an executive at Lockheed Martin and had spent the last two years in the United Arab Emirates living the life of an international playboy. He always wanted to be James Bond, so he took a certain delight in hob-knobbing with the upper echelons of society. His recent brag was that he was rubbing elbows with the crown prince. It was a lifestyle he wouldn't give up so easily.

"Did someone say beer?" A guy dressed up something like a pseudo-Rambo had turned in our direction. The other players were slowly leaving the room, many of them pressed down by the weight of defeat. Only a few stayed behind. "Man, I could use a drink."

Another man left his seat and walked over toward us. He was dressed like Morpheus in *The Matrix* but, other than sharing the same ethnic background, he looked nothing like him. "Are you guys in the finals?" He seemed to be addressing all of us.

Burt turned to look in his direction. "I am and she—"

"Don't tell him. He may have a sword hidden in that trench coat. He's probably just waiting to eliminate the competition by lopping off all our heads." I shot a sly grin in Morpheus' direction.

He countered with an equally cheeky Cheshire cat expression. "No, that's not my style. Besides, I'm Morpheus, not Connor Macleod. And besides, *Highlander* is so passé."

"Oooh, well la tee da! I take it you are in the finals?" I figured he was okay, even if he did say that *Highlander* was passé.

"I sure am. My name is Reginald Hudson. My friends call me Regi."

"Nice to meet you. I'm Kylie Rayne and this is my old friend, Roburt Blakeney."

"I don't know if I like being described as old."

"Not that kind of old. Besides, you're only as old as you feel."

"Great, feel me and see how old I am." Burt's laugh was maniacal.

"Not as old as that joke," I countered.

"Yeah, that was pretty bad." We all turned in the direction of the comment. A girl came up on our left and remained standing. She was very tall and slender, and her face had a childlike quality. I don't know where she was from, but if I had to guess it would be the Steppes in

Mongolia. Her hair was not black, but dark brown, with slight hints of red. Long eyelashes framed eyes which were almost green. She wore a black Kung-Fu outfit with a turquoise dragon embroidered on the front. Part of the dragon's body was on the left side of the garment, while the face and tail were on the right. The costume was perfect for her. "Hi, I'm Aliya Cahn."

"No way, Man." Rambo obviously had a lot of tact.

I had to stifle back a laugh myself, but at least I wasn't that conspicuous.

Aliya seemed to sense my uneasiness, "It's okay; I get that all the time. But mine is spelled with a C, not a K."

"Oh, yeah, that's different." His sarcasm was unbelievable.

"Okay, Rambo, what's your name?" I was hoping it was something that I could rhyme with a number of inappropriate words.

"Cole Turner, but you can call me anything just as long as you call me." This guy was a walking cliché. He looked at me like I was the last Coca Cola in the desert. *Gross.* It didn't take me long to realize that he wasn't dressed up either. No, this was his normal attire. The *Semper Fidelis* tattoo on his upper left arm told me he was a Marine, although I wouldn't have needed *that* to figure it out.

"Well . . . Cole . . . that's real . . . uh . . . redneck." *Nope, no inappropriate rhymes. Damn.*

He didn't seem bothered by my comment. "Look, is anyone else here thirsty? Cause I could murder a beer right now."

"Sure, I could use a drink." Burt's eyes gleamed at the prospect. He wasn't a big drinker, but he took a certain pride in having tasted ales from every corner of the globe. His recent discovery was Jackson's *Autumn Ale.* It was a local favorite made right here in Atlanta, and they just happened to have it on tap at the *Parasol.* "Shall we head over to the Hyatt?" You could almost see Burt salivating at the prospect of native hops. His eyes examined the others. They all nodded in agreement, and he knew I wouldn't say no. We made our way over to the Hyatt from the basement of the Sheridan. The streets were laden with sci-fi and fantasy's greatest heroes. It was like an interplanetary Mardi Gras. I was mesmerized by all the costumes. Was it just me or were they getting better? I remember when painted cardboard and a roll of duct tape would win you the star prize, now you needed an engineering degree just to participate. I felt underdressed in my jeans and black T-shirt.

I pulled Burt aside as we neared the front entrance of the Hyatt. "Did you really mean what you said back there?"

"What do you mean?"

"I *mean* about letting me win the tournament, cause if you did, you can't. *I* can't let you do that for me."

"Look, I don't want this. You do. Besides, when the officials see the hot little number who's competing, they'll probably fix the scores in your favor."

"Very funny." It occurred to me that he may not be joking. "Hey, what's that supposed to mean?"

"You tell me. You're the only enlisted person I knew in the Air Force who could have the officers eating out of her hand."

"That was because I was the best aircraft mechanic in the business. Pilots like to know they're in good hands."

"Oh, they wanted to be in good hands all right."

I gave Burt a playful slug in the arm. "You're just jealous because I'm a better mechanic than you."

"You think so, huh?" He bumped his shoulder into mine and shot a playful look at the revolving door. We raced to the entrance and fought our way into the same cubicle, pushing each other as it turned. We stepped into the lobby and put on our best "we're normal" look. Our caravan of finalists followed.

After the long process of vulturing over tables and waiting for people to leave, we finally landed a spot at the edge of the giant parasol. Burt and Regi took the drink requests and went up to the bar. I watched Burt walking away and couldn't help thinking that he fit in here much better than I did. This was his first DragonCon, but he looked like an old vet. He had always shaved his head, but the goatee and silver hooped earrings were recent additions. His leather pants gripped his legs tightly, leaving very little to the imagination. Burt had often been described as "John Luc Picard in his biker phase."

He was one of the few men of fifty who could wear leather without looking like an advertisement for *Guitar Rock*.

I, on the other hand, looked nothing like a cool space pirate. I had always been described as *wholesome*. My long, layered locks hadn't changed in ten years. And I felt self conscious in tight clothing. Although I wanted to be one of those girls who was brave enough to sport a spiky, multi-colored hair style, or wear a skintight spandex spacesuit, unzipped down to the navel, it just wasn't me.

"Hey, where the hell are they with our drinks?"

"Oh, that's rich, Rambo, considering you aren't buying. Why don't you go and see if they need help?" I was starting to get annoyed by his very presence, but at least he left.

Aliya looked puzzled. "That was a little too easy."

I didn't quite understand it either. "Yes, he's oddly accommodating."

Burt and Regi returned with our drinks. Rambo trailed behind.

"I would like to propose a toast." Burt played sophisticated very well. "I wish you all the best of luck as we enter this final round. I am glad we had this opportunity to meet. You all seem very nice— which will make it all the more difficult when I kick your asses later tonight."

A round of *boos* and *hisses* rose up from the table and napkins were hurled in Burt's direction. A commotion from the table next to us pulled our attention away from Burt.

"Hey, watch where you're going, Tentacle Boy! That *thing* just hit my girl in the face." The disgruntled patron pushed and Tentacle Boy went flying. The latter was dressed similar to Jabba the Hut's toadie in *Return of the Jedi* although his costume was far superior to anything George Lucas could create without the use of some serious CGI. The *Star Wars* theme suddenly became very appropriate as this place started looking like the space port at Moss Eisley.

Tentacle Boy was still trying to catch his balance and nearly tumbled into me. "I'm terribly sorry." The voice came from all around, like surround sound, but his mouth didn't move. His translucent, cellulose skin did nothing to hide the veins underneath. It reminded me of the legs of those oversized bathing beauties on the beaches in Nova Scotia. Obviously, a lot of work went into getting the skin to look just right. But the crowning glory was the tentacles. There were three of them on the top of his head and they moved on their own. We couldn't take our eyes off of him.

He turned to face us. "I have been looking all over for you."

We all looked baffled. I tried to think of anyone I knew with the ability to put together a costume like this. "You have?"

"Yes, you are all the *Voo Dong Privateers* finalists, are you not?" *Again with the surround sound. How was he doing that?*

"Yes, we are not . . . I mean . . . yes, we are." Cole was so easily confused.

"Good, I have come to tell you that the final competition has been moved to a different location and the time pushed forward . . . "

We looked at one another, turned our attention back to the alien and began shooting questions at him.

"What?"

"Where?"

"When?"

"Upstairs in this hotel, room 555, in ten minutes."

A number of expletives erupted from the group as we all scrambled to our feet. Cole knocked over his stool while reaching for his drink. "Oh, shit, I haven't even touched my drink."

"What are you complaining for?" Burt said. "You didn't pay for it."

Cole knocked it back despite the time constraint. *That's right Rambo, drink up. Loosen those reflexes. Minus one in the competition.* "You can have mine, too." I batted my lashes innocently. I wasn't planning on drinking it anyway. I would do nothing to compromise *my* reaction time.

We raced toward the elevators. There was a crowd of people all waiting to get to their prospective destinations. *This was going to take forever.* Without missing a cue, Burt and I ran toward the stairs. After all it was only five floors. The others realized our intentions and quickly followed suit.

I came to a screeching halt in front of the room. Burt practically slammed into me. Tentacle Boy was already there waiting.

"Wha?" Before I could form the rest of the word, he waved his gangly, three-fingered hand over the door handle and opened it. I hadn't actually seen him use the card key, but guessed the card was hidden under the bulk of his costume. We piled into the room. The lights were off, and the curtains must have been closed. The blackness was so thick I couldn't see an inch in front of my face. Although I didn't think it could get any darker, it somehow deepened. My heart started racing.

"Hey, what kind of crap is this, man?" Cole yelled. "Turn the damn lights back on."

Burt brushed against me. "Yeah, what is this?"

"What the . . . Oh, shhhhhhhhh!"

The floor gave way. I thrust my arms out and felt nothing. My stomach rocketed to my throat. Threads of electricity pulsated through me. A deafening, high-pitched, whine rang in my ears. Nausea racked my gut. I was getting dizzier by the second. Then, as quickly as it had begun, the sensation stopped. A red glow penetrated the darkness, and the surroundings slowly took shape.

This was no hotel room.

It was obvious we were in a simulator of some sort, but it looked like the set of a sci-fi movie. I was astounded at all the detail. *All this just to test a computer game?* As the shock wore off, I began to take in the particulars of the simulator. Through the constant pulse of red light, a CGI picture of the earth filled a giant display. It gave the appearance that we were orbiting. A large control center housed three smaller displays with various high-tech switches and dials recessed under a glass table top. Jets of air hissed up from the grated metal floor. As the crisp air shot up my pants leg, I was grateful that I'd left my Marilyn Monroe dress at home.

Three pseudo art-deco chairs lined the control center, each one of them in front of a prospective display. The chairs were black leather; although it was hard to be sure in the low, red lighting. Three of the walls had an iridescent luster and were designed to look like bulkheads but, rather than being made out of metal, they seemed to be made out of some type of fiberglass. The other was completely taken up with the picture of Planet Earth. There were two more control panels recessed into the bulkheads. No expense was spared.

"This is some cool shit!" I had almost forgotten about the others until Rambo piped up.

"You have such a way with words," I said sarcastically.

"Yeah." The nodding head and prideful gleam in his eye told me that this guy actually thought I meant it.

"We must begin, now. We have no time to waste." Tentacle Boy stepped to the front of the room and faced us. "As I am sure you have all realized by now, the final round of the competition will be different from the games you have played until now. You are in a simulator which has been designed to test your abilities as a crew in space combat."

"You're changing the rules?" Regi suddenly looked very worried.

"Well, I don't care what we do as long as I get to blow shit up."

The instructions continued. "You will all be given different assignments and ranks on the ship. Mr. Blakeney, because of your high score, you will now be the Captain."

"Hey, how'd you know my name?"

Our speaker ignored the comment. "Ms. Cahn, you will be the navigator. Mr. Turner, you will be the ship's security officer."

"What does that mean?"

"You will be in charge of . . . blowing up the shit."

"Right on!"

"Ms. Rayne, will be the ship's engineer and Mr. Hudson, the ship's doctor."

"Why do you need a doctor on a simulator? What sort of game is this?"

"That . . . is a very good question, Mr. Hudson. You see, the simulator was designed to be as accurate as possible. No ship could function in combat conditions without a doctor. "

"Yes, but what will he *do* if it's just a game?" Frankly, I was a bit nervous about the prospect of simulating injuries.

"If you will look around, you will notice five display monitors. Each monitor correlates to a different job on the ship. For example, the computer will come up with problems the ship may encounter and relay it to the prospective monitor. If there are incoming enemy ships, it will be displayed on the security officer's monitor. All information about the ship's navigation will be displayed on Ms. Cahn's monitor. Mr. Hudson's display will mainly have statistics on life support and atmospheric conditions. All information will then be duplicated onto the captain's monitor. The captain will be able to make decisions based on *all* collected data."

"Captain Blakeney, will you take your position in the left chair at console? Mr. Turner, you will be on the right side, and Ms. Cahn will be in the middle."

"Sandwich time!"

Aliya shot a piercing gaze in Cole's direction. Burt looked equally disgusted.

"Dr. Hudson," the alien pointed to the chair along the left side wall, "if you will please be seated. And you, Ms. Rayne," pointing to the one on the right, "will sit here."

We all took our places. "The battle will commence in approximately twenty-seven minutes. Until then, take the time, please, to study your displays."

I sat down in front of my monitor and examined it. This was like using my computer at home. I was able to view three dimensional schematics of the engines along with electrical and pneumatic diagrams. A lot of thought went into coming up with this program.

The silence was broken by a low pitched, pulsating horn signaling something important was about to happen. Small dots started to move slowly across the planetary display. "We've got six bogies headed our way!" Cole was really getting into this.

"How long until they are within range?"

"3.5 minutes, Captain," Aliya answered. Her voice was stoic but her expression was very playful.

"Raise shields, Mr. Turner." I had to admit, I was impressed. I looked over at my monitor. A pop-up appeared on the screen. Pressurization had dropped but was still at 97%. This was just like playing *Sub Commander*. I relayed the info to Burt.

"Thanks. Got it."

The ships on the planetary display grew larger with every second.

"One minute, Captain." I wondered if Aliya remembered this was just a game. "Ninety seconds . . . eighty . . . seventy . . . " She continued counting down. " . . . ten seconds . . . five seconds—"

"Whoo-hoo! Here we go!" Cole began laying on rapid fire that would easily have won him top score in *Voo Dong*. "Eat shit and die you sorry son of a bitch." There was a big CGI explosion, as two of the ships disintegrated. "Yeah, baby! Whatya think of that?"

"Oh my God, it's just a game." *I felt like Jane Goodall in a* National Geographic *special*. More expletives poured from the mouth of our resident chimpanzee. "How are you even managing to fire that thing without an opposable thumb?"

"Skill, baby, pure-d-bonafide, grade-A skill." He shot at another one. The damage to the other ships did seem to be pretty bad. "Check it out, man; they're gettin' their asses kicked." Then he looked annoyed. "Spoke too soon. Our shields just went down to 50%."

"Kylie, what can you do to fix the problem?" Burt looked proud of himself. He was in his element.

The simulator gave a violent shudder. A chorus of "cools" and "wows" started to echo through the room, but were stopped short. The force had shattered one of the bulkhead panels and sent it flying across the room into pieces.

"Oh, God, oh God, man, What the fu—" One of the pieces made contact with Cole's right arm and the other embedded itself into his chest.

"Oh, God, please help me." Cole crumpled over in the chair and then hit the floor. No sooner had he made contact with the hard metal when Regi bounded out of his chair and raced over to examine the injured crewman.

"Don't worry, I'm an EMT."

But Burt saw the concern in Regi's face and spun around to face the alien.

"What in God's name have you gotten us into? This is no game. This is *really* happening."

The alien looked very nervous. "But he will be okay."

"Okay? *Okay*? I don't know if you've been paying attention, man, but I've got a big hunk of spaceship sticking out of my chest."

"Pipe down, Cole." Burt turned back to the alien. "That's just it, he shouldn't even be in this mess, and neither should the rest of us."

"You tell him, man," Cole whined in agreement.

"One more word from you and I'll have Regi sedate you the old-fashioned way."

Regi packed the wound with pieces of Cole's mangled shirt. "This is just a quick fix, but this man needs a doctor."

"I hate to break up the party, but we've got trouble." I noticed the other four ships circling back like sharks going in for the kill. Aliya grabbed the firing mechanism from Cole's control panel. She made ready to shoot the first thing that came into her view. Burt sprinted up to the platform where the alien was standing. "I want an explanation, *now*."

"Please, there is no time. If the enemy gets through, he will destroy your planet."

Burt turned in the direction of the helm. "Aliya, how confident are you about firing those things?"

"No problem."

"Good, don't let any get through." He turned to face me. "Kylie, can you do anything about those shields?"

"I don't know. I'll have to see if I can steal power from somewhere else." *After all, it worked in Star Trek.*

"Do whatever it takes." He continued the interrogation of the alien. "How much power do we need in the shields to take these guys on?"

"At least 70%."

"Did you hear that, Kylie? We need at least 70% shield capability."

"Working on it . . . Captain." I had always wanted to say that.

Another ship exploded on the display. Without batting an eye Aliya announced, "Only three more left, Captain."

The alien seemed very relieved. "We have a few minutes before their return."

"Good, start talking."

I listened while scrolling through different screens. I pulled up the statistics and viewed them. I was able to drag and drop from one stat to the other. I didn't think something so simple would even work. Eventually I was able to borrow enough power from the ship's other systems and transfer it to the shields and get the shields back up to 73%.

"Shields are at 73%."

"Good work, Kylie."

The alien continued his explanation of his planet's history and explained that they had been at war for many years. "Our technology far surpassed that of the enemy, but their tactics were much more brutal. One of our bases was infiltrated and the enemy got away with vital equipment. Our scientists had just developed the means for achieving deep space travel. We soon learned that the enemy would use this technology in order to conquer other planets.

"Our intelligence reports indicated that they were bound for a planet in a nearby solar system, the one you call Planet Earth. The journey would take 125 of your earth years, and none involved in the expedition would be able to return. I, along with four other comrades, volunteered to go. When the ship reached its destination, I found that I was alone. All of the stasis chambers, with the exception of my own, had malfunctioned. Without a crew, I knew I could not defeat the enemy. I decided to take drastic measures. I converted the spaceship by using technology that I borrowed from your planet."

"You mean stole . . . "

The alien ignored Cole's snipey comment. "Although there were more skilled people on earth which could have crewed the ship, there were none I could approach. Only at this convention would I be able to mix among your people with relative ease."

Aliya spun around in her chair, "Captain, the ships are returning."

"Everyone get ready." For Burt, that meant *battlestations*.

Regi sat Cole up in his chair and strapped him in. He checked the bandages once again before returning to his seat. Aliya fired off more rounds at the enemy ships. I turned back to my monitor. The ship shuddered a few times, but didn't seem to be in any immediate distress. I kept watch over the vital statistics. Another *thud*. Despite all the excitement, I was fighting hard to stifle a yawn. My ears began to ache and I couldn't seem to get them to pop.

"Oh shit!" *How could I be so stupid?*

"What's going on over there?" Burt diverted his attention from the display.

I pulled up another screen on the monitor. "We're losing pressure—fast." I jumped out of the chair and moved toward the alien. "Where are all the tools?"

"There." He pointed to a panel near the floor and to the right of the engineer station. Fortunately, he had the forethought when he remodeled to "borrow" a toolbox. I took out the biggest, flathead screwdriver I could find and began to rapidly remove panels. I started near the one which had blown off earlier. I listened carefully for the unmistakable *hissing* sound. One thing I learned from working on C-130's was how to find a leak. The ship jolted.

Burt's voice rang with excitement, "All right! Two at a time. Now you're talking."

I didn't have time to look up, but it was clear that Aliya had just demolished two of the enemy ships. I continued my search. After about the fifth panel, I spotted the culprit. The blast responsible for the injury to Cole had also managed to damage one of the ducts. Warm air escaped out the sides.

I darted over to my monitor and pulled up the engine diagram. I overlaid the pneumatics diagram. The air going to the duct in question was coming off of the 23rd stage of engine compression. That is, if I was even reading this thing correctly. I wondered why the air wasn't hotter. I went back to the screen with the pressurization statistics. "Hey, Regi, come here."

Regi rushed over to assist. "What can I do?"

I pointed to the monitor. "Tell me when these numbers go up." I went back over to the panel and tugged at the two sides of the duct until the ends met.

Regi called over to me, "Kylie, your numbers just shot up from 50 to 73."

I released the two sides of the duct. Air blew around inside the panel with even more force.

"Captain, the shields have just gone down to 39%." Aliya didn't miss a beat.

It was just as I thought. "I think there is a correlation between the pressurization and the shields." It didn't make sense, but it was the only explanation.

"Can you fix it?" Burt's concern was mounting.

"Sure, if I can repair this duct the shields should come back up." I wish I was as confident as I sounded.

"Hey, that thing is coming back for us." Cole's voice had lost its cocky edge.

I looked around for something to use for a patch job.

"Kylie . . . " The ship was getting closer.

If only I had a roll of duct tape.

"Kylie, I don't think they're going to wait."

Aliya glanced at Burt. "They'll be in range of our shields in less than a minute."

I opened the panel below and felt the duct. No air flow was going through it. I addressed the alien. "What does this duct go to?"

"It goes to what you would call the safety valve."

"Great, let's hope we don't need it." I took a blade from the toolbox and cut off a piece of the duct. I slipped both sides of the broken duct into it. *Oh God, Please make this work.* I slipped the piece down to bridge the gap between the ducts and secured it with pieces of Cole's shirt.

"Thirty seconds, Captain."

"Well, Aliya, let's hope you're a better shot than he is."

"Wait. Captain, the shields are coming back up."

"You did it, Kylie. Great job."

The ship came in for a quick fly-by and fired. There was a violent jerk. My head banged against the bulkhead.

"Everyone OK?" Burt gave a concerned glance over in my direction.

"I'm fine." *Just love being whacked in the head.*

"Here he comes again, man." Even injured Cole just couldn't help playing back seat shooter. The enemy ship grew larger and larger in the display.

"Aliya, why aren't you firing? Aliya?" Burt jumped from his chair, gripping the console. "Aliya!"

"Oh, shit, what are you doing?" Just as Cole grabbed for the firing mechanism, Aliya fired. The display was filled with a firework display as the ship exploded.

"Whoo-hoo!"

"Way to go!"

"Yeehaw!"

We all leapt out of our chairs, jumped up and down, and hugged each other. I even gave Cole a hug. "You did a great job."

I prepared myself for the smartass comeback, but all I got was a humble, "Thanks."

Burt addressed us all. "Congratulations, we did it."

There was a sound from the platform like someone clearing their throat. In all the excitement, we had forgotten about the alien. "You have not done it. This is not the end. It is only the beginning. They will send more, many more."

Burt's excitement turned to concern, "How long do we have?"

"Five years, maybe ten at most. You must prepare your planet."

Fear gripped my heart. "But no one will believe us."

The alien extended his arm and raised three fingers. The tentacles on his head began to undulate, "They might not believe you, but they'll believe me."

DRAGONCON:
TRAILS AND TRIBULATIONS
(with apologies to just about everybody)

Todd McCaffrey

I found her at a bookseller's, near Artist's Alley. I remember when I first met her, last year. We met at the Drum Circle.

She was just seventeen, you know what I mean. And the way she looked was way beyond compare.[1]

In fact, she was dressed in a huge lizard outfit with the letters "K-A-M-I-L-E-O-N" stitched across it and she was holding a Tony Soprano doll with a stake in its heart under her arm. The stake was decorated with four little oblong triangles. It took me a moment to realize that the four little triangles were sails. And when I got that, I got the whole thing and did what any proper punster would do: I groaned in punishment.[2]

Me? I was carrying a Terry Pratchett book and occasionally throwing it in front of my feet and tripping over it.

"That's got to be Pratchett's *The Light Fantastic*," she said as she watched me. And that's when I knew: even if she was the only one who could see me, I had found my perfect one.

Well, the decision was easy. I mean, how could I dance with another, when I saw her standing there?[3]

And now, years later, with the spell still not broken, she was

[1] With apologies to the Fab Four.
[2] With apologies to Piers Anthony and *A Spell for Chameleon*.
[3] Again, sorry, John, Paul, George, Ringo.

pawing through stacks of used books when I came up behind her. She held a romance novel in her hand and was reading the back cover.

I reached around and grabbed it from her, shaking my head. "Repent!"

I took a quick glance at the book, threw it back on the stacks, tapping its spine at the imprint. "Harlequin!"

She made a face at me, then turned back to the stacks. I glanced at my watch, and shoved it in her line of sight. We were running late for our shift.

"Tick-tock[4]!" I said as I waggled the watch in front of her nose. She ignored me, pushing my hand away as she spotted an old magazine and grabbed it.

"It's Astounding," she exclaimed.

"Time is fleeting," I reminded her.

She shook her head at me just as we heard a commotion from Artist's Alley.

"Madness takes its toll," I murmured. I cupped my ear, trying to decipher the sounds over all the gabble. "But listen, closely."

"Not for very much longer," she told me with a sigh.

"I've got to keep control[5]," I said, moving closer to the noise. It was, after all, our job as undercover security and how we paid our way at the con.

As often happens, it was a new fan arguing with an old star over the price of an autograph.

"Time for the stars[6]," I sighed.

My partner shook her head, saying mournfully, "Star Tracks! The wrath of con.[7]" She pursed her lips, as she added disdainfully, "Star wars."

Fortunately, the fan calmed down and got his autograph. Nearby I

[4] Sorry, Harlan.
[5] With apologies to every Rocky Horror Picture Show.
[6] With apologies to Robert A. Heinlein.
[7] Sorry, Gene.

noticed one of the new, up-and-coming younger stars happily dashing off a signature for a toddler, glancing with apprehension at the older actor. I nudged my partner, pointing. "A new hope[8]."

The toddler's father was standing behind her, grumpy. On his shoulder was a smaller girl, dressed in a princess outfit. I smiled, pointing her out to my partner, "Sleeping beauty![9]"

She smiled and nodded back, saying in agreement, "A little princess.[10]"

I searched around for the children's mother and found her seated against a column, with a bunch of fabric draped around her and a needle in her hand. I patted her partner on the shoulder and pointed out, "Lie low, and stitch.[11]"

She scanned past and spotted a neat outfit: obviously a believer in furry fandom. The owner was in a very short skirt, so my partner nodded in her direction, indicating the skirt, "Mini!"

I glanced disapprovingly at the girl's costume: it was not to my tastes and I said so, disapprovingly, "Mouse."

Suddenly, around us, the lights flickered. This was the sort of thing we were self-assigned to handle, so I looked around the room, scanning. There was a maintenance man working in a corner. I jerked my head toward him, catching my partner's attention, suggesting him as the cause. "Lord of Light?[12]"

She shook her head, having spotted someone attempting to plug in another power strip to the overloaded wall and gestured toward him. "The lightning thief.[13]"

I gave her a disbelieving look, pointing up at the lights, my mouth working in a silent, "How?"

My partner grinned and responded in her best Holmesian manner, "Electrodirection, my dear Sam."

[8] Sorry, George.
[9] Sorry, Brothers Grimm.
[10] Sorry, Ms. Burnett.
[11] Please don't sue me!
[12] Hey, if the fit hits the Shan!
[13] Sorry, Percy.

When she'd first found out my name, she used a lot of fantastical references; it took me a long time to break her of the hobbit.[14]

Her explanation didn't leave me convinced. "Let's look around some more."

We started back towards Gaming. My partner paused as she noted a seller with old Mattel dolls. She was always looking for a partner for her other dolls. She was particularly impressed with the Wizard of Oz set and held up the Ken doll dressed as the Cowardly Lion for my approval.

"Dandy lion," I told her sarcastically.

She pouted at me. "Whine![15]"

"Oh, buy one Ken!" I relented. She glared at me, so I started angrily, "Oh, be—[16]"

I stopped, my eyes goggling as a large group of people dressed in clown suits entered the room. My security senses came on alert. "Attack of the clowns?[17]"

"Clones," my partner said dismissively, handing over her money to the eager seller.

I kept searching the crowd, and spotting a guy on stilts, I cried, "Look! Skywalker![18]"

My partner glanced toward him, awed at the special rig he wore which gave his steps an extra spring-like floating affect, and murmured appreciatively, "When gravity fails.[19]"

Unfortunately, at that point, one of the cleverly hidden rubber bands that provided the spring snapped, slapping the stilter hard in the thigh and eliciting a loud curse.

"The force is strong with him[20]," I muttered, shaking my head in sympathy.

[14] Just a short joke.
[15] Apologies, Mr. Bradbury.
[16] Did anyone get this?
[17] Sorry, George, it was too easy.
[18] Ditto.
[19] Apologies, George Alec Effinger.
[20] What can I say, George?

Overhead, the lights flickered once more and we looked at each other, startled.

"Come on, come on[21]," I urged my partner. We had not gone more than a few steps when we both stopped, our jaws agape in awe at a brilliant display of large spheres colored like the planets of the solar system.

My partner reached for the large, earth-like sphere and asked the red-haired seller, "How much for just the planet?[22]"

I grabbed it out of her hand and placed it back, telling her in my best Yoda voice, "Forbidden: planet.[23]"

Beside the seller was a pretty young girl who playing a hand-held video game. I could see the title: *Harlie*. She played for a while. When *Harlie* was won[24], she looked around for something else to do. She started looking in the cash box longingly, like she wanted to play with the money. Her badge read: *Maggie*. My partner noticed and pointed, saying, "Pretty Maggie, money eyes.[25]"

Seeing how hard it was for her to resist further temptation and remembering our jobs, I tugged her out of the Exhibitor's hall towards Gaming. At the exit we joined the throng filling up the hallway.

"Space, the final frontier[26]," my partner intoned but I barely heard her, peering back as I was into the Exhibitor's Hall, declaiming, "Thieves' World.[27]"

And we wended our way into Gaming, my headset beeped and I was advised by the head of security to keep an eye out for a small person dressed as a unicorn, seen in the company of a very old man.

"Mything persons,[28]" I told my partner as I pointed to my headset

---

[21] This one you've got hum, Mary Chapin Carpenter.
[22] Fondly recalling John M. Ford.
[23] Hey, George, you can't complain! I tied you into a classic here.
[24] Hi, David! (And Harlan)
[25] Hi, Harlan.
[26] Sorry, Gene.
[27] With apologies to Bob Asprin and Lynn Abbey.
[28] Again, sorry Bob!

and filled her in on the description.

"Is she carrying a sword or a wand?" my partner asked. There were several little girls wandering around, looking a lot alike, dressed in different costumes.

"A dagger," I told her.

"Ah," she murmured knowingly as she glanced around the hallway, "the warrior's apprentice.[29]"

"Yeah, they've already seen the sorcerer's apprentice," I said, "and he's not with her."

As we entered Gaming, my partner pointed out some women dressed in Greek garb, serving a man dressed as Dionysus, intoning with a raised eyebrow, "Ethos of Athens?[30]"

"I think you've got that wrong," I told her, my brain spinning. "I'm pretty sure it's supposed to be someone 'of Athos'."

With a disapproving glare, she let it slide, turning instead to a group of card players huddled over a table. One was gathering in his winnings, crowing, "Ace of Aces![31]"

One of the losers, a pear-shaped man, was shaking his head, muttering sourly, "Wild cards![32]"

The third was looking at his own hand disgustedly. "Bloody Jack![33]"

A loud commotion further inside attracted our attention and it was a moment before my partner spotted it and pointed, "See! Three P.O.![34]"

I suppose she should have said "pissed-offs" but hers was the superior way[35].

The three were grouped over another table. One was very young and short, the other of middling size and the third was tall and hairy.

---

[29] Apologies to Lois!
[30] Sorry again, Lois!
[31] Gotta be a gamer to get this one.
[32] With apologies to the pear-shaped man himself.
[33] Sorry, Mr. Meyer.
[34] George!
[35] Gene!

The young one had the manual in his hand and was pointing at it, declaring loudly, "Are two D2![36]"

The tall hairy guy growled. My partner and I exchanged glances and then she started forward, ready to disrupt the dispute. I wondered if maybe I should go with her, so I offered, "Han?"

"Solo![37]" she declared, holding a hand upright behind her, ordering me to stay put. She oozed the charm over the three of them and they were shortly transfixed, in awe of her. With a smile and a pleasant wave, she left them, telling me, "Phantom menace.[38]"

So, also, was a group of four arguing vociferously as they played: a father, son, daughter, and mother. I took a quick look at the game they were playing and told Han knowingly, "Family Business."[39]

By about now, I'm sure you're all curious as to how we got this wonderful gig. I mean, attending DragonCon year in, year out, for free is the fantasy of many.

Well, I'll tell you: we don't know.

Han (in preference to Hannah) has this theory that it was a little girl who tried a curse that worked; I have this theory that it was the little boy who was showing off his phaser—"It really works!"

What we do know is this: we're here for set-up, we're here for tear-down and everything in between. And after? There is no after: we're here from set-up through to tear-down and then we start over, with a new con.

We figure we've been through about twenty DragonCons so far and we're always hoping that the next one will be our con—the one where we met the little girl and the little boy.

One thing we're certain of—if we want to get out of this time warp, we've got to be certain that nothing interferes with all the DragonCons that have gone before—or we'll never get back to our own.

[36] George.
[37] George.
[38] Again, George.
[39] Gotta be a gamer.

So Han and I walk the nights and guard the con. Han had more right than I: her old job was policeman.

We gave up on gaming and headed out to the main hotel, the Hyatt. Out back, as usual, were several smokers. As we passed, one lit up and I muttered, "Firestarter.[40]"

Before Han could react to that, someone flicked another lighter near a candle, causing Han to intone, "Something wicked this way comes.[41]"

Fortunately, a girl with black faerie wings artfully decorated along the edge with small lights walked by, and I pointed, "Nightwings.[42]"

I trudged on into the ballroom concourse, determined to find our missing persons and doing my best to pretend that I hadn't heard her.

Just as I got near the escalator, I saw a streak of something small and white dart on, followed immediately by an old man who reached for her but failed to grab her.

"Han!" I cried, pointing toward the pair but by the time I turned around, they were already several people in front of me. Han hoofed it over and we both got on, anxiously eyeing the pair as they reached the top of the escalator.

Apparently, from the commotion ahead, the little girl bowled over some people as she struggled to slip from the old man's grasp.

We got there as the old man broke out of the worst of the throng only to find himself cornered in the center of a group of the 501st Imperial Storm Trooper Battalion.

"The tactics of mistake[43]," I said, shaking my head triumphantly as Han came up beside me.

"What?" one of the stormtroopers asked.

"Soldier," Han intoned, with a glance my way, "Ask Not.[44]"

---

[40] Apologies to Stephen.
[41] Apologies to Mr. Bradbury.
[42] Apologies to Silverbob.
[43] With apologies to Gordon Dickson.
[44] Again, sorry, Gordy!

I reached for the old man but he turned, one hand outstretched toward where we'd last seen the little girl.

"You have to get her!" he cried. "You have to get her before it's too late!"

And before I could say anything, he let out a surprised cry and collapsed to the floor, hard. It was then that I got a good look at him: his clothing was odd and he didn't seem to fit in at all. A stranger in a strange land.[45]

"Make room, make room![46]" Han cried, seeing that the situation was critical.

I knelt beside the man and he whispered to me urgently, "The wand or the horn, whichever she has—"

"Take it easy," I told him calmly.

"No!" he cried. "I came all this way, all this time looking for you. She's got it, get the horn and get back before it's too late."

"Too late?"

"The fabric of the universe is tearing," he whispered. "We should never have done it, never knew. She's your daughter, you've got to find her, get her back. Her wand's made of thiotimoline[47], dip it in water and drink."

"Our daughter?" Han asked, kneeling on the other side of him.

The old man's lips twitched as he pointed at each of us in turn, "Han, Sam,—" and he pointed off towards the vanished girl "—witch.[48]"

He looked at me with one final, anguished expression, whispering, "Sorry Dad, sorry it took so long." His eyes focused to the distance as he added, "The lightning. I had to ride the lightning."

Around us, the lights flickered. Han and I exchanged glances and when I looked back down again, he was gone.

Numbly, I led her out of the crowd, towards the doors to the evening air, watching her carefully.

---

[45] Sorry again, Mr. Heinlein.
[46] Sorry, Harry!
[47] Isaac, see? I worked you in, too.
[48] This one's all mine.

"Our son?" she wondered, glancing back toward the now-full atrium. She looked toward where the little witch had disappeared. "Our daughter?"

I could see her tears brimming, threatening to fill her eyes.

"Han?" I said quietly to her, going to one knee and putting a hand on her leg soothingly. "Are you crying?"

"Flow my tears," the policeman said[49].

"He was old," I told her.

She tilted her head up, caught my eyes with hers as she explained, "The doors of his face, the lamps of his mouth.[50]"

Her eyes lit with determination as she said, "We'll have to find her."

"Before it's too late," I agreed.

After a moment she stood and I followed wordlessly, circling behind her back and leaning her against me. For a long while we stood: Sentinel[51], against the fall of night[52].

The sliding doors opened and noise from the rest of the con flowed over us, beckoning.

"Come on," I said to her, pulling her around so that she faced inwards once more. "Once more into the breach.[53]"

She smiled at that but shook her head, correcting, "Back to the future[54]."

---

[49] With apologies to the late Mr. Philip K. Dick.
[50] Acknowledgements to Roger Zelazny.
[51] For Arthur.
[52] For Isaac.
[53] And how can you not do something like this without one poke at the Bard?
[54] With apologies to both Mr. Zemeckis and Mr. Spielberg.

ARTIFACT

Teresa Patterson

"The art show is on fire!"

I spun in the direction of the shout to see people running toward the brilliant orange and red flickering light coming from the ballroom that housed the DragonCon art show. My heart froze for a moment at the thought of that room, of all rooms, going up in flames. Even now, before the official start of the convention, the room was filled with irreplaceable works by Maitz, Eggleton, Whelan, and many others. They were still setting the show, so the ballroom would be crowded with cardboard boxes, shipping crates, and packing paper—all even more flammable than the art.

"Ohmigod, Kari! My art is in there!" Mozelle Funderburke, one of my clients exhibiting in the show, turned and sprinted for the ballroom. She had been speaking with Michelle Poche, Jean Marie Ward and me in the foyer outside the ballroom when the shout went up. The rest of us were soon in hot pursuit, despite the fact that we were all wearing high-heeled shoes in preparation for the pre-con party.

Jean Marie, a stunning red-head and DragonCon regular, published an on-line magazine. The convention was a major source of material for her writers. Michelle, author and screen writer, was new to Dragon, making her debut as a guest after the success of her first screenplay. A statuesque blond, she had been a model before becoming a writer and her long legs allowed her to easily outdistance the rest of us. She dove into the ballroom, only to stop so suddenly that I narrowly avoided piling into her. I can run in heels, but stopping is a little more difficult. I recovered my balance and stared in disbelief.

The huge ballroom exhibited the usual chaotic disarray of pre-con art installation with boxes, crates, hanging materials, and art scattered haphazardly around the hall, all illuminated by angry flickering orange and red lights. The roaring lights and shadows glowed on every wall and surface, just as they would if there were a fire raging in the room, but I could see no flames. It sounded like fire, even looked like fire, but nothing was actually burning. Everyone else converging on the show appeared to be equally baffled. After it finally sank in that the art show was in no immediate danger, I started looking for the source of the "fire." The amazing light show appeared to emanate from one of the displays near the center of the room. It was a very realistic simulation. Despite the lack of actual heat or flames, it looked as if we were walking into a raging inferno. The effect appeared almost three-dimensional.

"It's like being in a Star Wars hologram." Jean Marie held out her hand in wonder and watched the "flame" lights dance on it.

"Is this a normal part of the convention?" Michelle asked as we joined the crowd of artists and staff gathering around the apparent source of the light show. I had warned her that DragonCon was an event unlike any other, and to be prepared for anything. But, though I was a multi-year veteran of the con and its art show, I had never seen anything quite like this.

The imagery appeared to be projected from a strangely shaped sculpture, approximately two to three feet in size, attached to a slender black pedestal. The sculpture itself, carved out of some sort of glowing amber, resembled stylized flames—except, unlike amber, this stuff was moving, almost like melting and reforming wax. We watched as it undulated, flames caught in liquid and then animated in slow-motion. The pedestal had a wide base that narrowed to a thin pillar about three and a half feet tall before widening to a broad curved top that seemed to be connected to the glowing sculpture in an almost organic pod—sort of the way a rose is connected to its stalk.

"Normal? Nope. So far as I know no one's ever pretended to burn down the art show before—although there were times in the old days when some of the jury-rigged electrical wiring threatened to do it for real." I leaned in to take a closer look, trying to see where the amazing light projections were coming from. "I've seen a lot of unusual work, but this artist is new to me."

This was a major admission, since I had begun my fannish career as an artist and art show volunteer. I had worked my way up to art show director before branching off to become an art and then a literary agent. As a result, I knew—or had at least heard of—pretty much every artist who had ever worked in the science-fiction and fantasy genre. For me to be unaware of an artist that could produce something as impressive as this sculpture meant the artist was either brand new—or had been hiding under a rock.

"New to me, too, Kari." Rob Patrick, the director of the art show, came up behind me, startling me. Tall and broad, he loomed over my petite five foot three inch frame. He also had a big, jovial presence, which, combined with his size, normally made it impossible for him to sneak up on anyone. But normally he wasn't competing with a raging forest fire light show. Standing between Rob and Michelle, I felt like a dwarf.

"So who is your new wunderkind?" I gestured at the glowing sculpture. "Do you know if they already have an agent?" My official purpose in attending DragonCon was to sign new clients and make deals for existing clients—which made a great, tax-deductible excuse to attend my favorite show. But to pay the bills I had to actually do the work. And any artist that could produce art that could move and spit holographic fire would be a marvelous addition to my client list.

"I have no idea."

"Well, then, pass me their info and I'll ask myself." I batted my eyes persuasively.

Rob shrugged. "No. You've got it wrong. I have no idea who the artist is. Whoever brought this hasn't checked in yet."

That wasn't surprising, since the show was still getting set; there were a lot of artists who had not yet officially checked in.

"Then look at your list and see who reserved this space." I knew the art show always sold out, so there should have been a name to go with every space.

"That's just it. This space was never reserved. It was supposed to be left open as floor space for the performers. Whoever brought this in just set it up and left. I'm hoping they remember to come back and check in."

"Performers?" Michelle looked perplexed. "I thought this was an art show."

"It is. But one of the things that make the Dragon art show different is the addition of the performing arts," I explained.

"Yeah, we bring musicians and dancers in at specified times throughout the show to entertain. That way, people are more likely to stick around for the show and then spend money on the art. That," Rob added proudly, "was my addition to the show's legacy. The artists love it."

"Us starving artists love anything that will bring buyers in to keep us from starving," Mozelle quipped. She had rejoined us after having checked her display. "All the people in the world won't do any good if they're not in the show."

I grimaced, remembering past DragonCon art shows, some under my watch, when the art show had been relegated to a ghetto in a building several blocks away from the rest of the convention. Back then I could not afford the luxury of worrying about performance art. It had taken most of my team's time and effort just to make sure the attendees knew the art show existed. A light display like this one would have gone a long way toward convincing fans to walk a few blocks to see the show.

"I'm going to have to figure out a new spot for the performers, because I'm not about to try to move that thing." Rob gestured at the strange sculpture. "The worst part is, they left without even putting a bid sheet out. We have no idea what to charge if someone wants to buy it!"

"Well, in a way the light show *is* a performance." Michelle pointed out. "You could probably even dance to it."

Just as suddenly as it began, the light show stopped. The sculpture stopped moving, frozen in a form that resembled dull, partially melted caramel. Jean Marie moved in to examine the piece, running her hands over the sculpture and the base.

"It feels like glass or smooth ceramic. But I can't find any source for the projection or any kind of switch to turn it on or off."

Rob and I joined her, making our own examination of the piece, but she was right. The surface of both sculpture and base were completely smooth. It had no openings or projections of any kind. Rob even tugged on the sculpture to lift it from its base, but it didn't budge.

"Whoever made this was certainly thorough. It appears pretty tough."

"So what are you going to do, Rob?"

"Not much I can do. I'll put the performers somewhere else and hope this artist checks in soon. In the meantime, I have a show to set."

"If you're done with that, I've got some artists that need to talk to you."

I looked up to see John, the art show second, standing by with a clipboard and a line of artists. "No rest for the wicked," I whispered. Rob rolled his eyes at me, then put on his art show happy face to greet the first artist. "Hi, what can I do for you?"

"There's not enough light on my bay and one of my paintings is missing!"

"Missing? I'm sure it's just misplaced. The area is controlled by security. It can't have gone far. Where did you unpack it?" Rob took the artist gently by the arm and led him towards his display bay.

I had heard it all hundreds of times before. It was one of the reasons I retired from art show administration. I love the art and the artists, but the work was always grueling. The art show was arguably the most difficult area of any convention. Between administrating the registration of artists, sales of space, set up and tear down of the show, sales of the art, the auction, shipping and receiving art, and paying the artists after the show, the art director also had to deal with fragile creative egos and desperate artists. That often meant twenty-hour days during the show as well as months of work before and after—and all for free. As in most SF conventions, Rob and his entire art staff volunteered their time, busting their butt for a free pass to a convention they never had time to see. You had to love the art and the artists to do the job—either that or you had to be crazy. As for me, I plead the fifth.

And the artists they served? Most lived on the edge. They often epitomized the classic "starving artist." Many of them were at the mercy of the art show staff to ensure they made enough sales to get home, much less have food or shelter. That desperation could be difficult to face, especially in the pressure-cooker environment of a four-day show. I missed the adventure—but not enough to go back. As an agent I could pick and choose whom I wanted to represent, and I only picked artists and authors whose work I knew I could sell. Not only that, as an agent I actually got *paid* for helping creative people. And if I got bored? I could always write.

"Well, looks like the excitement's over. We need to get to work. The meet and greet pre-con party should be underway." I smiled at Michelle. "Time to introduce you to some of the other denizens of DragonCon."

"Fresh meat!" Jean Marie laughed an evil laugh as we left for the meet-and-greet. Disguised as parties, these events were a crucial part of the convention, giving me needed access to the clients and buyers that kept me in business, and giving Jean Marie access to celebrities for her magazine.

We arrived at the hospitality suite, high up in the Hyatt, to find the party in full swing. Later in the convention I knew the parties would fill the room and spill out onto the balcony. But many of the two hundred-plus guests would not arrive until later in the show, making the pre-con party sedate by comparison. We showed our credentials to the security volunteer at the door and went inside. I waved at a few familiar faces and led the way to the buffet.

"Kari, can I talk to you for a moment?" Bill Foss, a dapper silver-haired gentleman, intercepted me. His tailored business jacket and button-down shirt always made him stand out amid the T-shirts and spandex favored by the convention crowd. He said he wore them to blend in—but in this crowd they had the exact opposite effect.

Now a high-powered Hollywood agent, he was also a good friend. He had helped me get my start and had taught me a lot about running an agency. When any of his actors decided they wanted to write, he sent them to me. Whenever any of my writers wanted to sell scripts, he helped pave the way for them. He was also a consummate ladies man. I figured this was a good time to introduce Bill to Michelle, since she was both a scriptwriter and a gorgeous woman, two of Bill's favorite things.

"Hi, Bill, glad you're here. I have someone you need to meet. Michelle . . . ."

"Oh, yeah nice to meet you." He interrupted before I could even finish the introduction, not even looking at Michelle or Jean Marie before grabbing my arm to pull me aside. "Kari, I have a problem. Do you have a moment?"

Baffled, I shrugged apologetically to the girls and let him pull me away to the relative privacy of the outer balcony. I knew it must be something serious if it made Bill forget to flirt. "What's up? You OK?"

"No. I can't find Peter."

"Peter?" My brain fogged as I tried to guess which of the many men named Peter he meant.

"Peter Gerard. The actor."

"Oh!" Peter Gerard played the lead in a hit sci-fi show called *Babel Six*. He was also one of Bill's best clients and was planning to do a book deal with me. "*That* Peter." At Bill's look of exasperated distress, I tried to think of something to calm him. Like most who breathed the California air, Bill could be quite high strung. "Are you sure he's arrived? A lot of the Hollywood crowd won't be in until tomorrow."

"He was already in. We spoke this morning. He had a meeting with me late this afternoon, but he never showed. I phoned his room but no one answered. I even had the maid check it. His luggage is there, but he's gone. He's never missed a meeting before."

"He probably just ran into some fans and decided to give them some quality time. You know how generous he is. I'm sure he'll turn up." I wasn't sure of anything. But I knew it wasn't good for Bill to get wound up about a missing actor—especially at a convention.

"I'm just concerned." He took a deep breath. "If you see him or hear anything, let me know."

I agreed. Bill said he was too tense to stay at the party and left. I rejoined my friends, mildly concerned about Mr. Gerard's absence. If he missed a meeting with Bill, his primary agent, that didn't bode well for his meeting with me.

I tried to put the matter aside, making apologies for Bill and bringing the girls up to speed about what had happened. I promised Michelle another round of introductions when Bill was more focused, and we proceeded to attempt to enjoy the rest of the evening.

The next morning, Jean Marie met me outside my room.

"Did you hear? They found Peter Gerard. He apparently spent yesterday and most of the night at the Old Mill Inn getting soused at the bar. The news is all over the convention."

"That doesn't sound right. Peter doesn't drink."

"Are you sure?"

I was positive. "Remember that con in Chicago I told you about where they took all the guests and VIP fans on a gambling boat cruise the night before the convention opened?"

"Yeah. It was called something like Big Cosmos or something."

"That's the one. Well, Mr. Gerard and I were both guests at that one. The cruise consisted of several hours on a casino boat filled with gambling machines and free drinks. And do you know where Mr. Gerard spent the cruise? While most of the guests were playing the slots and sucking down free cocktails, he was on the top deck with a bunch of fans, drinking diet coke while teaching them how to play a dexterity game with empty soda cups. Does that sound like a man who would go out and get drunk the night before a convention appearance?"

She agreed that it did not. Something was not adding up.

I made my way downstairs and spotted Bill at breakfast in the restaurant tucked into one side of the vast Hyatt atrium. He immediately waved me over.

"Please join me. I was supposed to have breakfast with Peter, but he said he didn't feel well. At least if I am having breakfast with a pretty girl I won't ruin my reputation."

I had already eaten a breakfast bar in my room, but I slid into the chair across from him. "Ah, the flatterer is back. You must be feeling better—either that or you want something."

"Can't I just be appreciative of your beauty?"

"You are never *just appreciative* of anything. But it doesn't hurt my ego." I ordered a cup of tea from the attentive waitress. I noticed she was wearing some alien-looking makeup, probably in honor of the convention. "Seriously, though, is Peter OK? I heard they found him in a downtown bar."

"That part is true. But Peter says he has no idea how he got there. One minute he was in the Hyatt, the next minute he was on the floor at the Old Mill. He says he has no memory of the time in between. Everyone seems to think he was upset about the end of his TV show and went out to drown his sorrows. But you know that Peter doesn't drink. And he has no sorrows to drown. He was here to announce a deal for a new show. He is very excited about it." Bill took a drink of his orange juice. I stirred cream into my tea and waited for him to continue.

"I saw him shortly after they brought him back to the hotel. He was certainly disoriented, but not from booze."

"Then what?"

"I don't know. But I've been around far too many alcoholic actors to misread the signs."

"How are you going to handle damage control?" We both knew the con rumor mill was in full swing.

"I think he's just going to let it ride. As long as Peter is funny and accessible to the fans, they'll just chalk up the episode as a new part of his legend: the hard drinking party animal."

"That's going to be tough to swallow. I know I'd resent the heck out of it if people thought I was a heavy drinker." I sipped my tea, the strongest thing I ever drank.

"Well, Peter is an actor and a professional. He'll play the role because he knows that trying to deny it will only make things worse."

I left the table feeling bad for Peter. It didn't help that the only things I could think of that would cause both amnesia and disorientation were all worse than being drunk. I didn't mention any of them to Bill, but I was certain he already had the list running through his mind, too.

This DragonCon was shaping up to be even stranger than most. But I still had a job to do. As a successful agent and part-time writer, I was scheduled to speak on several panels. The parties were important for my business, allowing opportunities for networking and making deals, but the panels were for the fans. And it was the fans who made all the machinery turn for the entire industry. They bought the books, saw the movies and played the games that kept the rest of us working. It was their admission fees that made the convention possible. This first panel promised to be fun. Jean Marie was on it and my friend, best selling author Roxy Caine, was the moderator. The topic involved vampires and sex—a surefire crowd pleaser.

The panel room was buried deep in the lower levels of the Hyatt. Despite struggling with the overloaded elevators, I managed to arrive right on time, sliding into my seat beside Jean Marie. The room was filled to capacity with fans, most in spandex, leather, and goth style makeup, despite the early hour. I felt underdressed in my jeans and blouse, despite the fact that my outfit would be club wear anywhere else. It was obvious that most of the fans were there to see Roxy Caine.

"Where's Roxy?" Jean Marie asked. "Isn't she moderating?"

"I haven't seen her yet, but I'm sure she'll be here."

But Roxy never arrived. We did the panel without her, sharing the moderating duties among us, while making apologies to Roxy's fans. It wasn't unusual for writers to miss their panels, but it was unusual for Roxy. She took her convention commitments very seriously. It was that professional work ethic, along with a brilliant mind and a gift for storytelling that had taken her all the way to the best seller list.

After the panel, I tried to call Roxy on her cell phone, but the call went straight to voice mail—hardly surprising since the mass of concrete and steel in the convention hotels made cell phone signals notoriously unreliable. I gave up, resolving to try again later. In the meantime, I had to get to a meeting with an illustrator about a lucrative magazine cover deal.

The illustrator, Dan Mais, had a table in the artist alley area of the art show. I arrived at the ballroom to find it unusually crowded for the first morning of the convention. The boxes, crates and packing material from the night before had all been stowed away out of sight. Paintings and sculptures filled the bays and covered the tables of the central gallery area in an inviting display of imaginative imagery. Artist Bazaar sales booths belonging to individual artists lined the walls of the room. A four-person Celtic music group played a rollicking jig for an appreciative crowd in one of the open areas between the display bays. As I pushed through the crowds, I noticed the piece that had created such a stir the night before. It rested, still and cold, on its pedestal near the center of the show, surrounded by a mixed group of costumed attendees, most in leather and spandex. I had a few moments before my meeting, so I decided to give it another look.

The staff had erected a rope barrier around it to create a viewing perimeter. Someone had scribbled a hand-written sign and taped it to the base where the official big sheet normally would have been attached. It read "Unknown Alien Artifact." Something else seemed different about the sculpture itself, but I couldn't decide what it was. There was still no obvious machinery to explain its behavior.

Rob must have seen me come in. He met me at the display.

"Hey, Rob, the show looks great. You'd never guess there'd been a fire in here. How's business?"

"It's booming. Word has gotten out about the light shows. I had to put up this rope to keep people off of it. Everyone wants to know when the next show is scheduled. Of course we can't tell them anything because we don't actually know anything. We just tell them to stick around and see." He gestured expansively at the unusually large crowds milling through the show. "Apparently they're listening. Now if they just bid on art while they're waiting, we should break some records."

"So there's still no sign of the artist who left this?"

"Nope," he sighed, "not yet."

"Wait. I just realized you said shows, as in more than one?"

"Yeah, the thing has gone off on us a few times now. The last time was a little over an hour ago."

"Same thing?"

"Not really. Oh, it still produced a light show, but each time it created a completely different effect. And when it's over, the sculpture seems to take on a different shape."

I realized that was what seemed strange. The ragged flame-like edges I had seen before no longer existed, leaving the thing looking more like a smooth river-rock.

"When you find the artist, we've got to find out how he made this. It's odd that no one has turned up to enjoy its popularity. In the meantime, you might as well enjoy the attention it's generating."

"Well, I think the artists are enjoying the added traffic, especially if it gets some sales as well."

As if on cue the sculpture lit up. This time, it was as blue and tranquil as it had been red and fiery before. Waves and water seemed to ooze out of the sculpture while blue and green lights, shimmering like sun reflected off of water, filled the room. Every surface within sight looked like it was underwater. A sound that reminded me of surf and waves echoed gently through the room, creating an interesting counterpoint with the musicians. People started pressing close to see it. I decided to escape to my meeting before I ended up crushed in the crowd.

On the way out the door I spotted Anne McCauly, the Granddame of Fantasy, nestled in her wheelchair. She spotted me and waved. I waved back, and her convention-appointed assistant obediently pushed her over to meet me. Anne introduced me to her minder, a cute young volunteer named Claire. She was one of the few celebrities who rated a twenty-four hour companion to aid her throughout the convention.

"It's amazing, isn't it?" Anne indicated the lightshow going on around us. "It's just marvelous to see what artists can do with technology these days."

"That it is," I admitted. "Are you going over to judge the dragon egg contest?"

"No. I think the actual judging is tomorrow." She looked to Claire, who quickly checked the schedule and nodded agreement. "But I want to get a look at the rest of the art show while I have a chance. Perhaps we can chat later?"

"Love to."

Anne and Claire continued on into the show. I looked after them for a moment, thinking the wheel chair was very misleading. Anne McCauly wrote the first fantasy genre novel to make it onto the *New York Times* bestsellers list, and she had been setting the standard ever since. Though bound to a wheel chair much of the time, her mind remained razor sharp and her will, iron.

I made it to Dan's booth, but Dan wasn't there. That was unusual for him, especially since he had chosen the time to fit in with his schedule. No one knew where he had gone. I pulled up a chair, enjoying the special effects show while I waited, but Dan never showed. I finally gave up, leaving him a note. I hated trying to squeeze in rescheduled meetings at a convention, but this deal was lucrative enough for both of us that I would have to make the effort. By the time I left, the light show had ended and the sculpture was still again.

Jean Marie met me at the Art Show entrance. "Hey, Kari. Did you hear about Robert Hutch?"

Robert Hutch was an actor and a DragonCon regular. He had been on a reasonably successful sci-fi show in the seventies and now did guest roles on the new version of that series. I knew him, though not well. But Jean Marie had interviewed him several times for her magazine.

"No. What about him?"

"He went missing, right before his talk. They're saying one minute he was in the green-room, and the next minute he was gone. He turned up about twenty minutes ago claiming he was kidnapped by the Cylons. Everyone else seems to think he was lured away by some sweet young fan."

"And what do you think?"

"I don't know what to think. So far as I know he has never missed a guest appearance before. He knows the fans helped get his show back on the air. I feel he would never knowingly stand them up."

"Well, my appointment stood me up, so I've got a little time to kill."

"Great, let's hit the coffee bar."

Nestled into one corner of the towering atrium, the coffee bar not only provided great gourmet coffee and tea, it also provided a great view of the Hyatt Atrium concourse, one of the premier people-watching spots in the convention. In the evenings, the concourse was like an off-world red-carpet event, but even in the daytime it was an amazing amalgamation of people and costumes. From a seat in the coffee bar, or in the adjoining restaurant, it was possible to watch the entire convention pass by. Over the years, the coffee bar had become our favorite hang-out spot—especially since they made a mean Chai Tea Latte.

I called Michelle on her cell to invite her to meet us, but she wanted to attend the Crossed Swords live combat performance. Fannish costumes and medieval sword-play were all new to Michelle, and I knew the Crossed Swords always put on an excellent show. Since Michelle hoped to eventually write a medieval fantasy to go with her more contemporary work, I though the demo would be a perfect introduction to the genre. I had done my time swinging a sword as a member of the Society for Creative Anachronisms and had even performed on a sword demo team in my youth, so I felt no compelling need to watch the show myself.

"Enjoy. I'll catch up with you later."

We had only been at the coffee shop a few moments when I spotted Roxy Caine sitting in the back of the adjoining restaurant swathed in one of her elegant embroidered saris. I hopped the rail between the restaurant and the coffee shop and went over to check on her.

"Hey, Roxy, we missed you this morning."

"Oh, hi, Kari. Look, I am *so* sorry I missed that panel this morning. I don't know what happened." Normally poised and extremely self confident, she looked very distressed.

"It's OK. No problem. Everyone oversleeps once in a while. The panel went fine." I tried to reassure her.

"But, I didn't oversleep." She insisted, grabbing my hand to emphasize the point. "I have a book due next week. I was in the coffee shop writing by 6:00 a.m. I stopped about ten-fifteen, in plenty of time for an eleven o'clock panel. I remember stopping to look into the art show on my way to the panel. The next thing I knew I was standing in the pet shop in the Mall several hours later."

"But you're allergic to cats and dogs."

"I'm allergic to everything with fur! I have no idea what I was doing there or how I got there. Somehow I even left my computer in the art show."

Now I was certain something was terribly wrong. Roxy's life—all her manuscripts and edits for the new book—were on that computer. There was no way she would let it out of her sight. Yet, she herself was telling me it happened.

"Please don't tell anyone outside of the other panelists. I don't want anyone to think I'm losing it. But I wanted you to know I didn't stand you up on purpose."

I didn't know what to say. I reassured her as best I could, then made my way back to my stool at the coffee shop. I passed on Roxy's apology to Jean Marie.

"Poor Roxy. That must have been unnerving. At least she's OK."

We mulled over theories about Roxy's strange excursion, but none of our conjectures made sense, even to us.

"Hey, guys."

Michelle captured an empty chair and pulled up to our table.

"I thought you were going to watch the Crossed Swords?"

"I was. But they never showed. So I decided to join you."

We spent the next hour "people watching." Even by day, DragonCon boasted more spandex and leather per square foot than anything outside a fetish convention. Add to that the Storm Trooper Cadres, Brown Shirt contingents, Predator beasts, and medieval warriors and wenches, and it made for better entertainment than satellite TV. But I couldn't stop thinking about Roxy's strange memory lapse, or Peter Gerard's unorthodox excursion.

"Hey, guys!" I looked up to see Lisa and Tyler, two fans from my home town who were also DragonCon regulars. "Mind if we join you?"

Lisa, a short, buxom redhead, grabbed the powerfully built Tyler and directed him to get more chairs. While we struggled to squeeze two more people around the already-crowded tiny bistro table. I introduced them to Michelle.

"*The* Michelle Poche?" Lisa gushed. "You wrote *The Furies*! I loved that movie!"

"Thanks. Glad you liked it." Michelle flashed her dazzling smile. "I saw you guys at the Crossed Swords demo."

"Yeah, we saw you there, too. But it's nice to officially meet you."

"I waited for fifteen minutes, before giving up. Did they ever show up?"

Tyler shook his head while Lisa answered for both of them. "No they never did. But," she leaned in close "it was the strangest thing. They found all their swords and stuff lying in the back hall."

Jean Marie and I exchanged startled glances. We both knew that no self respecting swordsman would leave his weapons lying around unattended. And these guys were pros.

"Something must have happened to them," she said.

"They've got security out looking for them," Tyler assured us, "but some of the staff said they saw them in that hall about twenty minutes before the demo."

"Curiouser and curiouser," Jean Marie shook her head "this is shaping up to be one strange con."

At Lisa and Tyler's blank looks, I brought them up to speed on the unusual events to date—omitting Roxy Caine's unplanned trip to the pet store. They had no theories either, but were planning to make a point of viewing the "art show artifact" as it was being dubbed, for themselves.

I had to excuse myself for another meeting, so we agreed to try to get together later to attend the parties—I had to reserve the evening meal for a publisher. Tyler and Lisa agreed to show Michelle around the convention.

Throughout the rest of the day I continued to hear about various guests missing their events, or showing up in strange locations. Some of the stories were typical behavior for that particular guest, but too many did not make sense. When I finally met up with Jean Marie and Michelle later that night in the hospitality suite, we decided to compare notes. It turned out they had been hearing a lot of missing-in-action stories, too.

"Wow." Michelle shook her head. "If all these stories are true, an awful lot of people have gone MIA. And almost all of them are well-known celebrities."

"And, so far as we know," Jean Marie added, "most of them are turning up in unexpected places with no memory of how they got there."

We had gathered out on the balcony, away from the noise and crush of the party in full swing behind us, where we had a better chance of talking without being overheard.

"Yeah, if this was anywhere other than DragonCon, they'd have a full scale investigation in place," I grumbled. "As it is, everyone expects strange behavior from us sci-fi geeks, so no one's going to take this seriously."

"I think Pat Henry is taking it seriously," Jean Marie insisted. Leaning in and keeping her voice low. "I saw him outside Convention Operations headquarters a little while ago. He was on the radio with security, looking very pissed and ordering them to beef up protection on all VIP's."

Pat Henry was the head honcho of the entire convention. If he was worried, things were serious.

"There you are! You'll never guess what happened!" Lisa came bouncing through the door, sporting an elaborate leather and silk corset that showcased her ample assets. Tyler followed close behind her, also dressed to the nines in a goth-inspired suit. We made room for them on the now-crowded balcony, forcing Tyler to stand pressed up against Lisa's back. But he wasn't suffering. I could tell he was enjoying the view afforded by her steel-boned garment.

"No, I can't guess. What happened?"

"We went to the Dethhead concert—and they disappeared! Poof! Right off the stage!" Lisa illustrated by waving her hands in what was apparently meant to be a poofing motion. Dethhead was one of the more notorious bands that played the DragonCon stage. They were known more for their garish costumes, piercings, and on-stage antics than for their music.

"They came back," Tyler quickly added. "We thought the concert was over but they came back only a few moments later. They announced that they had been abducted by the alien mothership, but the aliens had taken one look at them and thrown them back."

"Do you think they were taken by whatever caused the other disappearances?" I could tell Lisa wanted that to be true.

"Knowing Dethhead? I think they found a way to capitalize on the events of the day and showcase a new stunt at the same time." Jean Marie had done an in-depth article on the notorious band for her magazine. They were all about the spectacle.

Lisa was clearly disappointed by Jean Marie's pronouncement, but Tyler nodded agreement.

"So, aside from the Dethhead stunt, do we have an idea how many people have been affected?" Michelle asked

We really didn't. After mulling things around, we finally agreed the best course of action was to let Pat Henry and con security handle things—much to Lisa's disappointment. But we would all keep our ears and eyes open just in case. We agreed to meet again the next day in the art show, mostly because it was centrally located and the site of my rescheduled afternoon meeting with Dan Mais. It was getting drafty on the balcony and I was wearing a strapless dress, so I decided to call it a night, leaving the others to party on at will.

Truthfully, I hated puzzles, and this whole disappearance thing was looking more and more like a giant puzzle. DragonCon was crazy enough without complications—though I was sure it was much worse for the people actually involved. I couldn't stop thinking about Peter Gerard, now stuck with a reputation as a lush, or Roxy Caine, shaken with the feeling that her brilliant mind had somehow betrayed her.

The next day, I was busy enough with meetings and several back-to-back panels that I managed to avoid thinking about the disappearances until it was time for my meeting with Dan. He was waiting at his booth this time.

"I'm sorry about yesterday. I really seriously overslept—by hours, apparently. I've never done that before. And I had the strangest dream. It was about Captain Martin and purple waves."

Dan had created the image of the iconic Captain Martin for the Rum of the same name, so that part of the dream didn't seem that unusual to me. As for purple waves? Well he was a sea Captain on a rum label. Dan clearly didn't want to talk about it further, so I didn't press the issue. I wanted him to sign off on the contract, and making him more uncomfortable than he already was served no purpose.

After the meeting, I decided to see how Rob was doing with the rest of the art show.

"So how's it going today? Any artists gone missing?" I meant it as a joke, but he didn't take it that way.

"Actually, quite a few," he growled. "Apparently many artists no longer believe in honoring their commitments."

"What do you mean? What's happened?"

"Well, some artists are just blowing off their panels and slide shows. They all received the schedule in advance, just like always, but some of the big guys, the ones you'd most expect to be professional, are just not showing up."

The room lit up around us as the sculpture chose that moment to begin another light show. This time the colors were bronze, gold and green. It reminded me a little of jewels, or a summer morning in the country. The sound it made reminded me of wind—or maybe a flock of birds.

"And I still don't know who dumped that sculpture thing here. We spent an hour last night trying to figure out how to turn it off. I guess I just have to hope the damn thing will eventually run out of batteries or something."

Rob was almost always cheerful, even under the extreme pressures of the art show. The fact that he was complaining at all showed that events were getting to him. I knew from experience that if he lost it, his whole staff would be affected.

"Well, it can't be as bad as the year I got stuck with the dead horse."

He grimaced. "Yeah, I remember that. It was a prop from a battle scene in that Mel Gibson Movie, *The Patriot*, wasn't it?"

"The artist never came back to claim it. We were stuck trying to figure out what to do with a very realistic, revolutionary war era, dead horse. Fake blood and all. We ended up loading it on a huge dolly and wheeling it though the halls on Monday morning, freaking all the business types. We finally managed to load it in a truck and transport it to the DragonCon warehouse for storage. I swear it was nearly as heavy as a real dead horse."

"Well, at least it didn't smell like one." Rob laughed. His good mood was back. I had done my job.

Behind us, just as suddenly as it began, the light show ended.

"Just remember, it can always get worse."

"Help! I need help!" I turned to see who was shouting and saw Anne McCauly's assistant Claire running frantically though the art show. "Someone help!"

"Claire! What's wrong?" She spotted me and allowed Rob and me to intercept her. "Has something happened to Anne?"

"Anne's gone!" Claire was wide eyed and obviously upset. "She was there and now she's gone!"

"She can't be gone," Rob insisted gently.

"Start from the beginning." I grabbed her shoulders to help her focus. "Take a deep breath."

A small crowd started to gather around us. I was relieved to see that Michelle and Jean Marie had arrived. They quickly assessed the situation and helped keep everyone but security back, while Rob and I focused on Claire.

"From the beginning, Claire. What happened?"

"I took Anne over to judge the dragon egg contest. Then I turned my back for a moment—and she disappeared!"

I felt a sense of relief. Anne was notorious for taking off on her own when her minders weren't looking. She could be a speed demon in the wheel chair when she put her mind to it.

"I'm sure she's around," Rob insisted.

"I know Anne." I tried to be reassuring. "She probably just decided to take off on her own. Don't worry, she can't get far in that wheel chair, and she'll be easy to spot."

"But that's just it!" Claire sobbed, "Her wheelchair is still there!" She pointed, stiff armed, across the room where an empty wheel chair sat in front of a display of dragon eggs. Claire dropped her arm and burst into tears. Rob and I looked helplessly at each other.

"I think it just got worse," he whispered.

He quickly alerted security to send teams to comb the convention and surrounding areas for Ms. McCauly, then questioned his own security people posted on the art room doors. None of them had seen Anne leave, and they all knew her. Jean Marie examined the empty wheelchair and reported back that all of Anne's possessions seemed to be in place. I tried to calm Claire and think. Anne could walk without a wheel chair, but not well and not far. How did someone disappear from what was arguably the most secure room in the convention? Because of the value of its contents, the art show was under guard twenty-four hours a day. No one got in without a badge, and no one got out without getting checked by security.

Claire got her breathing under control and insisted on joining the search. I let her go and went over to see if I could help Rob. The damn sculpture lit up again, but this time I didn't even look at it. It was only on for a moment, with no sound at all. That seemed strange.

"Does it do that, often? The shorter display, I mean, with no sound?"

"Yeah. It seems to do that about every other time."

"Weird."

About ten minutes later a young man in a security shirt raced over to the control desk to report to Rob.

"They found her!" he gasped, out of breath from his sprint. "They just found Ms. McCauly. She's OK. I came to get her chair."

"Where was she?" I asked.

"Sitting on a couch in the atrium."

"Upstairs?"

"No. The atrium at the Hilton. I just came from there."

That explained why he was winded. The Hilton Atrium was two city blocks, and a hotel and a half away, a brisk ten minute walk away for a healthy, athletic person. There was no way Anne made it there on her own.

"How did she get all the way to the Hilton?" Rob asked

"She claims to have no idea. She though she was still in the Hyatt, and that someone had taken her chair."

I rejoined Jean Marie and Michelle, who were looking at the sculpture.

"You know," Jean Marie crossed her arms and stared at it. "It's kind of funny that it lit up just before Anne disappeared and again right before they found her."

Something shifted in my brain. I hate puzzles.

"Well, I think we've had enough excitement," Michelle announced. "I'm hungry. Let's go eat something."

It always amazed me that Michelle could eat anything she wanted and still keep that amazing model-thin figure. I had to starve myself to even come close. But food did sound good. I realized I hadn't eaten since my breakfast protein bar. "Great idea. Calories be damned. I'll wear the spandex another time."

At the door to the art show, I spotted Lisa and Tyler. They waved and came over to join us. Behind us, the light show started up. I glanced back for a moment and that thing in my brain suddenly clicked into place. "Ohmigod! It's the sculpture!" I turned back to my friends in time to see Michelle's eyes roll back in their sockets. She started to collapse.

"Get her!" I yelled and lunged to catch Michelle. I felt Jean Marie's hands as she grabbed her from the other side. There was a wrenching sensation, and then nothing at all.

I awoke to find myself sprawled, in a most unladylike fashion, on something hard and warm and lumpy. I opened my eyes, but all I could see was a dim purple haze. Purple? Where had I heard that before? I had a splitting headache and felt like I'd done one too many extreme yoga poses.

"Where are we?"

It was Jean Marie. Squinting to force my eyes to adjust to the dim light, I looked toward the sound and spotted her, about ten feet away, lying in an equally inelegant position across a pile of what appeared to be machinery. The dim light made it difficult to pick out details, but we appeared to be in a chamber about twenty to thirty feet across. The walls were rounded, almost organic, lacking true corners or any obvious doors or windows.

Michelle was between us, but she was laid out like the princess from *Sleeping Beauty*, on some sort of raised support that looked a good deal more comfortable than my resting place. Unfortunately, like Sleeping Beauty, she wasn't moving. Shiny tubing that resembled umbilical cords ran from Michelle's resting place to the ceiling, and piles of machinery covered most of the floor.

"I don't know, but somehow I don't think we're in Kansas any more."

"What you doing here? You no be here! Just that one!" The voice, high-pitched and whiny sounded like a badly broken power drill. I managed to focus on its source, a glowing shape at the far side of the room that slightly resembled an oversize octopus. Also, like a disturbed octopus, it was changing color—not unlike the sculpture in the art show—flashing white and blue and purple and waving what appeared to be arms. I hadn't seen it come in, but the fact that it was here meant there had to be a door of some kind.

"You ruin all! You go! Is bad! You go!

That voice was definitely not helping my head. And my eyes were failing, too, because the thing seemed to be growing arms and legs until it looked almost human—in a squishy sort of way. Apparently upset, it waved its lengthening arms in an agitated manner and continued to yell.

"Hey, take it easy! We didn't ask to come here!" I snapped, struggling to get to my feet.

"Wherever here is," Jean Marie added, climbing gingerly off her own resting place.

"Want that one! Not these ones. These ones go!"

I finally dumped the heels and managed to get to my feet. Jean Marie moved to Michelle's side and started checking her over.

"Is she OK?"

"She's breathing. I can't tell much other than that."

"No touch that one! No touch! Just go!" Our host started forward toward Jean Marie, raising its arms in a threatening manner.

I stepped between them, my hands in what I hoped was a placating gesture. "Look, we'll be happy to go. Just give us our friend and send us back."

"We cannot do that."

The second voice, with much better grammar and volume control, sounded almost normal. I looked up to find our host had a companion. This one looked almost human—except for the rainbow of color changes racing over its skin.

"Why not?"

"Because you are awake. The others think it was a dream. You know it is not. You will tell them about us."

"As if anyone would believe us?" Jean Marie commented under her breath.

"I'm afraid we will have to kill you."

"What! Now wait a minute. Don't you think that's a little extreme?"

"No. Secrecy must be maintained. You must be eliminated."

"Eliminate! Must eliminate." The shrieky voice gleefully joined in.

I had to try a different tactic. "Look, we know you've been abducting people. Can you at least tell us why?"

The two beings looked at each other. Lights raced in rapid patterns over their skin.

"If you're going to kill us anyway, it won't hurt to tell us why." I pressed.

Jean Marie glared at me. The light show continued for a few more minutes.

"It doesn't matter." The cultured one finally responded. "The project has failed, anyway."

"What project?"

The being seemed to sigh. "Unlike the people of your world, we lack the ability to create entertainment. We cannot make stories. But we have been watching your old broadcasts for many years and our people have become addicted to your entertainments."

"Is that why you speak so clearly? From watching our old broadcasts?"

The creature spread his hands in an apparent affirmation.

"Then what happened to him?" Jean Marie pointed at shrieky voice.

"He is an engineer. Engineers spend all their time with machinery. That is enough entertainment for them. They don't like fiction. But most of our world does, and they are addicted to it. Now that your world has changed to digital media, there is no longer enough residual broadcast signal on the airwaves to satisfy them. Without the calming effects of entertainment, our people are rioting. The situation threatens to destabilized our government and destroy our civilization. Our mission is to find and collect the source of the entertainment and bring back something to pacify our people. Our engineers designed a machine to tap into your 'creatives'' minds, and collect their energies to bring back. With that energy, they are sure we will be able to create entertainments of our own."

"But why pick DragonCon?"

"According to our research, it has one of the highest concentrations of creative energy on the planet. The final decision was made based on the fact that the people of DragonCon already believe in life on other planets. They make up stories about them all the time. This makes it easier to hide our 'footprints' as you might say. Even those who remember coming here will believe they invented it themselves. We also knew we could place the transport device among the other artifacts you display where no one would notice it."

"The sculpture," Jean Marie blurted. "We were right. So you were abducting people. But why were they ending up in such strange places?"

The alien seemed to visibly deflate. "The mission has gone badly from the start. The transport unit was damaged during the journey. It has a flaw in the return circuit. We have been unable to repair it. We decided it worked well enough, so the mission continued.

"First we collected people we had seen in the 'videos' we collected, those called actors. But we discovered their energy did not work. They could not make the stories we needed. They were interpreters. We finally figured out that we needed other types of energy. So we started collecting those who made up the stories or illustrated them."

"That's why you grabbed Michelle."

"She wrote a motion picture, so we knew she had the creative energy in her."

"So you collect this energy, and that gives you what you need?"

The being colored. Dark browns merged with the blues to create a muddy hue across his body. "That was the mission. Unfortunately the machinery doesn't work."

The first being became extremely agitated. It started flashing red and white and waving its arms again. "I fix. I fix. These go."

"What do you mean it doesn't work?" I pressed, trying to keep his attention focused on me.

"The machinery collects the creative energy, but so far, we have not been able to turn it into anything we can use. We started collecting different kinds of creatives, hoping that would make the difference. We even tried using musicians—until we collected the Dethheads. Whatever they were, they were not entertaining. We sent them back immediately."

"The problem," Jean Marie suggested, "may have something to do with the fact that your engineers do not understand entertainment, yet they are the ones building your entertainment machine."

"For whatever reason, the machine has not performed as hoped. I am afraid we will have to declare this mission a failure. I am truly sorry you have to die."

"Wait! You are saying that all you need is fresh entertainment? That your people simply lack the ability to make up stories and movies and such for themselves?"

"Yes."

"Then I have a proposition for you, Joe. Can I call you Joe?"

"Joe" sort of nodded and flashed in confusion.

"Lots of people here can't make up their own stories, either. I am what is called an agent. It is my job to get fresh stories from their source, the creatives brains. I can do it for you without a machine. I can get you as much entertainment as you want. And you won't have to abduct anyone. Your secret can even be protected because writers and artists don't have to know who they're working for. I can tell them it is a new overseas cable channel or something. You can have our creatives write thousands of new stories just for you. Your mission doesn't have to be a failure."

"You can do that?"

"For the right price." I looked around at all the alien technology. I always wanted my own spaceship. "I'm sure we can find *something* for you to trade. You can even use Jean Marie's magazine to pick out your favorite creative artists." I looked over at Jean Marie who was nodding emphatic agreement.

Our host suddenly started flashing a bright array of rainbow colors across his skin. He appeared to commune with his fellow for a few moments, before turning back to me. "It is, as you say, a deal."

It took a few hours to iron out the contract, but we soon had an arrangement that would keep my writers and artists working long into the future, no matter what happened to New York publishing, and our new friend would go back home a hero. We shook on the deal and then prepared to go home.

Jean Marie and I took our places standing on either side of Michelle's couch. I couldn't believe we were actually going to beam down to our planet.

"Your friend will awaken when you arrive," the being reassured us. "We will send you to a secluded spot so your arrival will not be noticed and secrecy can be maintained."

He pressed something, and I felt that familiar wrenching sensation.

When my vision cleared, I saw several thousand people staring at us. We had materialized on stage in the middle of the masquerade. The MC looked at us in awe.

"So much for secrecy and seclusion," Jean Marie muttered, a large fake smile plastered to her face as she steadied an awakening Michelle.

Thinking quickly I grabbed the MC's mike, and announced, "You remember the classic movie Mars needs women?" The audience cheered assent. "Well, we've beamed to your planet to announce that we've taken care of that problem. We've given them all the women they can handle."

Jean Marie took the cue and we quickly vamped suggestively to more cheering while Michelle stood like a dear in the headlights of an oncoming truck. "But the problem is not over. Now, Mars needs writers."

The audience clapped and cheered as we quickly exited the stage with a very confused Michelle in tow. It was the truth, sort of, but now no one would ever believe it. The aliens' secret was safe as a DragonCon legend.

"I have no idea what just happened," Michelle glanced back over her shoulder as we hurriedly exited the hall, "but I'm famished. I could eat a horse right now!"

Jean Marie and I collapsed into laughter. It looked like it was going to be a successful convention after all.

LOST IN THE CROWD

———

Selina Rosen

They only really saw each other once a year at DragonCon. The rest of the time they just talked over the internet, maybe occasionally called one another. Cathy looked at Jason; he was doing a handstand on a stair rail.

"Get down, jack ass, you're going to get us thrown out," she ordered, but not without good humor.

He smiled at her, which would have been weird enough, him being upside down and all, but Jason was wearing the makeup he always wore to this thing that made it look like his face and right arm were melting. He wore the same tattered jeans and white "blood-stained" T-shirt with the sleeve torn off, too. Of course, she couldn't really talk, she'd been wearing a pirate costume for years.

Jason had such a good costume, and was such a regular at the convention, that people often wanted to have their picture taken with him like he was one of the celebrities.

"Come on, Jason, seriously. Get down," she said.

"Yeah, come on, dumb ass; forget security is going to revoke our badges. What if you fall?" Evan asked.

Jason nodded then and jumped off the rail to land in front of them. "I'm not going to fall. God! What a couple of old ladies." He pulled his shirt down quickly. "I told you I'm like a ninja. Come on, let's go get something to eat and then go back to the gawk of fame."

The gawk of fame was called the walk of fame by the people who ran the convention. It was where all the old movie and TV stars sat at tables with their head shots and other memorabilia spread out before them, waiting for fans to come by and buy their autographed pictures.

Jason's favorite thing to do at the convention was to go and just walk around and look at the celebrities. One in particular, Jane Sinclair, who used to star in his favorite sci-fi show ever, *Dirty Space*. The show had gone off the air ten years ago and she hadn't been in anything since. Jason was only twenty-five, and she was pushing all hell out of forty, but he was totally, stupidly infatuated. Every year he bought one of her pictures—though Cathy was sure he now had at least two of everything—and he always got them to take his picture with her for his personal "wall of fame."

She obviously never remembered him from year to year, which always gave Cathy a good laugh. How could anyone not remember Jason? In make-up that face was not one she would be likely to forget.

"Christ," Evan swore as they headed in the direction of the food court. "Have we got to go watch you drool all over Jane Sinclair, again?"

"Yeah. I haven't done it yet this year and it's a tradition. I think I'm going to get the picture of her running through Dirty Station again. I've only got two of those. You know . . . I think she wants me," Jason said, grinning.

"Come on, that's a face only a mother could love," Cathy said.

Jason frowned then grinned and said, "I'm pretty sure mother doesn't even love it."

"I don't get why you like her so much," Cathy said, trying to keep the jealousy from her voice as she followed behind her two friends. "I mean she looks older than I think she is, she's obviously doped out of her gourd, and she never even remembers you from year to year. Every year you go and worship at her feet and give her money you don't really have, and she doesn't even remember you."

He turned to look at her, walking up the street backwards as easily as most people walked forward, proving his ninja-like skills. "Ah, but Cathy, she always pretends to remember me."

"It's not her, it's the character she played," Evan told Cathy. "Dude, you think she's like her character and she's not. None of them are. They're just people like you and me."

Cathy remembered Jane Sinclair's character, Burnett. Burnett had been strong-willed and arrogant, but loyal. In season three, she'd fallen in love with an alien who had a face that looked like a butt. Jane wasn't Burnett, though. These days a better name for her would be Burnout.

Every year, Jane would tell them what great costumes they had, like she was seeing them for the first time and . . . well, Evan changed his costume every year, but she and Jason just always wore the zombie and pirate costumes. Cathy at least added accessories and changed pants and shirts. Jason didn't even do that. He said what he had worked why change it?

She adjusted her eye patch and ran her hand down the ragged scar that ran down her face and smiled. She felt sort of like Jason; she made a good pirate, so why change?

Evan had to do something different every year, though. This year he was wearing a Spartan costume. Cathy didn't mind that Evan felt he had to do a new costume every year, but she hated when it had accessories like a shield and a sword because it was a sure bet that she and Jason would be carrying them around as much as Evan was. As if on cue Evan asked Jason to carry his shield. Jason made a face, which made him look really hideous, but turned around and took the shield.

"Why do you always have to pick costumes that have props? It's such a huge pain in the ass," Jason said, voicing her thoughts exactly, which was why she had such a huge crush on him. They just seemed to have so much in common and they could just sit and talk forever. There was no one in her regular life that she felt as connected to.

The three of them had met here at DragonCon six years ago at one of the many concerts. The band on stage had sucked. They'd been standing together towards the back of the room that was just asses-to-elbows people, where they couldn't really see the sucking band, and they had started talking about how crowded it was and how much the band sucked and why were so many people crammed in there to listen to a band that sucked so bad? Then all at once they'd realized that they were doing the same thing. They'd laughed at themselves, left to go get some coffee, and wound up just sitting around talking. They'd been the best of friends ever since.

But it was when she'd seen Jason's picture on his MySpace account that the crush had first started. She guessed that made her shallow because 'til then she'd only seen him in the makeup and had concluded that he must be ugly, but when she saw his picture on MySpace, he was beautiful and she was in love. Unfortunately, because he was so beautiful she could never let him know how she felt about him because he would never return those feelings and, well, that was probably why his attachment to the actress stung so much. Even drugged out and let go, she was beautiful and perfect, which meant that Jason was at least as shallow as she was.

They ate at the food court, she and Jason going for pizza and ice tea while Evan went after oriental food, which took twice as long. In fact, by the time he joined them at the table they'd had to wait to get, they were mostly done eating and Evan was bitching.

"Why do we always have to eat in the fucking food court?" He glared more than looked at Jason. "Dude, you live here, don't you know where any decent restaurants are?"

"I told you. I don't work in the city. I never come here. Besides, do you really want to go to a regular restaurant dressed like this?"

"Oh, like the regular restaurants aren't serving anyone in costume during the con. And there is no rule that says we have to stay in costume for the entire con. What do you say we put on real clothes and go get some real food this evening?"

"Screw that," Jason said with a flip of his hand. "We can do that any time. DragonCon is the only time we get to let our inner selves out."

"So . . . your inner self is a burnt-up zombie and," he looked at Cathy, "you're a pirate."

"Yep, and this is the only place I can wear all the cool shit I buy here every year," Cathy said without missing a beat.

Evan looked at Jason with meaning, and Jason shrugged, then sighed and said, "I like being special, all right? It's why I never change my costume. I like everyone running up to me and going, Hey! It's the zombie dude."

"Well . . . " Even looked somewhat defeated. "All right, you guys do that, but tonight I'm going to put on real clothes, find a real restaurant, and sit down and eat food that doesn't actually suck."

"I saw a Hooters a couple of blocks back," Cathy said.

"We could do dinner there," Jason said. "They won't care if we're in costume."

"Hooters!" Evan said in disbelief. "Hooters?! I was talking about going someplace nice."

"Hooters is nice," Jason said, then added with a smile, "Dude, I like hooters."

"I do, too, but I don't want to eat there. Come on, chicken wings?"

"I love chicken wings," Cathy said.

"Great, it's settled then, we're having dinner at Hooters," Jason declared.

"I'm not eating at Hooters," Evan objected.

"Why the hell not?" Jason asked angrily.

"I want to go to a real restaurant like an adult, sit down somewhere there isn't any filth, and eat something that doesn't come in a fucking Styrofoam container." He shoved his food away from him then and stood up. "I was standing there in line between a Klingon and a fairy, and the fairy was talking to a guy dressed like Wolverine about a God damned D&D campaign like it was real life and . . . I'm twenty-four years old and I've never been laid. I work in a book store and live on Star Trek chat rooms. Ever since I got here this time . . . I just don't feel like I fit in any more because I look around and I don't want to be one of these people.

"I don't want to be doing this when I'm forty. I want to get married and have kids and get a good job and if I keep doing this . . . well, then I'm never going to have a real life. I'm dressed like a Spartan. I spent two-hundred and fifty dollars on a costume so that I can look like a geek in a Spartan costume, and I'm hanging out with you two, and neither of you are even interested in having a real life and . . . . That's it; I'm done." He stood up and started to walk away.

"Evan, come on, man," Jason called after him. He picked up

the shield and held it up. "Dude, you forgot your really grown-up shield."

"Keep it!" Evan screamed back and continued to stomp off.

"Should I . . . should I go after him?" Jason asked, sitting back down.

"No, let him go. He's been mostly a dick all day anyway," Cathy said. She had noticed the change with Evan first online, when they were talking. "He's been sort of upset ever since his mother died."

"Go figure," Jason said lightly, and started to eat Evan's discarded food.

Cathy laughed. "That's not what I meant. Of course he was upset about that, but then you remember he started talking about how he felt like he needed to make some real changes in his life?"

"Well, it didn't help that all his silly-assed gamer friends started basically living with him and eating all his food. Cathy . . . well, I could be wrong, but I think he lives in make-believe land all year and DragonCon is just the pinnacle of that for him. Maybe he wants to live in reality now. I can't speak for you, but me, I have to deal with reality three-hundred and sixty days a year. Four days a year I get to come here and live in make-believe, and I'm not going to let Evan or anyone else ruin that for me."

"Amen!" Cathy said with a sigh. She smiled. "So, you think we can get enough for that shield to buy dinner at Hooters?"

"At least a couple of drinks. Come on." He stood up, took her hand, and then they were walking through the maze of tables. For the moment, Cathy just pretended like he was as taken with her as she was with him. After all, that was what DragonCon was all about for her, leaving the real world behind for four days. Like Jason, it was what helped her get through the rest of the year.

Of course, when they wound up at the gawk of fame, she had to deal with the "traditional" fawning over Jane Sinclair, who looked even older and more drugged-out and whose canned responses still hadn't changed. And of course—yet again—she didn't remember Jason, but pretended to as he gave her money for a picture he already had and got Cathy to take his picture with her for his collection.

Cathy looked around at the sea of humanity and the utter chaos all around her, and for a minute thought maybe Evan was right. The celebrities pretended to be happy they were there. The fans shelled out big bucks for autographed pictures so they could go home and prove they'd really seen this star or that one. They'd tell their friends how nice the star was in person, when most of the time they had interacted with them for less than five minutes.

Cathy knew there were writers here, too, writers whose work she admired and who she'd love to meet, but finding the programming for their panels was nearly impossible. Even on the gawk of fame, the writers were stuck off behind a curtain at the end of the room, away from the media stars and mostly hidden from the general population. They were the people who wrote the books and shows the fans adored, they created the characters that TV and movie personalities played, yet they were ghettoed. Writers would sign books, even program books, for free, but when Cathy looked into the writers' area the lines in that room were short or non-existent.

People were all so superficial; it was all about the way things looked. It always came down to the appearance of things. No one seemed to care about how things really were as long as they looked good. It was always about who was the most visual, who had gotten the most attention from the right people, and who was the most beautiful. Right in that moment, it was hard for Cathy to pretend that people weren't as shallow as she knew they were.

Jane Sinclair's line had shrunk over the years until now there were times when she just sat there, yet she still wanted them to get their picture, spend their money, and move on. She'd been out of the spotlight a long time and now only a few of her die-hard fans—like Jason—even remembered who she was. Still she was here year after year, no doubt because it made up half of her yearly income, and she hadn't gotten any nicer. In fact, the truth was that she'd just gotten progressively more bitter.

They were both marching in the parade, though she'd be marching with the pirates and Jason would be marching with the zombies.

"Great make-up," a fellow pirate, whose badge said he was named Parker, announced.

"Thanks," Cathy said.

"My patch," he took it off and handed it to her, "I got it from a fellow in the dealers' room. See? You can see right through it."

"Very cool," she said and handed it back.

"Don't you usually hang out with the zombie guy?"

Cathy smiled. "Jason, yes."

"He your boyfriend?"

Cathy didn't know what to say. If she said yes, Jason might find out and figure out she had a crush on him. If she said no, this guy was going to start hitting on her and she just wasn't interested. "Yes," she answered, quickly deciding that if Jason found out and asked her about it, she'd just explain that she didn't want to have to fend off the guy's unwanted attention.

"Took you awhile to answer," Parker said.

Cathy shrugged then smiled. "I was trying to listen to what the parade coordinator was saying."

As luck would have it the zombies were just ahead of the pirates, and Jason came running back to her. "Guess what?" he asked excitedly.

"What?" Cathy asked, caught up in his enthusiasm.

"I get to lead the zombies and we're going to be right behind the car Jane Sinclair is riding in."

"That's great," Cathy said, forcing a smile she suddenly didn't feel.

From her place in the parade she could barely make out the back of Jason's head as he stumbled zombie-like down the street, but she had a clear view of the back of the actress riding like a high school homecoming queen perched on the back of the back seat of someone's convertible.

She ignored Jane Sinclair and just enjoyed being a pirate surrounded by her fellow buccaneers 'til she saw Jason take off running. Now Jason was in character and zombies don't run, so she knew immediately that something wasn't right. A man was running at the car carrying Jane Sinclair, a knife in plain sight, and Jason was running towards him. Cathy found herself running through the pirates and the zombies, untying her "peace-tied" sword as she went. She saw Jason grab the knife-wielding lunatic and the knife slice into Jason's chest. Cathy's sword was a cheap, dulled show blade, but when she smacked the attacker in the wrist he dropped the knife and Jason wrestled him to the ground.

Security swarmed them all.

Blood was running out of Jason's chest.

Cathy didn't take time to think. She dropped the sword, grabbed the sash she'd been wearing around her waist, wadded it up in a ball and held it against Jason's wound.

There was screaming and people running in fifty different directions at once, and then a stretcher and paramedics and somehow Cathy got separated from Jason. Her heart was pounding, and she felt like she might puke. She ran back to her hotel room, quickly showered and changed into normal clothes. She looked in the mirror and looked quickly away; there was no time to worry about such crap.

She found her keys, grabbed her purse, and headed for her car.

At the hospital, it seemed to her like everyone was staring at her. They told her Jason was fine, that he was being stitched up. His wound was mostly superficial, but they were still going to put him into a room for observation for a few hours. They gave her a room number and told her she could wait for him there. Her guts were rumbling and she was a nervous wreck. She started to just leave and call a flower shop to bring him flowers but . . . . She needed to see him, to see that he was all right, and if the tables were turned she wouldn't want him to send her flowers, to not be there. He was her friend, really her only friend, now that Evan had stormed off to become an adult.

Still, she couldn't bring herself to go to his room to be waiting when he got there. She was hungry and realized she hadn't eaten since the day before so she followed the signs to the cafeteria.

How sad was it to say that her best friends were guys she talked to online and only saw once a year, always in costume. She'd say Evan was right, except the truth was that Jason had been right. Cathy lived on her own. She worked, she paid her own bills, and every day just seemed to be about getting her job done so that she could go home, feed her cat, clean her apartment, pay some bills, and talk to her friends online. She had no social life; DragonCon was it, the only time of the year that she could just run the streets and have a good time. Put on a costume and just be someone besides Cathy Reagan.

She stood outside Jason's door. Her palms were sweaty. She knew he was in there because she'd asked at the nurses' station.

Suddenly someone screamed, then there were some whispered words, and then Jane Sinclair was rushing out the door. She looked at her and almost jumped back. "Damn, well . . . Tell your friend how sorry I am. I just wanted to thank him for what he did. I didn't know . . . I didn't know." She walked away, mumbling, and Cathy's heart skipped a beat. How bad was he? What had happened? She didn't hesitate now. She walked quickly into the room. He was lying with his back to her.

"Jason, are you all right?" she asked, carefully staying at his back as she walked up to him.

"I'm fine." But he didn't sound fine. "Evan was right about her, Cathy, she's just a superficial bitch, not like her character at all."

Cathy put a shaky hand on his shoulder. "Are you really all right, Jason?"

"Yeah, I'm fine. They're just holding me for observation because the cut was deep and it nicked one of my ribs. It didn't get inside, though, so they are going to let me out in a couple of hours. Guess I should call my mom to come take me home."

"I could take you home," Cathy said nervously.

"You aren't going to want to take me home, Cathy." He rolled over and was startled. She looked quickly away, not wanting to see the look on his face. He reached up, grabbed her chin, and turned her face so he could look at her. "What happened?" he asked gently.

"There was a tornado," Cathy said, close to tears. "It ripped our house apart. I was just a kid so I don't know what happened. My mother thought maybe a board with a nail in it or a piece of glass. The scar actually runs all the way down the left side of my body, too, and not that you can't guess, but the eye is glass."

"Cathy," Jason said, slowly letting go of her chin and smiling, "haven't you noticed anything?"

She shrugged. "What?"

"Cathy, do you really think I'd still be in make-up now? Do you think they'd let me wear a bunch of plastic stuff stuck to my body while they're cleaning blood off me and sewing me up?"

It took a minute for what he was saying to soak in. "Your . . . Your scars are real, too. But the picture on your MySpace account . . . "

"Wallet model," he said.

Cathy relaxed. "What happened to you?"

"Mom had a skillet of hot grease on the stove. I guess I was just old enough to reach it. They said it was like napalm. They've told me over and over all my life how lucky I am to be alive, but I don't feel very lucky. People can't stand to look at me, but they can't help but stare."

Cathy knew exactly what he was talking about. When you were an otherwise attractive-looking girl with a good body and some guy whistled and you turned around and he saw you had an angry red scar that ran from your forehead down your face and to your chin with what was obviously a glass eye staring—usually the wrong way—in a mangled socket . . . Well, it was the same thing.

"It's why I work at home," Jason said. "So, no one has to see me. But once a year, once a year I come here and . . . "

" . . . don't feel like such a freak," Cathy finished with him. "How do you feel?"

"Fine." He smiled. "Good." Cathy leaned down and kissed him gently on the lips then stood up. "Even better," he said.

Jason and Cathy walked hand-in-hand through the parking garage, he dressed like a zombie, she like a pirate.

"Hey!" someone screamed out. They turned, surprised to see Evan walking towards them in street clothes.

"Evan! Man, we thought you'd fallen off the planet," Jason said. He let go of Cathy's hand long enough to hug their old friend. They hadn't seen him in three years.

Cathy gave him a hug, too. "What have you been up to?"

"You know what . . . When I left here I went home and I started cleaning house. I told all my friends to get the fuck out, sold all my *Star Trek* and *B-5* collectables on E-bay, closed out my MySpace account, and went back to college. I got a degree in computer science and got a half-assed job as a programmer. I still couldn't get a date, and I was lonely as hell, but by God I was all grown up. That's when I realized being a responsible adult isn't all it's cracked up to be. I started actually dreaming that I was playing D&D, and then one morning I woke up at like 3:00 a.m. and I had this idea that wouldn't let me sleep. I worked on it for three months straight, didn't do much of anything else. I sold the idea to a gaming company and the game premieres here this weekend."

"What kind of game?" Cathy asked, taking Jason's hand again.

"Well, get this, it's all because of you guys. It's called *Pirates Versus Zombies*." Jason and Cathy both laughed.

Evan seemed to notice them holding hands then. "So what's going on with you two?"

"I moved to Atlanta and we got married two years ago," Cathy supplied, looking up at Jason lovingly.

"We started our own business, too," Jason said.

"You did?"

"Yeah, turns out there's a huge demand for theme parties for adults and kids. We have a small catering company. I take the Night of the Living Dead parties, Cathy does the pirate parties."

Evan laughed. "So you what . . . just get to stay in costume all the time now?"

Jason patted Evan's cheek with his open palm, smiled and said, "Evan, we aren't ever in costume now."

Cathy chuckled and they walked away, arms around each other.

HERO MATERIAL

Jean Marie Ward

"I'm in need of a hero," a silky voice whispered inside Carmen Rhames' head. "Would that be you?"

The skin on the back of Cam's neck crawled under her hair. She stood in one of the few bubbles of empty space in the DragonCon Dealers Room. There wasn't anybody around close enough to whisper. Her sister Isobel was at the other end of the Elphame Jewels counter, trying not to drool while she haggled over a silver skull pendant she couldn't afford. Cam's best friend Megan skulked in the DVD booth across the aisle, pretending she was interested in slasher flicks so she could keep an eye on Cam and her sister.

Megs flatout refused to come any closer. At first Cam thought she was creeped out by the case of fetish gear or the freaky little silver critters skulking around the jewelry in the front counter. But Megs said that was only part of it. What really set off her psychic Spidey sense was the tall woman in green who ran the booth.

Reluctantly, Cam dragged her gaze to the woman's face. The woman winked. Cam could've sworn she heard the little bells dangling over the wooden and glass counters jingle like they were laughing at her. Only the bells weren't jingling. They weren't moving at all.

Okay, that did it. Cam was officially spooked. If it had just been her, she would've bolted. But she couldn't leave Isobel. At eighteen, Isobel might be the "adult" of the group, but she was also the Queen of Oblivious. She might as well have a big red "O" painted in the middle of her forehead. *And a target on her back.*

"Neither foolish nor foolishly fearful—that's good. The middle road is always best," the woman said. She sounded exactly like the voice in Cam's head.

The woman pulled a deck of tarot cards from under the counter and nudged it across the glass in Cam's direction. "Would you like me to tell your fortune?"

"Is this where you tell me there's a terrible evil in my future, but you can sell me the spell to fix it?"

"Carmen!" Isobel hissed, still trying to seal a deal.

The woman chuckled. "If I pulled stunts like that, the convention would kick me out on my ear. I'm a jeweler, not a gypsy. But I do like to look at the cards of people who interest me."

Carmen wondered if that made her some kind of psychic peeping Tom. But Isobel was the one who got mad.

"What about me?" she demanded. "I'm the customer here."

The woman flipped three cards from the top of the deck with her left hand. "First card: Knight of Swords, the one who rushes in where angels fear to tread. That's you. Your second card, the Moon, says people take advantage of that. They will again, tonight. The person who can save you is number three, the Page of Pence—the student."

Her gaze flicked to Cam. "That would be you."

Cam gulped. The words were way too close to the ones she'd heard in her head.

"Whatever," Isobel said. "If my little sis has to come to my rescue, we're both in deep shit."

"Are you done yet?" Cam was proud of how bored she sounded. Not frightened at all. Buffy the Vampire Slayer couldn't have done it better. "We're gonna miss the *Heroes* panel."

"Oh, all right," Isobel grumbled. "Everything's overpriced anyway."

The woman shrugged as Isobel flounced away. When Cam turned to follow, a puff of dust blew out of nowhere. She slapped a hand over her eyes, but it was too late. The grit burned into her right eye like ground jalapeno. Blinded by the sudden, searing pain, she lurched into the counter. The case wobbled against her ribs, then righted itself.

"Here, let me help," the woman said. Before Cam could stop her, the woman brushed aside Cam's hand, grabbed her chin and squirted something into her right eye.

The pain vanished. A pearly film washed across her vision. Panic jumped into her throat. What if she had to go to the hospital? That would ruin the weekend for everyone. The tears she could've used a minute ago squirted into her eyes.

Hot, lavender-scented hands squeezed her shoulders. Megs' voice shrilled in her ear, "What did you do to her?"

"She had something in her eye. I flushed it out."

"With what?" Megs spat.

Cam blinked her vision clear. Instead of getting mad at Megs, the woman looked like she was biting back a smile. The bells were ringing again, only this time Cam saw them move. The woman tilted her head at a small bottle of brand-name eye drops on the countertop. A single drop of clear liquid clung to the tip. It looked okay. Nothing freaky or hallucinogenic about it. Cam practically melted with relief.

"Oh, sorry. My mistake." Megs added in a tight voice, "Ma'am. Look, *chica*, we gotta book. People are waiting."

Only if you counted Isobel as "people." But Megs wasn't giving Cam the chance to argue. She put one hand on Cam's shoulder and the other on her elbow, and frog-marched her down the aisle like they had a date with a firing squad.

Talk about overreacting. It wasn't that she didn't appreciate her best friend charging to her rescue. To be honest, Cam had been scared silly—emphasis on the silly. But she couldn't help noticing the way Megs kept Cam between her and the counter the whole time. What made it even funnier was Megs was two inches taller than Cam and a lot more coordinated.

Did the woman think it was funny, too? Was that why she smiled? Cam stole another glance at the Elphame booth as they headed out the door. The woman was taking care of other customers, but something was off. It was like two women in green were standing in the same place behind the counter.

Cam shook her head. It must be the angle. The weapons booth

where she'd bought her katana Friday afternoon was about the same distance away, and everything there looked okay.

Things looked pretty normal in the *Heroes* panel, too. There was a point, when one of the dumber fan girls in the audience managed to piss off the moderator, when it almost looked like their shadows were about to mix it up. Cam put it down to bad lighting and an overactive imagination.

Things didn't take a sharp turn for the weird until they met Megs' mom for dinner in the Peachtree Centre Food Court. The scene should've been totally mundane. White tile and glass made the place so bright you couldn't find a shadow. Metal chairs scraped the floor. Plastic trays clattered. Everything smelled like cooking grease, including the people in costume and the ones who weren't.

But as Cam scanned the crowd to find their table, she noticed more double-image people. Not a lot, and not all in one place. Was there something wrong with her eye after all?

A guy who looked like Silent Bob from *Dogma* caught her squinting at him. He wiggled his fingers in a little wave and rolled away. He couldn't have been walking. His head didn't bounce. He zoomed over floor like he was riding a Segway under his floppy coat. Only he wasn't holding on to anything. He was working the mic on his headset and the buttons of the two-way radio sticking out of his coat pocket. Cam dropped her tray the last inch to the table, sloshing her Coke.

"What's wrong?" Megs asked as she helped Cam blot up the mess. "Is it your eye?"

"That again," Isobel said, disgusted. "Give it a rest. She got dust in her eye. End of story."

"Well, I'm sorry it's not all about you."

Isobel lifted one perfectly groomed eyebrow. Her eyes glinted like she was spoiling for a fight. "Excuse me, who found the paramedics? Who made them check her sister out? And who was standing around like a dork, freaking about fairies and magic eye drops?"

"I didn't say fairies. The booth was called Elphame. That's *Elf Land*." Megs bared her teeth as if she could barely restrain herself from adding "you moron" in front of her mom. "Didn't you ever read

'Thomas the Rhymer' or anything about *Lord of the Rings* that didn't involve Orlando Bloom?"

Mrs. Owens started coughing as soon as Isobel mentioned fairies, so it took her a few seconds to wade in. "Whoa, back up, girls," she said. "What happened to Carmen's eye and when were you planning to tell me about it?"

Cam, Megs and Isobel hunched into their shoulders like turtles. As parents went, Megs' mom was pretty cool. She'd been to DragonCon before, and she was the one who convinced Cam's parents to let her go with Megs. She let Isobel stay in the room with them, even though it meant she had to share a bed. And Isobel could've commuted from Georgia State.

But the three of them had an unspoken agreement not to tell Mrs. Owens anything that would make her think they couldn't take care of themselves. Cam and Megs were fifteen. They were in tenth grade. They didn't want Megs' mom running after them like they were kids or dragging them to all the "classic" Eighties TV panels she'd circled in her pocket program. They didn't want to be stuck with Isobel, either

What was worse, the story she screwed out of them sounded so lame. Cam would've forgotten all about it if she didn't keep seeing things like the girl with the bat wings sticking out the back of her Darth Maul costume. That was when Cam looked out of her right eye. If she looked out of both eyes, it was the double-image deal—a winged woman with hooves for feet superimposed over a short, round-faced Darth Maul. When Cam covered her right eye, all she saw was Darth Maul flipping a chair around so she could straddle it backwards . . . and leave room to spread the wings she didn't have. None of the *Star Wars* Stormtroopers at the table with her seemed to notice anything off. Everybody was laughing and having a great time, including the girl with the wings.

It was the same story wherever she looked. Weird and mundane rubbed shoulders like it was the most natural thing in the world. A fox hiding under the skin of an Asian-American guy who was dressed as a pirate teased the totally human girl stealing his fries. The forehead ridges on at least two of the Klingons in line at the chicken place were the real deal. Omigod, Megs was right. Something magic had happened to her. Oh wow! This was too cool—and it happened to *her*! She had to clamp her knees together to keep from wiggling in her chair.

Was it just DragonCon, or was the whole world a lot stranger than anybody let on? She wanted to run outside and check the street. She couldn't wait to see what things looked like in her neighborhood or her dad's office at Fort Stewart. She'd bet money his CO was some kind of monster.

If she still had The Sight—or any kind of sight in her right eye—by the time she got back. The little bit of pizza she'd eaten curdled in her stomach. Megs wasn't the only one who read too many fairy tales. *Folklore theme: fairy ointment. Stupid girl loses an eye because she admits she can see fairies at a fair.* Maybe if she didn't say anything no one would know. Telling Megs—like she was dying to—wasn't worth the cost of her eye.

Mrs. Owens rubbed her forehead and groaned. "Megan, please, listen to yourself. Even your grandmother doesn't believe in elves. I'm not thrilled a strange woman used her eye drops in Carmen's eye. But under the circumstances I don't know what else she could do. And it worked, right?" she asked Cam.

Cam nodded. Giggling hysterically was probably a bad idea. People would want her to explain, and even if she could, Mrs. O wouldn't want to hear it. If she had a problem with elves, think what would happen if Cam told her about the bug-eyed, egg-headed alien harmonizing "Scarborough Fair" with the guys in kilts over by the Information Desk.

"And if elves really did exist," Isobel said, "they wouldn't let that old d-bag in the club. Did you hear the stupid fortune she gave me?"

"You're just pissed because she didn't say anything about the guy from the *Werewolf* game you've been crushing on," Cam said.

"Am not. I mean, it's not like I'm going to see him again after Monday. He goes to college in Florida."

Isobel said "Florida" like it was on the other side of the universe, instead of the next state. It wasn't like she'd have any problem reeling him in. Cam would never say it to her face, but her sister was a knock-out. She could be pretty nice too, when she put her mind to it.

Something was eating her, though. She picked at her nail polish and chewed her lip gloss instead of her food. When Mrs. Owens asked if she'd be playing *Werewolf* again that evening, Isobel took her time answering.

"The game's going to start later tonight," she said. "The guys didn't want to miss the Dawn Masquerade."

"Oh, maybe we'll see them there. I'd love to meet them," Mrs. O said brightly.

Cam and Megs exchanged smirks.

"We might." Isobel didn't sound too happy about it. "If you get to meet them, could I head out after the show?"

"Depends on what time the Masquerade gets over. You know what I promised your parents: everybody in the room by one."

"But that was *before* you said I could stay with you," Isobel wheedled. "If I'd stayed in the dorm this wouldn't even come up."

"Yeah, you'd just have to find a cab at two o'clock in the morning. And pay for it yourself," Cam said.

"You're not helping," Isobel huffed. She turned back to Meg's mom. "Look, Mrs. O, it's not like I'm going to get drunk and crazy. We'll be down in the basement playing a card game. There'll be people filking in the room next to us the whole time."

Meg's mom shook her head. "Sorry. My room, my rules."

And that was that. "Mom" trumped "cool" every time. To give Isobel credit, she let it go. She even painted three perfect Dawn tears on everybody's cheeks so they could really get into the mood. By the time they got back to the Hyatt, she and Mrs. O were bonding over Johnny Depp like nothing ever happened.

Cam let them pull ahead, and covered her left eye. The Hyatt atrium was Con Central Station, and she wanted to see everything it had to offer for as long as she could.

Her breath hitched in her throat. The people (and others) were only part of the show. Strands of light in every color of the rainbow formed a dazzling cat's cradle stretching from the large, sectioned circle twenty stories overhead to the lacy metal parasol suspended over the escalators. More stained-glass ribbons fanned from the spars of the parasol. Others exploded from the branches of the metal tree in front of the lobby restaurant. Colored light shot through walls and floors like laser beams. But they didn't seem to be hurting anything. Not at all.

Dust motes glittered in the strands. People passing through the web picked up bits of the sparkle. Pixie dust? Cam wondered.

There had to be some kind of mojo at work on the crowd. Not changing them exactly—Elevator Hell was real and populated by asshats—but nobody was screaming, swearing mad. Anybody who was smiling when they entered the lobby usually stayed that way. Those who looked tense tended to relax a little by the time they made it from the door to the escalators.

But where would you get enough pixie dust to cover a crowd this big? How would you keep it in play? Wouldn't it run out or get blown out the doors? Unless there was some way of recycling or recharging it. Was that what the lines did? Was it possible to draw a magic spell in light and space?

"Trying out an eye patch for the Pirates Ball?" Megs asked.

Cam squealed and dropped her hand. Megs seemed to have appeared out of nowhere. The last time Cam saw her, she'd been trailing after her mom and Isobel, arguing about magic and super-powers. "Scare me to death, why don't you?"

"I'll do a lot more unless you tell me what's going on," Megs said. "Since when do you vanish and leave me to cover with Mom?"

"I was gonna catch up."

"When? The show's about to start." Megs narrowed her eyes, and Cam could almost feel the gaze drilling into the center of her fore-head. Even with the magic in her right eye, Cam couldn't see auras. But every now and then she caught a glimpse of a glistening, soap-bubble thin layer over a person's skin. She could see one of those layers hovering around Megs, but instead of hugging her skin, it flared and danced like flames around the sun.

Megs paled. "What's wrong, Cam? C'mon, talk to me."

"It's complicated. At first, I wasn't sure if anything was going on. Then I wasn't sure if I should talk about it."

"Oh," Megs said slowly, like the word was a mile long. "Yeah. Talking about it is how you get in trouble. Look at me."

"You look fine. Really."

"Really? Why do I get the feeling those words have a whole new meaning for you now?" Megs held up her hand like a stop sign. "No, don't answer that. Just tell me you'll dish when you can."

"Promise," Cam said, crooking her little finger.

They shook pinkies, and Megs sighed. "I know you didn't want to drag it around all day, but I really wish you'd had your sword with you in the Dealers' Room this afternoon."

"Why?" Cam asked.

"The blade's solid steel," Megs said.

Cam stared at her blankly.

"Hel-*lo*," Megs yodeled. "Earth to Cam. Magic can't stand the touch of iron."

Cam thought about the black spars of the big parasol and all the metal used in the elevators, and wasn't so sure.

The storm that had threatened all afternoon blew in sometime during the Dawn Masquerade. Back in their room in the International Tower, Cam pressed her nose against the glass door to the balcony and stared into the squalling night. Rain sloshed over the railing and spattered against the glass in spite of the concrete slab overhead and the sheltering walls jutting past the balcony's edge. Lightning cracked like gunshots. If she angled her head right, she could see low-hanging clouds painted gray and yellow by the reflected flashes.

There was nothing supernatural about it, but it was still intimidating. Only a few months before, the Westin Hotel down the street lost hundreds of windows to a tornado. People staying in the top floors were almost sucked out the holes. The winds—just the winds—shifted the whole building on its foundation. So tornadoes weren't exactly common in Atlanta; there was nothing to say it couldn't happen again. Cam pulled the heavy drapes closed as if that would shut the storm out of her thoughts.

Fat chance. The wind seemed to get louder when they turned out the lights. Cam didn't know how anyone could fall asleep through the thunder and the swooshing rain. On the other side of the bed, Isobel lay as stiff as a board. She must've been more scared than she let on. She was covered to the chin, but her deodorant and perfume and the fragrance of her foundation were so thick Cam could smell them all the way down the back of her throat.

Wait, when did Isobel *ever* go to bed with make-up on? She considered zits a bigger disaster than global warming.

Cam thought back to what Isobel wore to bed: Baby Phat shorts and her favorite knit cami, the one with the lace and the inset bra. *Oh shit.* How did Isobel expect to get away with sneaking out of the room with everyone wide awake from the storm?

Only everyone wasn't wide awake from the storm. Mrs. Owens was already snoring. She dropped like a rock last night too. That must've been what Isobel was banking on. The idiot.

She's going to screw up everything! Mrs. O would have to kick her out of the room. The weekend would be shot. Mrs. O would spend half the time fuming at Isobel and the other half wondering if there was some way she could've stopped her. Megs would be angry because her mom was upset. Cam didn't want to think about how her parents would react. Every time Isobel pulled some stupid stunt—and she pulled a lot of them—Cam had to work twice as hard to get her parents to trust her. Cam had to stop her, or at least get her back to the room before Mrs. O. took her 3 a.m. pee.

Perversely, once she made the decision, she started to drift off. Mrs. O's quiet whuffling was strangely restful. If the springs hadn't creaked when Isobel eased off the bed, Cam would've been a goner.

Isobel froze at the noise, a darker shadow against the dimness of the room. Mrs. Owens grunted and rolled to the center of her bed, away from the door. Isobel snatched her con pass and room key from the nightstand, grabbed her sandals and scooted out of the room.

Cam expected the momentary glow from the hallway to give her away. But Mrs. O didn't react. Her snores settled into their old rhythm before Cam found her flip-flops and the shorts she'd worn earlier.

Cam tip-toed over the carpet. Backed against the door to muffle the sound of the latch, she waited for a thunderclap to cover her exit. Then Megs lifted her head off her pillow. Cam almost died. Megs waved as if she didn't already have Cam's complete attention. She pointed to the corner where Cam's katana leaned against the wall.

Cam hesitated. Megs jabbed her finger at the sword. Cam gave in. It was either that or risk all the arm flapping waking up Mrs. O. Satisfied, Megs nodded and eased back under the covers. Her mom snored through the whole thing.

Cam sniffed. What was she supposed to do with a twenty dollar katana? Threaten her sister at sword point? Like that would work. Isobel would laugh at her—if Con Security didn't confiscate it first.

Assuming she could find Isobel. The elevator lobby was empty by the time she got there. There was no way of telling where Isobel was headed. Movie elevators might come with handy-dandy indicator dials. The elevators in the International Tower sure didn't.

Down was a safe bet. *Werewolf* was noisy. They wouldn't be playing on the sleeping floors. It would have to be one of the conference levels. But which one?

Isobel said something about filking. Yeah, the filking was going on right next door. Automatically, Cam groped for the pocket program in her back pack. *Aw man, why hadn't Megs pointed at her program instead of her sword?* Maybe the concierge would have one?

Something snorted, hot and wet, against her right knee. Cam froze. Biting the inside of her cheek to keep from making any noise, she lowered her eyes without moving her head.

The love child of Dumbo and Winnie the Pooh fluttered its eyelashes at her. The creature was about the size of a fat beagle with small perky ears, a short trunk, and black button eyes. White stripes and dots painted its tarnished gray hide. It was cute and funny, like a guy wearing spats in an old black-and-white movie—if you ignored the wicked big nails on all four paws.

Oh shit, was it here to take her eye?

Get a grip, she told herself. *You're the one with the big sharp pointy thing.* Besides, the creature wasn't making any threatening moves. All four paws were firmly planted on the carpet. All she had to do was keep them that way.

The critter butted a lightly-furred forehead against her calf. She choked back a shriek. The elevator at the end of the line pinged. She threw herself against the half-opened doors and fell inside. Frantically, she mashed the button to close the doors. Nothing happened. None of the floor buttons were lit. She whimpered.

Shaking its head and muttering, the critter waddled into the cab. Using the elevator wall for support, it propped itself on its hind legs and stretched toward the buttons, but it proved too short to reach the bottom row. It turned and wheezed at her again.

"Going down?" she squeaked.

The critter snuffled. Cam swore it looked disgusted.

"What floor . . ." Cam smacked her forehead. "Duh! Forget I said that. What if I run my finger over the buttons and you let me know when to stop?"

The critter snorted excitedly and patted the wall with its forelegs when she reached the very bottom floor. After she pushed the button, it settled back on all fours beside her right leg, swaying a little, like it was grooving to elevator music. By the time the elevator slowed to pick up a pair of very human vampire wannabes on the sixth floor, her heart had stopped trying to pound its way out of her chest and her breathing was almost back to normal. It didn't hurt they were all going to the same place.

The lowest floor of the International Tower was two floors below the lobby, too far down for Cam to hear the storm or feel the pressure of the wind. But the magical light she'd seen in the atrium had no problem going the distance. Brightly colored lines crisscrossed the open area between the elevators and a suite of conference rooms. Pixie dust spangled the costumes of the Goth-lolli chorus girls rehearsing their kick line in the corner. A burst of cheering from one of the rooms in the suite suggested it might be a good place to search for Isobel. The critter had other ideas. As soon as they exited the elevator it scooted around behind her and started butting her left leg with its fuzzy forehead.

"Hey, stop that," Cam hissed. The critter slobbered on her calf. "Eeew!"

She half-jumped, half-staggered to the right. The guys who'd ridden with her looked down their powdered noses at her like she was a total spaz before tromping away. She gave them the finger, hiding it behind her sword. She might be seeing striped mini-monsters, but she wasn't that crazy.

The critter cut in front of her, glanced over its shoulder and snorted. It took a couple steps toward the escalator to the conference level and repeated the over-the-shoulder look, like it expected her to follow.

"I can't," she said, hoping anybody overhearing her would assume she was talking on an earbud. "I've got to look for my sister."

The critter snorted again and bobbed its head toward the escalator. Cam chewed her bottom lip. Well, it wasn't as if she had any better ideas.

Ribbons of light angled through the muggy hallways connecting the basement meeting rooms with the Motor Lobby leading to the Hyatt parking garage. The light lines crossed at several places in the lobby. Those seemed to be the most popular spots for the people (and others) in Renn Fair costumes tuning old instruments. Guitar music and a loud baritone voice echoed from a room at the end of a crowded passageway to the left of the garage doors. That must be the filking room.

But where were the gamers? The Motor Lobby boasted musicians and card players and a lot of people posing for pictures, even though it was after one o'clock in the morning. But no Isobel. Nothing that looked like a *Werewolf* ring, either.

The critter snorted, as disgusted as before. Belly swaying from side to side, it jogged through the doors to the garage.

"You've got to be kidding," she said, but nobody paid any attention, including her gray and white striped guide.

If she hadn't seen the comforting threads of light bracing the pillars of the garage, Cam would've been tempted to cut and run, regardless of what might happen to Isobel or their weekend. Once they left the bright puddle of light and sound around the Motor Lobby doors, the garage was dead silent except for the slap of her feet, the click of the critter's nails against the cement, the sizzle of fluorescent lights and the grinding yawn of twenty-plus stories of hotel settling over their heads.

The garage hadn't been this spooky when Mrs. Owens parked there, but there had been lots of people around. Now the dim lighting and the shadows added a major creep factor to the unnerving sense of the whole building pressing down from above.

Cam checked the draw on her katana. What was she doing down here following a creature she didn't even have a name for? Why did she decide it was leading her to Isobel?

She risked a right eye glimpse at her surroundings. Dark silhouettes jigged on the distant walls. Their movements had nothing to do with the lights or the cars.

The critter ignored the shadows. It trotted briskly down the yellow strip in the middle of the main traffic lane, where the lights were the brightest and the colored lines were the thickest.

Screwing up her courage, she asked, "You sure Isobel's down here?"

The critter grunted something that sounded like an affirmative. Halfway down the next ramp, it stopped. It craned its neck forward as if to say, "You go on."

When Cam pulled up beside it, she realized some of the noises she thought were echoes were voices. She hesitated. The critter screwed up its nose like it was preparing for another slobber.

"No, no, no! I get what I'm supposed to do. I'm not sure what I'm supposed to say. You're only solid in my right eye," she said softly. "According to everything I've read, that makes the words really important."

The critter bobbed its head and brushed its ear against her knee. The hairs framing its oval ears felt surprisingly silky. Uncertainly, she crouched down to give its head a one-handed scratch. The critter stretched its neck and rumbled contentedly.

"I'm glad you like it," Cam whispered, deepening her massage of the stiff hair along the back of its neck. "You've been a lot better at leading than I've been at following."

The critter grunted once and started gacking asthmatically. It sounded like laughter. Its lips stretched back from its nose in something resembling a grin. Then it imploded like a party balloon after somebody stuck a pin in it. A faint clatter drew Cam's attention to the floor. A tiny silver version of the critter, a chain strung through a loop on its back, glittered against the stained concrete.

Cam looped the chain around her wrist. "O-kay," she said. She thought she heard a soft snort in reply but told herself it was the voices rising from the next level down.

The pillars framing the next bend in the traffic lane formed a rough pentagram. Thick ribbons of colored light outlined the shape and drew a star on the floor inside it. Cam guessed the star was almost directly under the metal parasol in the atrium lobby.

Isobel and four other people hunkered down inside the pentagram. The three guys ran the gamut from a chubby middle school nerd to a skinny ninth grader with superthick glasses, to a fit guy wearing a faded Florida Gators t-shirt. The guy from University of Florida looked like a Justin Timberlake clone with all the brains sucked out. Just Isobel's type. Apparently, he was the other girl's type too. Her gaze kept darting to him as she talked.

"Then the accidents started." The girl's drawl reminded Cam of the ones she heard around Fort Stewart, only a little faster on the turns. The girl paused for effect, looking at the guys, then Isobel. Cam guessed she didn't like what she saw. The girl had the kind of pretty that takes a lot of work, but her legs weren't that hot, especially compared to Isobel's.

"What kind of accidents, Laurel?" her sister asked breathlessly.

"The bad kind, of course. The kind where people lose legs and arms and eyes. The kind where whatever you build up falls down and drags your equipment down into the hole with it."

The two younger guys hugged their arms to their sides. If they were trying to keep their fear from showing, they were doing it wrong.

Gator Guy nodded, eyes bright and wide. He was totally into it, which was probably the real reason they were all here. Cam bet he was some kind of urban legend freak, and Laurel thought she could use that to get ahead in the boyfriend stakes. Isobel was too dumb to realize she was helping.

"The architect was at his wits' end. This hotel was supposed to be the crownin' jewel of his career. His reputation, his firm and everythin' he owned was on the line. Then one day, when he was in his office wonderin' if it might be simpler to swallow a bullet and get it over with, he heard someone knock on the door. Once." Laurel rapped her knuckles against the nearest pillar. "Twice." She rapped again. "Three times.

"When he opened it, there was no one there. But when he turned around, there was an old, old Geechee woman standin' in front of his desk, her head all wrapped in rags, and beads and bones hanging from her neck. Her eyes were white blind, and her voice crackled like dead leaves.

"She told him he was buildin' his hotel on the very heart of the Georgia slave trade, the very site of the Atlanta slave market . . . "

The guy with the glasses raised his hand like he was in class. "But according to our carriage driver, this part of town—"

Laurel dropped him with the mother of all glares. "Do you want me to finish this story or not?"

"Forget about him," Gator Guy said. "Go on!"

"Yeah," Cam chimed in, "get to the good part. You know, the part where they brick up one of the construction workers in the foundation or pour him into the concrete."

Everybody in the pentagram jumped, including the JT clone. Cam sauntered down the ramp, channeling Buffy for all she was worth. The Slayer would never be caught dead in flip-flops hauling around a sword she didn't know how to use. But from the way everybody was looking her, Cam figured they didn't know that. She grinned at the thought. The chubby kid flinched. Even her sister gulped.

Laurel recovered first. "So you know the legend?"

Cam shrugged, Slayer cool. "Maybe not the details, but it's the same old story they feed you at every castle and cathedral in Europe."

"And you've been to so many," Laurel sneered.

"Actually, yeah. Army brat. Her, too." Cam tilted her sword hilt at Isobel.

Her sister squared her shoulders. "What are you doing here?"

"Trying to find out why it was so important for you to get down here tonight. You don't really believe this crap, do you?"

The JT clone put his arms around Isobel. "Of course, she does," he said.

They exchanged goofy smiles. Isobel cooed, "Oh, Dean."

Laurel's mouth thinned. The energy hugging her skin bucked and roiled. That couldn't be good.

"So what's the deal?" Cam asked. "You're going to taunt the spirit or call him up to do what, exactly?"

"Cam!" her sister objected.

"If you don't believe in the Hyatt ghost, why do you care?" The guy with the glasses asked, honestly curious.

"Because we need to get this over with before our roommate's mom wakes up and ruins our weekend. Unless, of course, my showing up like this screwed up the ceremony?" Cam asked hopefully.

"No," Laurel said. "In fact, we need a *virgin* to complete the spell to lay Old Tom to rest."

Cam sputtered, "You're kidding!"

Nobody else was laughing. She couldn't believe it. Chubby was what—thirteen? Not to mention his BO qualified as a weapon of mass destruction. When and how did he lose his cherry? The sox rot alone was enough to kill any girl who got close. Glasses Guy didn't look much older. He might be okay when he hit high school, but right now he looked like a bug. Besides, he was blushing. His dusky olive cheeks had darkened to brown as soon as she started to laugh. Then there was Isobel, who had turned bright pink from the top of her forehead all the way down to her boobs. Cam was surprised all the heat didn't blister Dean's hands.

"Trust me, you're not going to have any problem," Cam said wryly. "Just go back to what you were doing, and pretend I'm not here."

"Don't you want to join the circle?" Laurel asked. "It might be safer."

"Circle jerks really aren't my thing."

Now if this ritual really does involve virgin sacrifice . . . Cam slipped her sword a few inches out of its scabbard. That got their attention. "Besides, cold iron and magic don't mix."

Laurel didn't disagree. Apparently, the geometry in this part of the garage wasn't lost on her either. She lined up the members of the group with the points of the pentagram, positioning Isobel between BO boy and the guy with glasses. (Surprise, surprise.) But if Laurel's plan was to use the circle to split Isobel and Dean, she outsmarted herself. Isobel and her stud muffin stared soulfully at each other across the circle and made mushy noises about laying a troubled soul to rest.

Cam couldn't wait to tell Megs. The two of them would never let Isobel live this down.

Laurel pulled a stick of pink chalk from the pocket of her baggy linen shorts. She was really going all the way with this nonsense. And it was nonsense. If anybody died under mysterious circumstances when they were building the Hyatt, if there had ever been any hint of a genuine urban legend connected to the hotel—much less a slave market—Megs would've known. The girl was a ghost magnet. If there were ghosts anywhere around, she wouldn't just find them, they'd find her. So she didn't stay anyplace without Googling it to hell and gone to make sure it was clean of restless spirits.

Which didn't mean it was safe. Waves of energy snapped over Laurel's skin. It reminded Cam of Megs' aura in the lobby, only worse. Megs' aura didn't seem to react to the magic lines threading through the atrium. Laurel's aura grew more opaque as she drew her magic circle between the pillars.

Cam didn't believe in magic ceremonies. Any idiot could draw a circle with a five-pointed star inside and add the signs of the zodiac around the rim. Just because it looked mystical to the four nitwits inside didn't mean the symbols had power. It meant the dodos were dumb. More disturbing were the rampant hormones bubbling inside the pentagram. Two girls after the same dumb guy—with an audience keeping score. Cheerleaders killed for less.

Cam retreated a few feet up the ramp to an area where there weren't so many magic lines to contend with. She drew her sword and laid the sheath beside her feet. Gritting her teeth against the sound and the certain knowledge she was damaging the blade, she used the point to scratch a circle in the cement around her.

Who was overreacting now? She could've kicked herself for all the times she accused Megs of being superstitious. Megs totally believed. Cam pretended to believe because she wanted to, but she always thought she knew better. Now she didn't know what was real or whether it could hurt her. Her muscles twitched with fear. She held her sword in both hands, and it was all she could do to keep the blade from shaking. Buffy would've been so ashamed.

The magic lines seemed to glow brighter as Laurel closed her circle. A faint crackle from the fluorescents told a different story.

"Guys, this is turning into a bad idea," Cam said. "The lights are getting dim."

"It's just the storm," BO Boy said.

"That's right," she agreed, "it's just a big, fat, bad-ass thunderstorm that could turn into a tornado. Do you really want to be stuck down here if that happens?"

"If that happens, the parking garage is the safest place to be," Glasses Guy said.

"And if the power goes down and the lights go out?"

"If it frightens you so much, leave." Laurel lifted her chin and her arm at the same time. "We've got important work to do."

"I'm not going without Isobel."

"She'll be fine," Dean said. "I'll take care of her."

"If there aren't any more objections—" Laurel's expression dared Cam to interrupt, "—let's begin. Everybody face the star in the center of the circle. When I say go, we start walkin' widdershins, sayin' all together, 'I believe in Thomas Brown.' "

"Uh," Dean and BO Boy said together.

"Anti-clockwise," Laurel explained. They still didn't get it. "To your left, you . . . boys!"

Cam thought she heard Isobel choke back a laugh. But her sister's face was the picture of innocence by the time Laurel flashed another furious glance in her direction.

"Is everybody ready *now*?" Laurel drawled. "All right. We need to go nine times around the circle to lay Old Tom's soul to rest. All together now. Nine. Eight. Seven . . . "

The pillars and flickering shadows on the walls seemed to hold their breath. The cords wrapped around the hilt of her katana dug into Cam's palms. Her fingers throbbed, the echo of thunder in her pulse.

" . . . One. Now. I believe in Thomas Brown."

Everybody chimed in on a different syllable. The next chorus was less ragged. "I believe in Thomas Brown."

The auras of the people in the group grew more solid as they shuffled through the glowing star in the center of the pentagram. Cam no longer had to strain to see the filmy full-body energy bubbles. The different emotions coursing through Isobel and Dean, BO Boy, Glasses Guy and Laurel took on color and shape. They became so tangible, Cam could almost smell them. Thrilling fear, horniness, hope, cunning, sex, and fury.

"I believe in Thomas Brown!" they shouted together.

Laurel's energy was raging red and angry purple. It seemed to claw the light. With each circuit, it grew stronger, striking static through the lights. Tiny lightning bolts mimicked the massive thunderbolts searing the air outside.

Cam became aware of the weight of the building overhead. The fluorescent lights rattled in their sockets.

"I believe in Thomas Brown! I believe in Thomas Brown!"

Laurel's eyes slitted. She grimaced. Her chest heaved like she was running some kind of race. The rage enveloping her snagged the extended energies of the others. Its blackness stained everything it touched. It swelled and rose like smoke, coiling around the Hyatt's magical safety net.

" . . . Thomas Brown!" they screamed.

The lights blacked out.

Everybody started screaming for real.

Thanks to her right eye, Cam could still see. Magical geometry strobed through the darkness, but the pattern was warped. In less than a heartbeat, the snakelike ropes had pulled the lights out of alignment. Where the stained glass lines bowed, the pillars holding up the garage wobbled. Steel groaned and mortar ground together as the snakes tightened their hold. It sounded like the building was about to collapse. Fine white powder sifted from the ceiling.

She had to do something or they were all dead.

"Get down!" Cam shouted as she sprang forward. "All of you. Now!"

She slashed her sword at the nearest snake and cut it in two, then went after another. Nobody moved. They froze and screamed like a bunch of idiots. She had to kick the legs out from under Dean to get to the next snake. "I said down!"

For years she'd dreamed of wielding a katana like Renji in *Bleach* or Sango in *Inuyasha*. This was nothing like she pictured it. She didn't know how to use the damn sword. It was way too big for her. She practically fell over herself with every stroke, scraping her toes and the sides of her feet in her stupid flip-flops. The sword was heavy too. Her shoulders ached, not so much from swinging it, but from keeping herself from swinging too far. If she hurt somebody, nobody would believe she was trying to save them. If she didn't keep going everybody would die. And if she accidentally cut one of the hotel's magic lines . . . ?

She wouldn't let herself go there. Thank God she was fighting something that didn't fight back. The snakes parted in a hiss of steam. She barely felt them against the blade. She felt everything else, though. She squeezed the katana's sweat-slick hilt so tight, she thought her wrists would fall off.

The sense of a tremendous weight hanging over her head eased a little. But the strain of cutting the right thing and only the right thing got worse. Sweat popped out of her forehead and salted her upper lip. It rolled icy down her spine.

The emergency lights kicked in, almost blinding her. Through the pounding in her ears she heard Isobel whimper, "Cam?"

Glasses Guy took one look at her sword and dropped to the floor. BO Boy shrieked and did the same. Dean started to roll over. Cam jumped on him and cut another brackish line. The nearest pillar creaked back into place.

"What the hell are you doing?" Laurel yelled. Out of the corner of her eye, Cam saw her make a grab for her arm. Something streaked between them, and Cam heard a muffled thud.

"My sister said 'Down!' " Isobel added as an afterthought, "Bitch."

Smiling, Cam jerked her blade through another smoky worm. Another pillar groaned into place. "Just a couple more," Cam panted.

"Do it," Isobel said. "Nobody moves until you say so."

Cam wanted to laugh at the certain command in her sister's voice, but she didn't have the breath. She sliced through the final knot of dark. All the fluorescents in the garage flashed to life, and for an awful instant she couldn't see anything. She lowered her sword to the sounds of five people scuffling to their feet. By the time her eyes adjusted to the light, the guys were in full retreat.

Laurel would've probably tried to jump her again, but Isobel had her right arm twisted behind her back. Her sister wore a bloodthirsty smile. Laurel started to snarl something, then she froze, her eyes fixed on the katana.

A thousand smart remarks jockeyed for position in Cam's brain, but she was suddenly too exhausted to say any of them. She'd saved her sister—her *older* sister—and the rest of them. That was all that mattered anyway.

Blearily looking around for her scabbard, she happened to glance at her katana. Some kind of black gunk dripped off the blade. Carefully holding it by the hilt, she covered her right eye to be sure. But no matter how she looked at it, the blade was coated in slime. The oily gunk rolled sluggishly down the chipped and pitted edge of her brand new katana before plopping, drop by drop, on the stained cement.

"Carmen Sofia," her sister wheezed, "I think you've got some 'splainin' to do."

After everything that happened Saturday night, it wasn't easy for Cam to sneak into the Dealers' Room before it opened. But she managed. It was even harder to wait next to the Elphame booth clutching her katana, steeling herself for a fight . . . or worse. Cutting those energy snakes—or whatever they were—in the parking garage didn't make her a hero. It gave her a better reason to be scared.

The bells jingled. The woman in green breezed down the aisle, a cardboard cup of coffee in her hand. She set her cup on the counter and tipped her head at Cam, as if there was nothing at all strange about finding her there with a sword in her hand first thing on Sunday morning. Fluffing her skirts, the woman settled gracefully on the booth's single high stool. In a lot of ways she looked the same as she did yesterday—tall and gray-haired, with eyes older than the hills. But the face she kept hidden was young and beautiful in the same strange way as the silver creatures in her jewelry case.

Cam set the little silver critter who'd led her to the parking garage on the countertop. "I think this belongs to you."

The woman smiled and the bells sang louder. "Keep the tapir as a souvenir," she said. "You earned it."

"I'd rather keep my eye."

"What good would your eye do me?"

"But the stories—" Cam clamped her teeth on her bottom lip before she said anything stupid.

"Do you think we're frozen in time?" The woman lifted the lid on her cup and blew gently. Chunks of coffee-colored ice formed in the cup. Condensation dewed the cardboard. "Our technologies have advanced as much as yours. Those drops, for example. They'll wear off by Monday morning, sooner if you rinse your eye with a saline solution."

"Then why'd you do it?"

"It amused me."

Cam suspected the reason was as simple as that, but it disappointed her just the same. "Then you really are as heartless as they say."

The woman took a sip of ice coffee and considered for a moment. "Not quite. Some things are worth saving. This—" she gestured to the bright magic and mundane bustle gathering in the Dealers' Room "—is one of them."

"Then you knew what was going to happen in the garage last night."

"Not exactly. I had a sense of the way the wind was blowing, but I didn't know whose house—whose hotel," she amended, "it would blow down."

"I still don't get it," Cam insisted. "Even if you only guessed something was up, why didn't you take care of it yourself?" She pointed at the coffee cup. "You're the one with the power. Why put it on me? People could've died!"

The woman laughed like a flock of birds taking flight. "Look around you, Carmen Sofia Raymes. Look at my silver, my bells, my cases of wood, brass and glass. Now look at what you hold in your hand.

"Sweet child of man, I needed someone to wield the iron."

SIBLING RIVALRY

Bradley H. Sinor

As to why they stole the fire extinguisher, I didn't know and I
didn't care.

I had taken the redeye flight into Atlanta, and then discovered that
my hotel didn't run a shuttle service to the airport. At first, the only
choice that presented itself was the long line of car rental counters.
Spotting the MARTA (Metro Atlanta Rail Transportation Agency)
train sign presented a very workable alternative.

Hey, I've always had a weakness for trains.

Earlier today, I had returned from picking up lunch at the Greek
place across the street from my office to find that I'd had a visitor. The
interesting thing was the door was still locked tight.

One of my exes keeps telling me I should put in an alarm system,
but when you're in a building that would have been old in the Depres-
sion, it seems a waste of money. Besides, I didn't think that the wiring
could handle the additional load.

Even though I was on the 12th floor, I checked the window anyway.
It was locked tight, just like the door. Since there wasn't a fire escape,
someone would have had to know a few magic tricks to get inside.
Stage magic has always been a hobby of mine, bringing in a few dollars
when the P.I. business was slow, and getting in through the window
would be beyond me. Whoever my visitor had been, they had left a
manila envelope sitting in my desk chair. I opened it to find several
things of interest: a round-trip airline ticket, a hotel room confirma-
tion number and a membership in something called DragonCon.

"What in the hell is DragonCon?" I asked the empty office.

I've been a private investigator for eight years, so finding answers is my bread and butter. In this case it was easy; I just Googled the term and had the information in a matter of a few key strokes.

DragonCon turned out to be a large-scale sci-fi convention, with a lot of actors, musicians, writers, artists, and that sort of thing. It had been going on for twenty years and got a shitload of people who were apparently willing to come from far and wide to hang out with their fellow sci-fi geeks.

I had actually been thinking about taking a few days off to go fishing. It looked like the trout would have to wait, though, since included with the other paperwork were twenty pictures of Benjamin Franklin, all of them with non-sequential serial numbers.

This whole thing had piqued my curiosity. I've had more than one person tell me that my curiosity would be the death of me; one day they may be right.

I'd been on the train for a half hour, and had had the car to myself for the last few minutes. That was when the gang-bangers showed up, none of them any older than sixteen; dressed in baggy pants, do-rags and vinyl vests.

They stood in the door of the car, surveying the whole scene, before dropping onto one of the plastic bench seats that ran along one side. Three of them were pointing out the window and speaking in low voices; the fourth was lost in whatever was on his iPod.

We'd passed two more stops when iPod boy suddenly stood up and marched across the car. I shifted a bit, just in case there was trouble in the offing. He didn't make a move toward me. Instead, he went to the back of the car and began feeling around under one of the plastic benches. It took a moment for him to find and open a compartment that had been built into the thing. He pulled out a fire extinguisher that had been stored there. With a satisfied look on his face, iPod boy carried it back to where his friends were sitting and slid the thing under their bench without a word being said.

Two stops later, the gang-bangers were up and heading for the door before the train had come to a complete halt, iPod grabbing the extinguisher and hefting it onto his shoulder.

"There's something you don't see every day," I muttered.

"I'm sorry, sir," said the girl sitting below the sign that said Pre-Registration O-Z.

"This membership has already been picked up."

Ms. O-Z was dressed in a tee shirt that bore a cartoon-looking figure of a big-eyed girl in a mini dress and pigtails. Her own hair was dyed black, but had blonde roots showing, and she had a spiderweb tattoo peaking around her neck.

"Really?" I said.

The girl nodded and looked back at the laptop in front of her. I watched as she moved the mouse around and pulled up several screens. I could see my name in a list of other attendees, and the column next to it indicated that the membership had been picked up.

"Is there a problem here?"

The young woman who stepped up beside Ms. O-Z didn't look too much older than her. I did notice that her name badge, which featured a minipainting of a dragon curled around a rose, had the name Carla.

"No problem," I said. "Except your system says that they gave someone else the membership that was in my name."

"Indeed?" Carla stared at the screen over Ms. O-Z's shoulder for a couple of minutes before she finally looked up at me. I had the feeling that Ms. Carla thought this was just a minor glitch, no doubt expecting much larger ones as the day progressed.

"Can I see your ID?" she asked.

"Certainly," I flashed my driver's license, voter registration and library card. I was careful not to show my PI license or gun permit; there are some things that people don't need to see.

"Okay, here's the deal. They did apparently give away your membership to the wrong person. That's not a problem. I can print and laminate a new badge for you. I'll meet you at the Special Services area with them in fifteen minutes." She gestured toward a desk in the far corner of the hall with a half a dozen people standing around it.

"That sounds like a plan to me," I said.

Carla was as good as her word. Fifteen minutes later I had a badge that was still warm from the laminator and a manila envelope full of papers. I decided to celebrate this small victory with coffee from a vendor's cart just outside of the hotel.

I had just taken a swallow of a large double latté with triple chocolate chips, when *she* came stomping through a crowd of people in Star Trek uniforms, with an expression on her face that looked about Category Four angry and reaching for Category Five. The girl was maybe an inch shorter than me, dressed in a black tee shirt, cargo shorts and hiker boots, her hair tied in a ponytail.

In no more than three seconds she was in front of me and growling something that sounded like "You son of a bitch" before she drove her fist into my chin.

I didn't go down, but only because I managed to grab the edge of the coffee cart. There were a few stars flying around my head and a flash of light that filled up the world for a couple of seconds, but I don't think I lost consciousness. The next thing that I knew, a Good Samaritan had me by the arm, steadying me.

"Easy there, mate," he said with a distinctive Australian accent. "That's not exactly the way to start the day."

Out of the corner of my eye I caught a glimpse of someone pushing my attacker up against the wall, pinning her between the cart and a big concrete planter. It took a minute or two for me to recover. When I did, I looked back toward where the girl should have been, but saw no one; the only thing next to the planter was a crushed up fast food bag.

"So, what the hell did you do to her, mate?"

The pain in my jaw had faded into a dull ache. My newly-made friend, "just call me Reg" had suggested that we go find a good stiff drink, strictly for medicinal purposes, to help me deal with the pain.

That sounded like an idea I could live with, but the rumbling in my stomach presented an argument for a different course of action. I hadn't had anything to eat that morning; the free continental breakfast being offered in the lobby of my hotel had been less than appetizing. Since the main hotels where DragonCon was centered were in downtown Atlanta, there was no shortage of food possibilities.

So Reg led me through a covered skyway bridge to a large food court, which suited me fine. From the size of the place, it seemed intended to serve the needs not only the food needs of hotel guests, but a good portion of the daily business population of downtown Atlanta. People in costumes ranging from Spiderman to SpongeBob Squarepants were mixing with tourists and shining examples of business casual dress.

"I wish I knew what I did to her, or at least who she was. Maybe I would feel like I deserved that whopping," I said finally.

"Well, if you've forgotten her, then you must have done some heavy-duty drinking. She was a nice looking Sheila," he said. Reg was an older guy, mid to late fifties was my guess. His pale hair and skin give him a kind of ethereal appearance. It sort of fit with everyone else I had seen at the convention.

I grabbed a piece of pizza from an Italian fast food place, along with a replacement container of coffee. Reg did the same, taking a Dr. Pepper instead of coffee, and pointed toward some empty tables at the far end of the food court. Garish signs, announcing *Coming Soon*, covered over several unoccupied store fronts in that direction.

Before he had a chance to sit down, Reg's cell phone rang. After a few quick words he announced that the call had been from his office. Apparently, there was some kind of crisis that only he could solve. He apologized, suggesting that maybe we should meet for a drink later and then hit a couple of the convention parties tonight.

So I dropped down into the chair and looked back toward the hallway. From the corner of my eye I noticed someone come through a maintenance door just to my left and up to my table. Just when I thought things were not going to be getting any weirder, I looked up into my own face.

"I think we need to talk," I heard myself say.

"So, are you my evil twin Skippy?" I asked Alright, I know that remark scored rather high on the flippant and stupid meters. It was honestly the only thing that I could think of to say right then.

My other self grinned. I'd like to think it was because he understood my reaction. Hey, coming face to face with your identical twin brother, especially when you don't have any brothers, is not business as usual.

He took the seat opposite me with his back to the wall, keeping an open path to the doorway he had come through, and laid a canvas messenger bag on the table between us.

"Why don't you call me Bucky? That will keep things from getting even more confused than they already are," he said. Nobody had called me Bucky in more than twenty years. To the best of my knowledge, there was no one alive who even knew that had been my nickname.

Now that I got a closer look at him, I could see that Bucky had a black eye, some cuts, and, I suspected, a nice collection of bruises. Obviously I was in better shape than my "brother." Damn, even with the nickname, terminology was going to be a bitch.

"Okay," said Bucky. "Let's get down to it. The easiest way to explain this is to be up-front with the fact that I am you, and you are me."

"And we are all together," I said. "Right?"

Bucky chuckled at the reference. It was reassuring to know that my "brother" was a fan of the lads from Liverpool like I was.

"The long and the short of it is that somewhere along the line I made one choice and you made a different one," he said. "We don't have time to compare personal histories, just know it happened and has happened thousands of times. There are a lot of us, a lot of everybody when you get down to it."

At the other end of the food court someone dressed as Hellboy had been deep in conversation with a rather anorexic looking girl in a Wonder Woman costume. Apparently, the lady did not like what the big red guy said, since she dumped the contents of her drink over him and stomped away.

At the sound of the ruckus, Bucky's hand pushed inside his jacket, exposing the butt of a pistol. I've never cared that much for guns; the results of using them are far more final than I like. After a moment, he relaxed and turned back toward me.

"So how did you end up here?" I asked. "And what am I doing here, anyway?"

"About two years ago I discovered I could slip between possibilities. I've developed a little sideline of handling cases in different timelines. Only problem is, one of them has gone more than a bit wrong," he said.

Just then a racking cough shook Bucky. I had a feeling that, in addition to the bruises, we were dealing with some broken ribs, not to mention a possible punctured lung. Bucky boy there was going to need to get himself to a doctor as soon as possible.

Once the coughing jag was over, he reached inside of the messenger bag and pulled out a long wooden box that he laid on the table between us. The workmanship was highly-detailed with inlaid ivory designs in swirls and geometric patterns. Obviously a lot of time and skill had gone into making it.

"What's in it?" I asked

"Not my business. This was supposed to be strictly a courier job. Pick up the package and get it to my client. Unfortunately, someone took umbrage at the idea of my possessing it; otherwise, I would have taken this thing back home, pocketed my fee and then headed to Bora Bora for the weekend."

"Would, by chance, one of those people who got in your way be a good looking girl with dark hair and a hell of a right cross?" I asked.

"You met her, did you?" Bucky grinned. "She's a bit of a hellion, I'll give her that. I'm surprised you didn't notice the family resemblance."

"A family resemblance?" I didn't like where this was going. "Are you saying she's another version of the two of us, from some other timeline?"

"Nope, though I have run into female versions of us, but she's not one of them. She's our sister, Elaine."

Oh, damn! I felt my stomach twist in a dozen different directions. My older sister Elaine had been killed in a hit-and-run accident when she was in the sixth grade.

"Let me make an educated guess," I sighed and pointed at the box. "She is one of the crew that tried to stop you from getting that."

"Give the man a gold star for getting it right on the first try. Not only is she part of the crew, she's their boss. I stung them badly, but," he shrugged painfully, "they gave as good as they got. Unfortunately, during our little 'family reunion,' the compass unit I use to find my way home to 'my' exact world got smashed."

"And without that you can't go home again?"

"How very Thomas Wolfe but, unfortunately, accurate. I could go 'home,' but the odds on it being the exact timeline that I came from are pretty slim. The thing is, *that* is where my client knows to find me. I would like to get paid." Bucky said it all with the same faux Boston accent that used to drive one of my ex-wives bonkers when *I* did it. I was beginning to understand her point of view.

"I'm not exactly a mapmaker."

"That's alright, because I had a spare unit. Unfortunately, during our little commotion, I had no time to use it. I had to hide it to keep Elaine from getting the thing. It's none of her business who I'm working for, client confidentiality and all that. Problem is, even though I got away from her and her bully boys, I'm in no shape now to try and get the compass unit back."

"So, that's where I come in," I said.

"Yep. It wasn't hard to arrange for your membership and plane ticket. I've visited this time line before, so it wasn't a problem to call in a few favors and lay a trail to get you here. You're the only one I could trust with the truth."

"Thanks, I think. So where is it?"

"You're going to love this; it's on exhibit in the convention art show."

It was time for me to come out of the closet.

According to my watch it was 10 p.m. The art show had been closed for two hours. I, on the other hand had been in the maintenance closet for just over five hours.

I twisted one way, then another to work out the kinks in my leg and back muscles. Squeezing my five-ten frame into a small, smelly space for an extended period of time was not fun. For around the hundredth time since I had left Bucky, I found myself wondering what the hell I was doing. Why should I believe him? This whole thing sounded like something from a bad drive-in movie. Okay, he did look just like me, but they do say that everyone in the world has a double. He just happened to be mine.

The art show took up two large ballrooms, crisscrossed by pegboard and wire frame walls that formed a complicated maze winding hither and yon. I had wandered around the place for some time, trying to orient myself on what was where, and how best to get out once I had secured my prize.

I spotted the compass unit as soon as I walked in the main door— exactly where Bucky had told me it would be. A small metal tube, marked with gauges and dials on the surface, lying with a number of other items in a very large treasure chest. That chest was wrapped by the tail of a large metal dragon sculpture.

There were too many people walking in and out, not to mention more than a couple of rent-a-cops prowling the area, so just grabbing it and running was not an option. So, instead, I hid out in the main-tenance closet for five hours.

Outside of the room, I heard a mixture of laughter, conversations and that low ambient sound that crowds of humanity seem to make anywhere and anytime. I didn't see any sign of closed-circuit televi-sion and it was more than reasonable to guess that there weren't any high-tech alarm systems or sensors waiting to be tripped, not on a temporary show like this one. I knew that there would be security of some kind. More than likely it would be the rent-a-cops, probably checking the place every couple of hours. That would be quite long enough for me to grab the unit and retire to my hiding place to wait for the show to open up tomorrow morning. Then I would just walk out with the regular visitors.

"I'd hold it right there, if I were you," said a muffled woman's voice from just behind me. I took a deep sigh and turned. I'd been dreading this moment ever since Bucky enlightened me as to who had busted my chops that morning.

After all, as far as I was concerned, she had been dead for two thirds of my life. I turned and looked at into the face that I could sort of see my twelve-year-old sister's features in.

"Evening, sis," I said.

"Good evening, little brother." She held a Styrofoam cup in her hands, and lifted it in salute to me. "I think we need to talk."

Bucky found me around noon the next day.

I had spent an hour wandering around the convention dealers' room; there were a hundred and fifty merchants set up, if there were a dozen. They had everything that the sci fi geek could dream of: an endless supply of toys based on everything from comics to movies, computer games, fantasy jewelry, has-been actors hawking their photos, and even one or two dealers selling, of all things, books.

I was looking at collectable trading cards when I felt a hand on my shoulder.

"I thought we gave up baseball cards when we were fourteen," said Bucky.

"Please," I tried to put the right sort of irritation in my voice. "These are the ones that my girlfriend's son is nuts about. I score major points with her for keeping him happy, especially since he may be my future stepson."

Bucky chuckled, glancing nervously around the room. He was wearing a leather motorcycle jacket, along with wraparound sun glasses. Not my idea of the best disguise, especially in late summer Atlanta, but who am I to criticize.

"Shall we," he said gesturing toward the room's entrance.

Just outside the door, where two escalators brought a continuing flow of people up and down, there were several large banks of pay phones. Thankfully, no one was using any of them, but in this age of cell phones, how many times do you actually see anyone using a pay phone? I've always been an advocate of hiding things in plain sight; if you're careful, major secrets can change hands in the middle of a crowd.

"You got it, then?" he asked.

"Of course, I did. Let's just say it was easy and leave things at that,"

I said. Instead of going back to my hidey hole after I had retrieved the item in question, I had slipped out through the hotel employee's hallway; easy and simple. Complicated causes trouble.

I pulled out the compass unit, holding it up in my best Vanna White imitation. The look of relief on his face was major. He twisted his lip in the same way I did when I was contemplating a check from a satisfied client.

"I was seriously wondering if I would see that again," he said.

"Happy to oblige, 'brother,' " I said. "Now, you haven't gone and misplaced the box, have you?"

Bucky shook his head and reached into his messenger bag to show me.

"May I?" I asked.

He shrugged and passed it over, as I handed him the compass unit. I trailed my fingers along part of the design, pressing down on an inlayed piece of ivory and on the corner of the box. Something moved and a drawer slid open.

"I'll be damned," Bucky said. I had a feeling that he had tried to open it but had failed and that was why he had been feigning indifference to the contents.

"I wouldn't move, gentlemen, and I would drop that box, if you please," said a tall figure in *Star Wars* storm troopers armor, standing a dozen steps away. Only, instead of a standard issue Imperial blaster, he held a .38 caliber police special.

Since I had no desire to add lead to my diet I did exactly what I was told. In the process I slid the drawer closed on the box and turned slowly toward our intruder, positioning my self so I blocked Bucky's view of him. In the process, I pushed the box back toward Bucky with my foot.

"You're a little short for a storm trooper, aren't you?" I asked

Then, in a move that I hope would have impressed my martial arts sensei, I twisted to my right, launching a kick at the gun. The trooper pulled back before my blow could connect, but he didn't retaliate. Behind me there was a distinct whooshing sound, kind of a mini sonic boom.

"Crikey, mate, that kick of yours was a little too close for my liking," said the storm trooper, as he reached to pull his helmet off.

"Reg, that was the whole idea," I said, looking back at the bank of phones where no one was standing now.

"So what am I going to do with you, little brother?" Elaine asked, speaking softly in spite of the background noise on the airport-bound MARTA train.

"You could always pull a gun and pistol whip me," I said.

"There is that option. As I recall, I never did get even for you putting your iguana in my closet during that slumber party when I was in the fifth grade."

"Hey, a little brother's got to do what a little brother's got to do," I said.

It was still strange talking to her. Part of me remembered that irritating older sister who was mine alone to torment, anyone else stay the hell away from her, whose departure from my life on a rainy street ripped a hole in my soul that didn't heal for a lot of years. The little brother in me I was very glad to have her back, even for a moment. Another part of me said who the hell is this woman?

"I still am amazed that you were able pull the whole thing off," she said.

As a matter of fact, I was, too, but I wasn't going to admit it. Right up until I heard the sound of air rushing into the space that Bucky had occupied when he phased out to his own timeline, I had been convinced that the whole thing would end up as major failure. I was not eager to see my other self mad; I know how I am when I get mad, and it isn't a pretty sight.

"It was just a matter of letting him see what we wanted him to see and making him think what we wanted him to think—basic Stage Magic 101. You keep the audience looking at the right hand while it's the left hand that is getting into mischief. Of course, if he knew that you and I had talked, that might have skewed the whole thing," I said.

Reg had come onto the train with us, though he had taken a seat several rows away, to give us the illusion of privacy. But I would bet my bottom dollar that he could hear everything we said and was ready to step in on her side, if for some reason she thought me departing from our little arrangement.

From my jacket I pulled a thin manila envelope. Inside were three foil-wrapped packages, with names written across them, featuring a familiar figure in a red cape with an S on his chest. Elaine nodded, confirming that these were the items that my other self had "borrowed" from her.

"What's so special about these particular ones?"

"They come from a timeline where the creators of Superman, Jerry Siegel and Joe Shuster, did not get screwed by their publishers and had very long, successful careers. You should see the other super-heroes they created. Amazing," she said, grinning. "Those cards are rare enough to begin with; there aren't that many timelines where they were actually produced. To have them signed by both Siegel and Shuster, well, to say the least, it quintuples their value. They are worth a fortune to my client, and that's why Bucky wanted them for his client," she said. "The madness of collectors; I have never understood it but, it has proved very profitable to me."

"What I didn't understand from the beginning was, why you just didn't grab Bucky get them from him, without involving me."

"There was no way to know if he had opened the box, and if he had, then he could hidden them anywhere. Face it, downtown Atlanta is big and has more nooks and crannies than I care to contemplate, especially when you are looking for things as small as trading cards."

I pushed the envelope toward her, but pulled it away before Elaine's fingers could touch it. Out of the corner of my eye, I saw Reg turn, and he was obviously ready to step in if things got out of hand.

"So, now, about my finder's fee," I said.

Elaine pursed her lips for a moment and then smiled. "I antici-pated that, little brother. If you check your bank account, you will find a substantial payment had been deposited. Your regular daily fee tripled, plus a bonus for your time."

"That sounds fair. Can I trust you?"

"I'm hurt. Of course you can trust me. After all, we're family," she said.

Just then the door between cars flew open and a couple of teenagers came in, two young men maybe sixteen. From their outfits, baggy pants, vinyl vests and do-rags, they could easily have been the same ones who had been there when I rode in from the airport, or at least of the members of the same gang. They were arguing about the relative merits of a rap group named *The Deep Ones* and a goth band called *Death's Big Brother*, and got rather loud about the whole thing. Elaine looked at them with some distaste and then turned back to me.

"I think this concludes our business," I said as I passed the envelope to her.

"It's been a pleasure," she said. Reg came back to where we were standing; they both produced small silver tubes similar to what I had given Bucky, and made some quick adjustments. They didn't fade away; they were just simply not there. The whoosh of air rushing into the space the two of them had occupied was in no way as a loud as when Bucky had shifted time lines, but it was noticeable.

"Damn," said one of the gang bangers who came up next to me. "Two people just disappearing, there's something you don't see every day."

"Indeed, you don't," I nodded and passed him another picture of Mr. Franklin, to go with the one I had given him and his friend earlier, when we made our arrangements. Cold cash does have a way of silencing any sort of awkward questions that might come up.

Once I was alone, I pulled three foil wrapped packages out from under my left leg and smiled at the figure in the red cape on their front. If what Elaine had said was even half true in this time line, then these should fetch a nice price, more so than the ones I had switched them for when she had been distracted by the gang bangers. I knew some crazy collectors, too.

But even if, in this timeline, these things weren't worth anything, I felt good about the whole matter. It had come down to whether I trusted my "sister" Elaine or my "brother" Bucky.

I learned to trust my gut a long time ago; that's how I've stayed alive all these years in this business. In this little matter, my gut had told me not to trust either one; they'd both been playing me and I doubted that I had gotten the full story from either one of them. Instead, the safest path was to trust one person and one person only. Me.

PAT THE MAGIC DRAGON

───

Jody Lynn Nye

"Mommy, why do they call it DragonCon?" a little girl asked as they followed the long, snaking line through registration. Pat Henry smiled to himself. The mother, somewhere in her middle thirties and fan-shaped, caught a glimpse of both the expression and the convention committee badge.

"Well, why do you call it *Dragon*-Con?" the woman asked him point blank. Pat nodded to her deferentially, but his only choice was to lie through his teeth.

"We're pretty fond of dragons down here," he said. "They're the biggest of the fantastic beasts, and even from the beginning we intended this to be the biggest and the best convention anywhere in the country."

"In the world," put in a stout, dark-haired man with a beard about five places behind the woman in line.

"Glad you think so," Pat said, pleased.

He glanced around. He didn't see any fire ants yet, but that didn't mean they weren't there somewhere. Better check with Security and see there had been any sightings. He scanned the long lines. Security and operations personnel, many from central Georgia, but many who came all the way from North Carolina and Virginia, browsed the room, checking for those telltale signs of trouble. This was their first contact with attendees, and hence, their first line of defense. Pat knew the signs well: eyes that were just a little too shiny, fingers that made a clicking noise when they moved, and that odd smell that human beings usually couldn't detect. Each of his people carried a Black Box. To the uninitiated, the Box looked like a walkie-talkie, and Pat was content to let them think so. Modern electronics had reduced reliable communication devices to the size of a matchbook. The real phone set was hidden inside a shirt collar or under long hair and attached by cord to the earpiece worn by each patroller. The Black Box contained a stun gun that could bring down a charging buffalo and a hypo loaded with formatoxin. Neither of those would do more than slow down a fire ant, but it would be enough to keep it immobile long enough for help to arrive. Pat hated to use the Boxes; there was a risk of collateral damage to human beings. Fire ants never went quietly.

The earpiece blatted out a burst of static.

"Looking for me, Bill?" he asked.

"We've got an arrival," his ops chief, Bill Mann, Jr., said in a calm voice, knowing that the walkie-talkie system was overheard by non-committee members. "You might want to get to the primary location."

Pat started moving, dodging among the rows of people waiting to register.

"Excuse me," he said, absently, his mind racing. None of the special attendees was due until the evening. What on earth were they thinking, coming in in broad daylight?

From the ballroom, it was a solid ten minutes' run up crowded escalators and through corridors until he was out on (street between hotels). Not for the first time he cursed the territoriality of the Atlanta hoteliers who, though they joined their establishments together at the second-floor level, refused to allow a tunnel system when the hotels were built. It certainly would have made his life easier. Not that he could have explained in plain language to the association or the Atlanta police why it was a good idea. On the other hand, he blessed the architect who built the Hyatt, designing two basements that didn't seem to connect to one another. The space between them provided a safe and secure location that only a select few knew about.

The security guard at the doorway that led down to the motor lobby almost stopped him, but she was an old hand at DragonCon, and recognized him. She waved him in. A dozen fans tried to follow.

Pat heard their protests as she halted them and sent them up the stairs to the entrance on the next level. Because of the heavy foot traffic, the route he was taking was one way coming in the other direction. Normally, he set a good example, but he had to get to the concealed door, pronto.

Pat fumed, though he knew Bill couldn't give him any more data over an open frequency. Who could it be? Didn't they know that they might be endangering the entire conference, arriving early?

He strode through the corridor, noting that the ochre paint had been recently renewed, as was the plain carpet underfoot. Everything was clean and in good repair. The Hyatt, glad to be a part of the annual DragonCon festivities, had done them proud. The surroundings weren't flashy, but the fan convention overhead provided all the color and visual distraction that was necessary. He wound through the labyrinth of meeting rooms, heading toward a blank wall at the end of the corridor.

To be honest, DragonCon had outgrown its location, and could really have used a dedicated facility that could hold the multiple thousands who came to enjoy the weekend, both convention and conference, but he couldn't fault the hard work and confidentiality that maintained it here in the heart of the largest city in southeast America. Still, he and the committee weren't ready to move. There was no place big enough that was ready to go. Pat pressed his lips together, formulating what he was going to say to the fool who had come in, forcing them to open the secret rooms up ahead of time, before all the protective cantrips and wards were in place. He took the key from his inner coat pocket and inserted it into the camouflaged keyhole at the end of the corridor of alphabetized rooms and muttered a familiar phrase. He felt the wards slide back. The door opened and he slipped inside, ignoring the curious glances of the few fans who were wandering around, checking the place out. He hoped none of them were fire ants.

A tapestry-covered partition had been set up across the entrance of the main hall to prevent anyone glancing through the door from seeing the occupants of the huge hidden chamber. Pat heard groaning and panting noises. If two of his guests had arrived early to make love and had attracted any attention from the humans upstairs, he was going to give them a piece of his mind!

He rounded the partition and heeled to a stop. The words he had been readying faded away, forgotten. He stared up at the slender female red dragon perched on one of the nesting boxes, her tongue darting between her teeth, her wings flapping in agitation.

Pat thumbed his walkie-talkie. "Who's up there?"

"This is Everette."

"Everette, can you send someone from first aid down here?" he asked, hoping his voice sounded casual in spite of his pounding heart. "We've got eggs."

"Really?" his ops chief responded, forgetting himself. "Who?"

"Everette!"

"Sorry. Switching over now. Back to you in a minute."

"Annette, someone's coming pretty soon," he called. "I'll help you until one of the midwives gets here. Are you okay?"

"I'm so sorry," she wailed, her long neck whipping back and forth. "I was too close. I couldn't hold back any longer!"

Hell of a time, he thought, stripping off his tie and jacket; they wouldn't survive his transformation. But that was why DragonCon existed.

With large brains, muscles and wings, dragons had held the upper hand for a good deal of prehistory. Since the evolution of smart predators, however, dragons had become an endangered species. They were at a particular tactical disadvantage with regard to homo sapiens. Though many human cultures had deep-seated respect for *draco draconis*, the fact was that very few human beings liked the idea of sharing territory with them. They were suspicious of large, smart carnivores that could fly. Then there was the problem with greed. Dragons had an affinity for gold and glittery minerals. They drew magical energy from those substances. Humans, not surprisingly, also valued these selfsame natural resources, but as wealth, wealth that often robbed them of what good sense they had. It took a considerable amount of effort to mine gold and cut gems, so if one happened upon a cache of treasure guarded by one large beast (dragons were solitary most of the time), one might think it cost effective to dispose of said beast and claim the treasure. Fighting a dragon was more momentarily dangerous than mining, and a good deal more glorious to talk about later on. Pat hated treasure hunters, but he understood them. Dragons weren't innocent in the treasure-hunting racket, either. Plenty of them had stolen their gold from humans, who'd gone to as much trouble as any dragon to mine, refine and cast it.

But over the centuries both dragons and humans had become more civilized, though humans had developed advanced weaponry, and dragons had kept only the armaments provided by nature: teeth, claws, wings, superior size, and magic. In the greatest part, humans had stopped believing in dragons altogether, a disbelief fostered and encouraged by dragons who had no trouble passing among humans in disguise. That growing disbelief enabled dragons to live on in secret, but it was no help to their continued existence. Their numbers dwindled over the centuries, largely because of vanishing habitat. With satellites surrounding the planet, there were few places, if any, that large winged creatures could fly without appearing on the next update of Google Earth. (Needless to say, one of the places that had been necessary to infiltrate was the geography wing of that ubiquitous online service. At that moment, four dragons were on the payroll in the home office as senior programmers.) Humans had also increased in numbers so spectacularly that the balance between them and dragons was irredeemable. The Internet, television, hidden cameras and other means of surveillance had driven the dragons underground, so to speak.

Hence the need to band together on a regular basis. True, dragons were solitary by nature, but safety in numbers was an undeniably useful concept. Any intelligent being would understand that. After endless decades of argument over where and how often they should meet, Pat and the other dragons of the Atlanta area declared unilaterally they had organized an annual moot. All were welcome to attend—if they followed certain rules, such as no blood feuds, settling of ancient scores, or eating the locals. DragonCon was for the future, not reliving the past over and over. There was an old saying, that a dragon may forget his name, but he'd never forget a grudge. Pat and his fellow founders were determined to make certain peace reigned.

Like any venture, the event had started small, with a few who believed and trusted the Atlanteans. The early meetings were a little on the formal side, no bad direction to air, considering. Gradually, other dragons had seen that DragonCon was a safe venue. As each year passed, more and more of them made the journey, and departed reluctantly at the event's end, vowing to return the next year. It came to be known as the place to air grievances and settle disputes, discuss the problems with ever-encroaching human habitations, and to lay eggs.

Unlike the human perception that dragons sat on their clutches forever, eggs hatched a mere four days after laying. During that time the females, who refused to leave their incipient offspring no matter what the peril, were vulnerable to attack. Infant hatchlings had to be protected during that time. Being in the company of numerous males obviated the fear of losing dragonets, since no human, no matter what his or her motivation—having a unique pet, entertaining a foolish notion of raising a mythological creature, opening a sideshow or starting some kind of scientific research—was going to steal an egg or a baby dragon in front of anything from a hundred to a thousand angry adults. With a little sunshine, a little gold, a suitably bloody first meal, and the baby dragons would be ready to spread their wings and follow their parents to the four quarters of the wind.

Knowing that they had ensured the safety of dragon young for over twenty years already pleased the Atlantean dragons. The fact that the convention above them in the three, now four, hotels was an increasing success as well was a bonus.

Not every human was ignorant of the true purpose of DragonCon. The spells that concealed the conference from prying eyes were the product of human wizardry. The mages, witches, priests and priestesses, self-proclaimed Jedi and other seekers after truth who helped to keep the protective spells in place considered the confidence of the dragons an honor and a sacred trust. If they couldn't return from year to year, they sent substitutes. Longtime human attendees felt like members of a special society, as indeed they were.

On the dragons' part, DragonCon gave them a controlled point of interaction with friendly humans. (Chinese dragons) and wurms from remote provinces were able to meet and get used to interacting with the strange little soft-skinned two-foots, to teach them to stop fearing humankind as a species, and learn to be wary only of the fearful, crazy or greedy ones. Pat had to admit there were plenty of those, and some of them came to DragonCon. You could never be too careful, but he thought he knew what he needed to about humans.

They had not counted upon the fire ants.

In the centuries before they settled in central Georgia, Pat and his mate had dealt with environmental hazards. Sometimes his nightmares were filled with the Italian volcano where they had set up housekeeping in the 18th century that abruptly came out of dormancy the night after she had set a clutch of five eggs. They had spent the day smelling the rising sulfur and accusing the other of noisome post-prandial digestive distress. (They both had a tendency to gorge on Italian food.) Only the warning rumble from below had given them enough warning to vacate their new nest, unwieldy large eggs in hand, so to speak, before half the landscape exploded below them. He had had to change the mind of packs of hungry wolves in Russia that thought a nice cave filled with warmth and tasty dragonets was a good place to spend January. But never had he had to face such a miserable environmental monstrosity, a pain and a curse, as the minute red insects that trolled in packs of millions below ground in this otherwise pleasant land. By virtue of their small size, fire ants could crawl right underneath a dragon's scales and inflict an acid-burn bite on vulnerable skin that left one feeling as if one had breathed flames on one's own flesh. The pain didn't subside in a day or two. It went on for weeks. The strongest possible healing spells were needed to dry up the acid and heal the bites. And it was never just one ant that attacked: it was anywhere from a dozen to a million. They could kill by overwhelming a being's immune system.

The nastiest thing Pat had learned about them was that they did it on purpose. Fire ants were capable of spite. What's more, they weren't of the low intelligence that most human scientists attributed to them. As the science fiction writers in the convention upstairs might say, they occupied a hive-mind, but not one with a single thought. It was more like a big, old-fashioned party line where they could all talk at once. They detested and resented the above-ground species, especially dragons. They relished a chance to discommode, injure or kill anything they could. Most horrifying of all, young dragons were especially vulnerable to the poison. Fire ants liked the taste of dragon flesh, and could easily muster the numbers to carry off a whole carcass. The dragon community lost a few hatchlings and a least one adult before they understood the danger.

They attempted to make peace with the ants, hoping to establish a détente, but once they made contact with the intelligence behind the swarm, they were sorry they had. The myriad voices that came through the link was as varied as Facebook and as full of vitriol as a Victorian spinster. The loudest and most persistently vicious was the queen ant, Hedaera. She considered dragons her lawful prey, and her millions, if not billions of followers agreed with her. The dragons had no choice but to keep them out of DragonCon any way they had to.

Trouble was, most of the poisons that humans used to repel fire ants were ridiculously toxic to dragons, too.

While dragons weren't native to that part of the continent, other intelligent species were. The council sent out emissaries to the nightwalkers, nocturnal species who could also take on human shape when they chose. They were eager to form a mutual protection pact. They offered to share what spells they had been using to keep the ants at bay, and received in return what the dragons came up with. The fire ants didn't take their exclusion quietly; hence the committee's need for constant vigilance. Luckily, the ants couldn't tell time and had no concept of the passage of seasons, so they didn't keep track of the calendar. They only knew DragonCon had begun when the dragons began to arrive. It was up to the council to keep them out until the hatchlings were safely awing.

Surrounded by human midwives, healers and security personnel armed with Raid and tasers, Annette finished triumphantly, setting her final egg. She settled down on the nest and feathered her wings about her, looking a little like a gigantic red hen.

"Six!" she announced.

"Congratulations," Pat said. It was a large litter by dragon standards. Two was a good deal more usual, and some females went years without producing any. "I've got to go. Will you need anything in the meanwhile?"

Annette showed him a mouthful of sharp fangs. "No, thank you, dear Pat. What a relief! See you at opening ceremonies?"

"You can count on it." Pat breathed out a thin stream of flame that tickled her jowl, a dragon's kiss. He returned to human form, his suit, tie and radio, and headed for the door. "I have to go back up and look out for more guests. They'll be arriving every which way."

The procession around the motorized chair was not as dignified or as slow-moving as perhaps the escorts would have wished, but they weren't the ones driving, so to speak.

"Make a hole!" bellowed the tallest man, at the head of the file by virtue of his very long legs, which enabled him to take strides that outdistanced the cart behind him by mere seconds. "Make it wide! Dragon lady coming through!"

The crowd parted hastily. Anne McCaffrey, author of the bestselling Dragonriders of Pern series, and favorite guest of DragonCon, sped across the floor toward the elevators. Her silver-white hair was adorned with an elaborate rondel of pheasant and peacock feathers impaled by a jeweled pin, and her green, purple and blue quilted jacket made a lively statement of color. Green eyes crinkled with amusement and pleasure, she smiled at the faces around her, some grinning, some astonished at finding her in their midst. Koolness, a tall, sharp-faced man with a clipped, fair beard, stayed close to her side. With cat-fast reflexes he gently handed out of her way a young fan who, overwhelmed by the sheer numbers and the exciting sights in the Hyatt lobby, was not watching where she was going. At last, they reached the elevator. Koolness held the door open while Anne reversed the chair and backed into the booth. As many fans as possible crowded in around her, their bodies held in a posture of respect.

Aranel, a fierce-looking redhead, was at Anne's other elbow. She, like many of the women clustered around Anne, was dressed in a pseudo-medieval style. On her shoulder was balanced a tiny toy dragonet with glittering opal eyes. Her tight-laced, wide-sleeved tunic had no pockets, but she had a large pouch laced to her belt. From it she took a handful of papers and a badge festooned with a long ribbon. She handed them to Anne.

"We have a little meet-and-greet scheduled for 4:00, if that's all right with you."

"Of course!" Anne appealed to Koolness. "Is anyone else here yet?"

He met Aranel's eyes over Anne's head. Not everyone in the elevator was in the know. He nodded briefly and closed one eye in what anyone else might call a sensuous wink.

"Just one so far," Aranel confirmed.

"Good," Anne said. "I've got something for the charity auction. Will one of you two make sure it gets upstairs to Pat?"

"It would be my pleasure," Koolness said with a courteous half-bow. The others in the elevator looked envious. Anne took a book out of the basket of her motorized chair and handed it to him.

"Just Pat-Pat, if you would be so kind. No one else."

"Of course, my lady," Koolness said.

To anyone else it looked like a copy of the newest Dragonriders novel, with the illustration of a handsome bronze dragon rising into the sky on the cover. Koolness's keen eye picked up the faintest movement of a wingtip. He put the book under his arm as he held the door open for Anne to pass through.

"Hey, Janny!" a tall man with a shaved head and a curled beard shouted across the motor lobby of the Hyatt. He flapped his arm frantically to get her attention.

Janny Wurts and Don Maitz glanced backwards. Janny, a tall, very slim woman with thick dark hair going silver, grinned and waved back. Don, just as slight, with wide eyes and an elegant mustache, turned to see who she was waving at.

"Hey, Steve! Later, okay? We've got to get set up!"

"Okay!"

The two artists kept going, pushing the tall standing crates along the corridor into the elevator. More friends hailed them as they emerged, but they kept going, steering the heavy boxes toward the ballroom that housed the art show. One of the art show staff seated in a folding chair at the door, a stout woman with bright carmine braids named Fran, recognized them at once and let them in. She stood aside as they eased the huge boxes down the ramp, then followed them eagerly.

As in years past, the large booth backed by towering pegboards immediately inside the huge room had been set aside for them. With the easy strength of a woman who had spent years breaking horses, Janny pulled an enormous framed canvas out of the first box and hooked it onto the holed boards.

"That's gorgeous," Fran said, admiring the handsome blue-scaled dragon who lay curled on a hearth rug in front of a fire. He was surrounded by books, alembics and other magical impedimenta.

"Thanks," Janny said. She and Don wrestled the next painting out of its crate and put it up. A shimmering, pale dragon whose skin looked like a living opal leaned over a stone balcony, a rose in her claws.

"Wow," Fran said. Janny gave her an impatient look.

"If you don't mind, we'd just like to get our stuff up. We have to concentrate to get everything right. It takes a lot of work to put everything where it will look the way we want it to."

Fran looked guilty. "I'll come back later and see if you need anything."

"Yeah. Thanks." Janny watched until Fran had gone back to guarding the door. "Okay, she's gone."

"Thank you for the ride, my darlings," the sibilant voice said from the right hand frame.

"Indeed, it was pleasure," added the figure in the left-hand frame. "May we request a return journey? It would be most helpful."

"No problem. Art show pickup is Monday morning," Don said.

"We're going to try to blast out of here right after lunch," Janny added. "We've got to get back ASAP. Our horse-sitter can't stay past Monday."

"That would be sufficient," came from the left-hand canvas. "Our thanks. We must leave you now."

"See ya later," Janny said.

She and Don stood a casual lookout as two slim shadows slid down the canvases and flattened themselves on the floor. Once there, they took on the same pattern as the carpet. As invisible as any creature that size could be, they flowed invisibly up the stairs and out of the room. The two artists returned to their work, arranging the paintings on the pegboards so they were both attractively arrayed yet not crowded. Janny attached bid sheets to the bottom or side of each one. Don stacked books and cards on the cloth-covered tables.

They had almost finished setting up when Fran returned, pushing a wheeled cooler filled with sweating cans and bottles.

"Do you want some pop or water?" she asked them.

"Thanks," Janny said, reaching into the box. She popped a can and let the icy, tingling liquid flow down her throat. "Ah. I was dry. You really feel the heat on the drive here."

Fran frowned. She scanned the display, her finger tracking from side to side. She pointed to the largest piece of art on the left. An elderly wizard the tips of whose sweeping mustaches touched the collar of his brocade robe tented his fingers over a crystal ball at a small table in the middle of the room. Tiny fairies in bright jewel colors flitted around his head, leaving contrails of light. "Didn't that picture have a dragon in it?"

"Heck, no," Janny said, pointing to the tag. "There's the name of it. 'Wizard's study.' There's no room for a dragon in there."

Fran glanced at the other major canvas, in which a pale-skinned demoiselle in a flowing silver robe was leaning over the stone sill of a castle window. She didn't even bother to ask.

All over the complex of hotels, dragons were arriving, in every size and by every means of transport. More scaled guests crept out of paintings in the art show. Some came disguised as sculptures in bronze, shrunk down into gaggingly adorable ceramic figurines, pressed into papier-mache plaques or concealed in ornately beautiful boxes. Half the artists in science fiction and fantasy were in on the secret. The dealers' room, too, was full of dragons in hiding, waiting for their chance to slip from their places of concealment and make their way to the conclave.

It would be a whole lot better, Director of Programming Regina Kirby mused, as she marched down the escalators toward the Regency Ballroom, if magic were easier and cheaper. Then she could teleport from one crisis to another, and not waste so much time running around! The hotel engineer reported that there was a power outage on the Mezzanine level, which might interfere with the first of the major convention presentations. She checked her watch. Only two hours to go. That was no time at all to handle things, and she had nowhere she could transfer the event. Anime and manga had become such a popular media form that thousands of attendees were showing up just to meet the guests. It would really bite if the first panel of the day was held up for lack of electricity. Maybe she could hit up one of the visiting wizards to put a temporary spell on the fuse box and keep it going, at least until the engineers could figure out what was going wrong.

She threaded her way through the growing crowd. A couple of rather handsome, black-bearded men in their thirties wearing black tights and poet shirts were playing guitar at the far end of the level from the escalators, providing a treat for the eye as well as the ear. Regina wished she could stop and appreciate them, but duty called.

She rounded the corner just behind a group of Goths. Most Goths were in their late teens or early twenties, but these looked older. Damn, but the woman in the skimpy black dress had a great figure.

Regina wondered what she did in her mundane life. The human visitors to DragonCon ran the gamut, from waitresses to astrophysicists, from infants attending their first convention to nonagenarians—also attending their first convention.

The musicians who occupied the booth near the tall glass doors leading to the patio were just setting up a pair of enormous speakers. A lot of indie bands whose themes involved fantasy came in to play for the fans, hoping to sell some CDs and gain a following. The very tall man in deliberately slashed black and white layered T-shirts noticed her Staff badge and gave her a casual nod. She waved and went on. The engineer said he would be waiting for her near the door of the ballroom. Regina looked around for a man in coveralls.

A bad whiff of something hit her nostrils. It was a faint scent, but its hot, acid tang was unmistakable. Fire ant. Furious, Regina looked around. Where were those lazy wizards? Nothing should have made it up the concrete steps from street level, or down from the lobby above. No one was complaining about having been bitten, yet. She scanned the floor, looking for the telltale trail of red specks. Then, she noticed him.

He crouched against the inner wall, facing the doors. Regina might have charged past him if she hadn't stopped to admire the male musicians. He was well-disguised, but his eyes were too round for a human being, and his skin had a bronze sheen to it that made her gaze deflect off it uncomfortably, as if it was too bright to look at. By his casual dress he was one of the attendees, but she knew he wasn't human.

Regina had seen bigger fire ants, but not much. This one had to be a soldier, six feet tall if he was an inch. He was sniffing the air. She could almost see the little antennae waving back and forth on his head. Darn it, the obscuring spells should have taken all the dragons' scent out of the air! She'd have to refer the matter to Everette and have him scare up the wizards, but in the meantime, this clown was a solid threat to the convention as well as the conclave. What could she do?

He spotted her. His mouth opened in a way that no human being's could and emitted a hiss.

Even if he hadn't had anything to do with the power failure, she couldn't leave him on the premises. Regina didn't want to alarm the ordinary fans who were filing in. Some subtlety was called for.

She let her eyes widen as if she was terrified to see him. His round eyes narrowed slightly. This small female wouldn't look like she was much of a threat.

Good, she thought. *Reel him in.*

She backed away slowly a couple of paces, then shot forward, heading for the ballroom. It ought to be completely empty at this hour. She could take care of him there.

The soldier stiffened as she ran past him. It would take a moment before the queen ant gave him orders through the ether, but the critters weren't capable of that much complex thought. Within a heartbeat or two he came hauling after her. She gave a glance over her shoulder and flung open the door of the ballroom. It slammed against the inner wall.

The emergency lights cast a grim yellow glow over the carpeted expanse. Luckily, the hundreds of chairs stored in there were piled up in stacks of ten and twelve near the back wall. Plenty of room, Regina thought, just as the door slammed open again. Regina turned and ran toward the intruder, changing in mid-stride from human to dragon.

She cursed at the sound of her favorite blouse tearing up the back as the scales of her spine thrust through the cloth. The fire ant reacted with typical insect swiftness. He dropped his own disguise and stood up on his hind legs, all four fore-limbs preparing to take on the enemy. Its eyes took up almost half of his head, and the mandibles took up almost all the rest. Impossibly narrow neck and waist joined the three segments of its body together.

Regina would have loved to crisp the creature into a slagged heap with a burst of flame, but she was afraid of setting off the smoke detectors. One of the biggest problems they had was playful fans setting off alarm after alarm that caused the big buildings to be evacuated and the fire trucks summoned, incurring increasingly large fees from an increasingly irritated fire marshall. DragonCon had fewer of them than most large conventions, partly due to the wizards' cooperation spells, but mostly to fandom in general being self-policing. If she started the weekend off with a false alarm, she'd never hear the end of it from the rest of the concom. Instead, she landed on the soldier's back and planted her rear claws solidly in the thick chitin.

It swiveled its upper portion around and bit her on the forearm.

"Ow! Dammit!" Regina let out a howl of pain that echoed off the ballroom's high ceiling. She swiped at the ant with bared claws.

It ducked, bent its knees and rolled over, dumping her onto the carpeted floor. Regina opened her wings and flapped up out of reach. Her foreleg throbbed like a hangover. She was dying to give the miserable monster a blast of fire just for spite, but she could not risk it. Instead, she flitted halfway around it and went for its narrow throat. It raised an armored leg into her neck, snapping her jaws shut. She jerked her head further up and knocked its jaw upward. The mandibles clacked.

Regina landed on all fours and lunged for the creature's left hindleg. She twisted her neck and threw the ant on its side. It curled around her head, tearing at her spine and ears. Every bite sent white-hot pain lancing through her nerves. She chomped deeply into its thorax. Ugh! Ants tasted terrible, like pancakes fried in axle grease. She spat out the first mouthful and went for a second.

The ant squealed, a shrill noise that caused the chandeliers overhead to dance in protest. It battered at her, snipping at her spines with its jaws. Regina tried to push the creature's jaws away from her. She decided to use its own ruse. She launched herself up, and came down on top of it with all her weight. She heard a snap! The ant let out one more squeal and lay still.

Moving tenderly to coddle the parts of her that ached, Regina levered herself up and sat on her haunches.

The ant's spindly limbs continued to twitch. The bronze sheen of the multifaceted dark eyes started to dull. She leaned close to see if it was really dying.

The ant's upper body jerked upward, its mandibles snapping. Regina moved her snout just in time.

"Damn you, die, already!" She swiped at it with a claw. The head flew off its skinny neck and bounded across the room. "Ugh."

Regina felt the bites on her head, neck and forearm. Someone was going to have to take a look at those. She refused to think of having them hurt for days the way an ordinary fire ant bite did. But what to do with the body? The engineer was going to turn up any moment. She was lucky he hadn't come already. She might have to eat the corpse to conceal it. The prospect made her feel sick. She'd already had a bite of it. Her wounds were making her feel woozy. Better to call for backup.

She touched the radio in her ear with the tip of a claw.

"Everette, I'm in the Regency Ballroom, and I need some help getting rid . . . "

The sound of voices reached her sensitive ears. People were coming toward the ballroom. Quickly, she kicked the remains of the ant corpse underneath the skirt of the table that held the lighting and sound boards at the rear of the ballroom, then struck a pose with one arm up and her wings spread.

"Hello?" Everette's voice echoed tinnily in her ear. "Regina? What's wrong?"

A half-dozen heftily-built fans in graphic T-shirts and jeans wandered in. Regina stood absolutely still.

"Nobody here yet," the first one said. He was a big boy with a scanty beard and wavy dark hair. "We can get the best seats for the show."

"Ah, cool," the second fan exclaimed, running over to look at Regina. The African-American teenager walked around and around her. "Look at the great dragon sculpture here!"

"What show is it from?" the first teen asked. "I never heard of a blue-green dragon. It's not even in D&D!"

"I don't know," the second said. "Maybe it's a movie prop. Look how real the eyes are. They seem to follow you!"

"Hey, you guys shouldn't be in here yet," a mellow baritone voice said from the doorway. Bill Mann, a stocky man of middle height whose small features left plenty of room for a high, creased forehead under his curly, dark hair. His radio cable was clipped to the neck of his 'WWGD?' T-shirt with the outline of a standing lizard breathing lightning superimposed around the letters. No doubt had often found himself asking in unusual cases the very question the initials stood for, which was a restatement of his own philosophy: *What would Godzilla do?* Since he never had much of a chance to trash Tokyo, Bill settled for putting his best efforts toward his assignments. DragonCon ops counted on his reliable nature and even temperament. "Show's not on until three. We haven't got it set up yet. You're going to have to leave right now."

Regina could have kissed him.

"If we help set up, can we stay?" the second teen asked, hopefully.

"Nope. Sorry. Hotel regulations. It's for your own safety." Bill stayed by the door until the cluster of teens retreated. He glanced over his shoulder, then addressed the statue. "All clear."

Regina waited a moment before hastily retransforming. Without the wings for balance, she staggered. In human form the bites hurt a little less than they did on sensitive dragon tissue, but they looked pretty bad.

"Oh, my," Bill Mann said. "That really is a mess. Let's get you to a medic. I'll have someone come and take care of that soldier ant ASAP."

He put his shoulder under her arm and started to help her out of the room.

"We have a bigger problem," Regina said. "The concealment spells are all breaking down. That ant got in, and none of the alarms went off."

"Everette," Bill said, touching his radio control, "someone needs to go and find the . . . operators. We've got containment breach."

Complaints were coming in from all over the convention venue. Pat Henry frowned over yet another report that spells had broken down in several places, and conclave business was overlapping into the convention. Fans were excited about having seen a two-legged red-scaled wyvern flying into the Marriott through a skylight in the atrium. Pat had started a whispered rumor campaign with the recipients 'sworn to secrecy' to counter the sighting with news that it was a special effect, part of a preview of an upcoming Lucasfilm fantasy movie. The wyvern himself, mundanely known as Stanley, was embarrassed to have been spotted and given a dressing down by the senior draconians present.

"We've got to find those wizards," Pat said. He got on his radio to the rest of his staff. "Find the . . . operators. Check anyplace that any of them have been seen. This is a top priority. And you'd better go loaded for bear. We've had some sightings and at least one encounter."

Subtly, among the growing crowds across four hotels, radio-bearing personnel started making inquiries, and the news that they were sending back weren't good. Janice left the autograph area and set out in search of Penelope Winton, a magician who was a major British media fan. She was almost always in the room set aside for that program track, sharing episodes with fellow enthusiasts. No one had reported seeing her. Janice checked at the Hilton and found that Penelope had actually been in town since the night before. It took some persuading, but she managed to convince the hotel security chief, Bob Askill, that it was important to look in Penelope's hotel room to make sure nothing had happened to her. Her luggage was unpacked, but her purse was missing. Janice hoped Penelope was with it.

For the fourth time in fifteen minutes, Everette Beach tried the cell phone number for the Fulbrights. James and Tera weren't on staff that year, though they had been in the past, but James had been good enough to use his talents to seal the multiple entrances to the Marriott. Those spells had shown fewer holes than others cast by less experienced magicians, but security personnel were starting to see wear and tear, especially where the weave intersected the tunnels that joined the hotels to the skywalk. James would never let anything get that ragged on purpose.

The phone rang four times, then a perky female voice came on the line.

"Please leave us a message at the tone!"

Everette hung up without adding another query to the ones he had already recorded. It might be that the Fulbrights had turned off their cell phone to avoid waking up their baby daughter. They could also be meeting with their fellow pirate recreationists, many of whom were in attendance. Or they were just out of cell phone range. He just had a bad feeling that none of these might be so.

"Can you take over for a little while?" he asked Sharon Tiedeman. Sharon wasn't in the confidence of the top levels of staff yet, but her silent assent as she sat down at the main console told Everette that she might indeed be worth trusting, and soon.

"Reports, everybody?" Pat's voice crackled through the earpieces.

"I've got nothing," Everette said. "James and Tera are nowhere. Their little girl's okay in the children's room. I'll ask my wife to pick her up if they don't come back before it closes."

"Susan Charnoff didn't make her three o'clock or five o'clock panels," Bill Mann reported. "She hasn't been in her hotel room since morning, either, according to the access records."

Other personnel reported the same thing: usually reliable wizards and magicians, program participant, fan or staff, had failed to show up at panels or other events. They had all gone missing, often just after checking in at the hotel. Calls to cell phones yielded nothing. John and Brenda Tackett started making cautious calls to the guests' home phones in case they had returned, or not even left yet.

"She should be there," Rajiv Bhatan said of his artist wife Ansri. "Her phone is very good. Do you want me to come down there?"

"I'm sure it's just a missed connection," John said, forcing a pleasant tone into his voice. "Perhaps she went out to dinner with some friends and forgot about her panel."

"Perhaps that is it. We are in a different time zone. Maybe she did not reset her watch when she arrived. Please ask her to call me when you speak to her."

"I will. Thank you, Mr. Bhatan."

"My pleasure."

John hung up, gnashing his teeth.

The dragons in the conclave were starting to get worried. A fierce Andean dragon who had only been persuaded to come this year after a decade of pleading by all the draconians in the American southeast was starting to make sharp comments about the poor organization. Pat refused to doubt the commitment of his staff even in the face of evidence. Why would all the magicians walk off the job at once? And where were they?

"Is there anyone left who can refresh the spells?" he asked John. "Anyone we know is still safe?"

"Well, there's Ms. McCaffrey, but we don't want to stress her out. Her bursitis, you know."

"If she'll put a glamour on the door to the conclave, that should be enough for ground zero," Pat said. "Anyone else?"

"Well, we're still waiting for a few to arrive. Their planes haven't landed yet."

Pat eyed him. "Are you sure they're on board?"

"No reason not to. I'll have a couple of dragons meet them at the airport and escort them straight to you."

"Don't let them out of your sight for a moment."

But that proved to be more difficult than it seemed. Three fans from the west coast whose powers only worked in combination, not unlike the witches in their favorite TV show, "Charmed," arrived and were whisked to the communications office by tenacious and nervous security people in a huddle of secrecy that intrigued and confused them. Pat gave them a quick briefing and sent them out, again under heavy guard, to shore up the defenses around the Hyatt.

Unfortunately, a horror writer coming in from New Jersey was not so lucky. She made it all the way by van to the turnaround in front of the Marriott. When her driver got out of the car to take her luggage out of the back, he stepped out of eyeshot for one moment. When he came back, she was gone. Searching the hotel and the surrounding area proved fruitless.

"Well, now, that is most peculiar," Anne said, as a cluster of her fans looked puzzled at the blank wall at the end of the corridor. She reached out and rapped it with her knuckles. "Now, I was positive I could get through here to the other side. I was sure there was a door."

"Everyone makes that mistake," one of the Pern fans, Steven, said politely. "We'd have to go down one level to get across. Or up two."

"Maybe we just took a wrong turn," Anne said, hopefully. "There's a shortcut here somewhere. If you just wouldn't mind taking a look—it's for motor-chairs and carts only, not a regular footpath. It's a door, just the same color as this wall. I used it last year." She gave them a winning smile. "I don't want to be late for my autograph session." Willingly, the group of fans spread out to look, leaving only Koolness, Aranel, Hisham and Angel around her.

Koolness waited until the footsteps were far enough away.

"All clear," he said. He and the others formed a screen so that casual passersby, of whom there were many, couldn't see what she was doing.

"Fine," Anne said, rummaging in her bag. "My heaven, if I'd known I was going to have to be casting spells I would have brought along a cat or two. Cats are very good for witchcraft, you know. Mine in particular." She brought out a handsome, purple-enameled fountain pen and unscrewed it. "They tried to take this away from me at the airport, but I told them that an author has to have a pen! Now, let me think . . . ."

She leveled the pen at the wall and began to draw upon the air. With her eyes closed, she began to sing softly to herself. Anne had a sweet, strong voice, trained for theater. The rich tones seemed to flow into the pen. From the point issued iridescent golden lines, like oil spreading out upon the surface of a pond. Koolness tilted his head, thinking that if he caught the pattern just right he might be able to read the words in it.

Before he could even absorb the shape of it, the pattern sank into the wall. For a moment the dull-colored paint seemed brighter and slightly shiny, like metal. He touched it. It felt like painted drywall.

"That ought to take care of it," Anne said. "Let Pat know when you speak to him."

"I will, my lady," Koolness said.

The rest of the fans returned, trying not to look as if they were thinking 'I told you so.'

"Sorry," Steven said. "None of the doors go through on this level."

"Well, my mistake, then," Anne said. "This hotel is a regular rabbit-warren. We'd better go the other way. There's little time left. It would be so much more convenient if I could just go *between* on dragonback."

"Don't we all wish," Angel said, with a grin.

As they followed Anne in her rolling chair, only Koolness could hear the sibilant voice behind them.

"Thank you, friends . . . ."

Anne outdistanced her escort easily in her motorized transport, leaving the others to jog behind her to catch up. Koolness came around the corner just in time to see an elevator open. A couple of large men in black T-shirts came out of it. He could scent the powerful tang of ant on them from across the room. Most humans would put it down to ordinary body odor, but it made his eyes water.

"Can we help you in, Ms. McCaffrey?" one of them asked. He leaned over to take hold of the handle at the top of her backrest.

"Why, that would be very kind," Anne said, but with a backwards glance filled with meaning. Koolness and Hisham put on a burst of speed.

"We'll take that," Koolness said, smoothly, moving into place at Anne's shoulder. "It's our honor. But you can hold the door."

The two men exchanged peeved glances.

"Okay," one of them said. "Nice to see you here, ma'am."

"Thank you!" Anne said. Fans piled in to take up the available space, since elevators ran slowly if at all during the long weekend, leaving no room for the two large men to board behind them. Anne sighed as the doors closed. "Did I ever mention that I do find safety to be in numbers?"

Koolness had to agree.

"Ah, well," Anne said, as if to herself. "It would just be nice to get to go *through* that door once."

The gopher, a brand of staff volunteer so named because they 'go fer' whatever was needed by senior staff members, rapped tentatively on the door of the mini-suite in the corner of the twenty-second floor of the Hyatt. Dale was in his middle twenties, but had gained a reputation for tact under Brenda Tackett's firm tutelage. Such care was required when dealing with the media guests, many of whom could be difficult in the extreme, such as this one. He'd never met Shawna Lacey before, but he'd seen all her movies. She starred in a series as a hell-witch who battled demons who escaped to earth from the pit.

"Ms. Lacey?"

The door opened a crack and a dark brown eye peered out of the blackness beyond. "Yes? What is it? I'm resting."

"Ma'am, Pat Henry sent me. We'd just like to make sure that you've got everything you need."

The gap widened and a very attractive, slim African-American woman not that much older than he smiled cordially at him. "That's nice of him. Yes, I'm fine."

"I wondered whether you wanted an escort to take you around the exhibit hall or the art show?"

"Maybe later," she said, patting a yawn delicately with a purple-taloned hand. "I have an appearance at the Fantasy Romance track later on, and I just wanted to get some rest.—Is there something else?"

Dale had strict orders from Pat not to impose, but to bring up the subject and leave it to her whether to volunteer to help.

"Well, ma'am . . . "

Lacey cut him off with a gesture of those sharp fingernails. "Not ma'am. It sounds so *old*."

"Well, Ms. Lacey, we've got a little problem brewing up," Dale began shyly. He explained the situation. "I understand that the spell takes a lot out of you, but it would help a lot if . . . well, Pat said you're one of the best. He'd consider it a big favor if you would help seal the place up. Just around the perimeter of the convention center. It's important. I know you did it once before—before . . . "

"Before I became famous?" Ms. Lacey smiled at him. "I'm flattered to be asked. Tell Pat that I promise to make sure that everything is sealed up in place and no one will get in where he or she is not supposed to be, if I have anything to say about it. Will you tell him that?"

She gave him a brilliant smile. Dale couldn't help but be dazzled. "I sure will, ma'am—I mean, Ms. Lacey. Thanks a million. You don't know what it means to us."

"Oh, I think I do," the actress said, with a little smile that brought out a dimple in her right cheek. "Go away, now. I've got to prepare myself." She gave a theatrical sigh. "You understand. Would you mind having someone send up a bottle of champagne?"

"Sure," Dale said, hopelessly star-struck. "Thanks, Ms. Lacey!"

"No problem," the actress said. She waited until he withdrew, almost bowing, and closed the door on him.

Dale ran toward the elevator, jabbing the stud on his earpiece as he went. "She says okay, Everette. Tell Pat Ms. Lacey's on board. I can't believe anyone said she's a problem. She just couldn't be nicer."

The soft voice chuckled in his ear. "Just likes to be needed, I guess," Everette said.

"Oh, yeah, she said she wants some champagne. Do we have that, or does the hotel bring it?"

"Room service can get that for her. I'll give them a call and put it on the convention's tab. Good job, Dale."

James Fulbright sneezed. Red Georgia clay dust sifted into the small storage room through leaking joints between slabs of concrete. The room had no windows. The only connections to the outside world were a painted steel door and a ventilation duct in the ceiling that kept belching cold air down on their heads. He wrapped his arm around his wife, Tera, who sat huddled against him for warmth. Their thin summer clothes were no protection against the air conditioning.

Several other people occupied the cramped space with them. James recognized some of them from previous conventions, among them a prominent former author guest of honor, a few fans and three media guests, whose friends in Hollywood would hate them for their talents, which had nothing to do with their skills at portraying characters in TV shows. He didn't want to let on that he knew about them in front of the others.

"But what are we doing here?" one of the latter, a tall, skinny twenty-something man asked for the hundredth time. He and his girlfriend were game designers. "Why us? Are we under attack by terrorists? They can't hold us for ransom. I haven't got any money."

"I don't know," James said.

"All we can do is wait to hear their demands," said the British woman seated beside Tera. Her accent made the last word 'demahnds.' She had very bright, dark-blue eyes and fine brown hair, and projected an aura of calm. She clicked the small phone in her right hand again. "My mobile still has no signal."

"I'm worried about our daughter," Tera said.

"She'll be fine," James said. "The daycare people are like family."

"I want to get out of here. Now!"

"We've all tried the door," the skinny man said. "No one's going anywhere unless you can walk through walls."

"Well, no one can do that," James said. They all laughed uncomfortably.

"I could use a drink," said the author.

"I second that," said the British woman, extending a hand. "By the way, my name's Anneli Madden."

"James Fulbright. This is my wife, Tera."

"Pierce," said the male game designer.

"Nan," said the female game designer.

Somehow, introductions helped make things feel a little less insane.

Clanking sounds came from the door. James rushed at it, and was thrust backwards by a couple of men in work shirts and blue jeans. He sat down hard on the concrete floor and sprang up again. They were strong for their size and build. James picked up a familiar, strong, acrid scent. He and Tera exchanged nervous glances, then he made another attempt to get past the disguised fire ants. One twisted his arm behind his back with no effort at all. James struggled, trying to raise enough power to fling the ant away. The damper that kept his spells from working was still in place. Who had cast it, and why?

Three more of the disguised ants came in, all but carrying a dark-skinned woman in expensive silk trousers and a lace, bead-trimmed camisole.

"How dare you treat me like this! Don't you know who I am? Bastards! Put me down!"

Obediently, they dumped her on the concrete floor.

"Ow!" the woman howled. She scrambled to her feet. James noticed her shoes were spindly and fragile-looking. "Not like that, you morons! No, don't close that door!" She stumbled forward. The ants pushed her back and started to pull the door shut.

The British woman moved more swiftly than they did. She blocked the door with her strong leather walking shoe. "I demand to be released at once. Release us all!"

"You don't give orders," the first ant said. James groaned. Soldiers. They were the biggest and strongest of the ants except for the queen.

"Who are you? Why are we here?"

"Please," Tera said. "I have a little girl. You have to let me go to her."

One of the soldiers lunged for her, hands out. Tera flinched. The British woman took her firmly by the wrist and pushed Tera behind her. "Don't tell them anything that will make you more vulnerable to them," she advised. "Ask them. We need information."

"What do you know about dealing with jerks like this?" the author asked.

Anneli smiled. "I'm in the Foreign Service."

But the fire ants were done talking. They kicked Anneli's foot out of the way and slammed the door shut.

"Curses," Anneli said. She tugged the door. It didn't move a millimeter. She sat down against the wall once again. This time she tented her hands and furrowed her brow in concentration. After a few moments she wove her fingers together in a different way. After a moment, she sighed.

James recognized the pattern, and smiled. "Your powers aren't working either, are they?"

She looked astonished, then smiled. "I should have guessed I wasn't the only one. You're a magician?" James and Tera nodded.

"Me, too," said the stout woman with dishwater hair and a *Shrek* T-shirt.

"Us, too," said the tall young man.

They all turned to the peevish writer. "It's got nothing to do with me. It's all a mistake. I just want to get out of here. Why did I tell my agent I'd come to this stupid convention?"

Tera shook her head. "Her, too," she said. James nodded. Tera's sense was never wrong. "And . . . and you, Ms. Lacey?"

The actress very perturbed. She got up and paced, the thin sandals rasping on the cold floor. "She took my *face*," Shawna Lacey shrieked. "Of all the balls! How dare she?"

"I'm so sorry, Ms. Lacey," James said. "Believe me, DragonCon apologizes deeply for anything that might have happened . . . ."

Shawna was not placated. "If I could do one single solitary spell I'd burn that bitch to a *cinder*." She snapped her fingers.

"Well, we might as well try practical matters," the British woman said, rising to her feet. "Would one of you gentlemen give me a leg up?"

James followed her eyes avidly. "Are you going to try to climb up through the ventilation ducts?"

"Heavens, no!" Anneli exclaimed. "You watch too many James Bond movies. I just want to see if I can't turn down the air conditioning. Americans always cool their buildings down to deep freezes."

James obliged. A reduction in the blast of chill air perked everyone up. The British woman brushed off her skirt and sat down again.

"Now, should we try singing a song or something, just to get to know one another?"

"I'd rather die," said the author from New York.

"You and me both," said the Hollywood actress.

"Not to worry," Anneli said, unperturbed. "I only wanted to raise the group's spirits. Chances are if we can raise some positive energy, we can mass together enough of a spell to alert someone as to where we are, or at the very best, open that door."

James liked her straightforward attitude. "Ms. Lacey, I love your movies. Tell us about the one you liked doing best."

Shawna left off her pout and thought for a moment. "Well, it pretty much has to be *Death to Zombies*. When my agent told me that I got the part . . . ."

James sat back. A trickle of good energy started to build. It wouldn't be long before they could take action.

"Champagne?" Pat asked, when Everette reported back to him.

"Yeah. Is it okay?"

Pat frowned. "Shawna Lacey never drinks champagne. She's a teetotalist. Never touches alcohol. Are you sure it was her?"

"Well, Dale seemed to be sure. He's seen every movie, knows everything about her—just everything."

"I don't know. Could she have sent her double?"

"No way. Dale wouldn't have been fooled by a double. He's too much of a fan-boy. What's the problem? Maybe she just has a guest in her room. None of our business."

"It is our business," Pat said, uneasily. "That just sounds wrong. I'd better look into it. Where is Brenda?"

"In the conclave center," Everette said. "The falk sing is starting. She'll probably stay all night."

Pat glanced at the window. Dusk was falling. Pretty soon the humans would start their filk sing. Both terms were misinterpretations of the word 'folk,' but each had come to have importance in its own cultural setting. Only the dragon song tended to be a lot louder, punctuated with gouts of fire instead of cigarette smoke. In the meantime, the lobbies of all four hotels were filling with human visitors displaying their hall costumes. DragonCon had a reputation for attracting master costumers. Unfortunately, the elbow-to-elbow crowds made it all too easy for enemy forces to infiltrate. Pat hoped the spells cast by the newly arrived magicians, Ms. McCaffrey, and Ms. Lacey would be enough to keep them from finding their way into the conclave.

"What do you mean, you haven't found the eggs?" Hedaera the Ant Queen demanded angrily, walking back and forth in Shawna Lacey's suite with her cell phone held between mandible and antenna. She had dispensed with the human shape and resumed her normal appearance, guaranteed to give a hotel worker a heart attack—which it had, incapacitating the room service waiter who had brought her her desired champagne. He'd made a nice snack in between gulps. The skeleton and empty bottle were tucked under the tablecloth of the service cart, waiting for pickup by whoever made up her room for the night. "It's been magic-free for days! All you had to do was follow the scent!"

The soldier-general at the other end sounded flustered and upset.

"The concealment *was* breaking down. We thought we were getting close to the target—but all the trails we were following have dissipated. Are you sure the dragons haven't all left?"

"They can't leave!" the Ant Queen exclaimed. "Not until their eggs hatch. And I want them *before* they do." Delicious, savory, rich eggs, with the embryo enveloped in the tender sac, waiting to be devoured in turn. One might be enough for her, but two would assuage her appetite even more. And the adults! When her small subjects had bitten them, the flavor made its way through the shared intelligence to every member of the hive. The Queen, at the top of the pyramid, experienced the sensation multiplied almost into infinity, and she craved more. After years of defeat, she had spent years laying myriad eggs to build up her army. Now countless fire ants occupied the underground passages beneath Atlanta, all born to one purpose. "Find them!"

Millions of her subjects wandered unseen through the convention center, creeping along walls, infiltrating ceilings and airways, hitching a ride on the clothing of the thousands of human attendees. It hardly mattered if most of them were killed; their shared intelligence was passed along to all those in its echelon. The echelons reported to thousands of captains, all identical, all female, and from there to the soldier-generals. The Queen could hear their thoughts without the telephone, but the electronic medium allowed her to shriek her orders directly to each.

"My scouts have found whole parts of the hotels blocked," the soldier said. "Some wizards must have escaped our attention."

"They have found some we did not," Hedaera said, not pleased about it. "They are under guard, but you are to try to capture or incapacitate each of those as the opportunity arises. Until the way is clear, we will not find the nesting ground. We have the force to overwhelm any opposition. All we need to know is where it is!"

"There is all that fresh meat wandering around aboveground," the soldier said, peevishly. "We could fill the hive for years with what is there, and easily captured."

"Don't think of your stomach!" the Queen raged, even though she had been doing just that. "I want dragon meat, nothing else. Swarm everywhere. Follow every single scent, no matter how faint."

The soldier did not argue. It, too, had experienced the savory taste. Its entire army wanted more. It clashed its mandibles. "We will continue to search, Mother."

The sensitives among the human attendees of the convention began to get headaches. Not overwhelming migraines or sinus headaches, but just the vague sensation of pressure as if two fingers were pressing on their temples. Tera clutched her head as the captive magicians concentrated all their efforts on sending a message to someone, anyone, who would come looking for them, filled the space around her. It was like being a ping-pong ball under a magnifying glass in the hot sun. Any minute, she felt, she would begin to melt. She hoped it would work before then.

What little power they had been able to raise in the dampening field the ants had shut them into would never be enough to open a door made of cold steel, so the magicians had to work on getting someone else to open it for them. At the behest of the British woman, who proved to be good at analyzing what move needed to be made next, and how to coax everyone else into helping her do it, they focused their gifts upon a point in the floor.

"Picture a beacon like a laser beam," James advised.

"What's it pointing at?" asked Pierce.

He and Tera exchanged glances. "It had better be Pat Henry," Tera said.

"Pat," James agreed.

"We haven't met him," the author from New York said.

"Then let me direct it," James said.

"I've always wanted to direct," Shawna said, almost automatically.

"Yeah, that's going to help," said Nan, sarcastically. "All right, mister. We'll drive. You steer."

"We're locked in and we can't get out," sang the Celtic band at the end of the ballroom lobby. "We're in a cellar down below. Where it is, we don't know. Oh, come on down and let us go. Oh, oh. Oh, oh!"

"I love that song," said one of the lanky twenty-somethings in the large crowd listening to the music.

"Me, too," said his friend, an equally thin girl with black leggings and a belly stud, swaying to the beat. "What album was it on?"

"I think it was on the Pat Henry anthology," the young man said. He frowned. "That doesn't sound right."

"No," the girl agreed. "Doesn't he do jazz?"

A middle-aged man with a gray ponytail smacked a card down on one of his opponent's.

"I play the Pat Henry on your ghoul," he declared.

The elderly woman across from him with the peacock feather medallion clipped to the hair above her left ear leaned over and peered at the pasteboard.

"That's not a Pat Henry. That's a wraith spell."

The man looked down. "Weird," he said. "I could have sworn I had one. Oh, well."

"We're not connecting with him," Tera said, concentrating hard.

"You try finding one person in the middle of fifty-thousand others," James retorted.

"Come now," Anneli said, soothingly. "Let's not lose our heads."

"I bet you were teacher's pet in school," Shawna Lacey grumbled, but they went back to concentrating.

Pat held up his taloned hands and appealed for quiet. The dragons reluctantly came to order. The females on their nesting boxes looked broody and bad tempered. Sitting in one place for five days was no one's idea of fun. He wished it was just that easy. The message he had received, relayed to him by more than a dozen cranky sensitives, both relieved and concerned him, but at least he had a pretty good idea where the magicians had gotten to. Trouble was, they weren't there where they could refresh the fraying spells, and he was worried about overstressing the enchanters that were still free and under constant guard. The key was not to wear down the spells in place.

"I know you all want to get out and look around Atlanta, especially since the parade is tomorrow morning, but we've got a real threat going on here. I have to appeal to your patience to stay put in this part of the complex until we've got it taken care of."

"We can help!" a huge, yellow-scaled dragon from Central Asia said, rearing up on his hind legs and brandishing a five-clawed hand. "You calling us defenseless?"

"We don't know the extent of the threat," Pat said. "The best thing you can do is stay in here and defend the nests and the youngsters. If you keep coming and going, then the fire ants are going to figure out where you are."

"I'm not afraid of a bunch of little bugs," the male exclaimed.

"You've never had them try to eat you," John Tackett said. In his dragon shape he was a slender, handsome bronze. "I nearly got killed by a nest of them a couple of years ago."

"Bugs *can* kill dragons!" an iridescent African green exclaimed. "We have many dangerous insects in our region."

The roaring became deafening as every dragon tried to be heard at once.

"But it's not fair!" a young female blue exclaimed. "I'm supposed to be in the Pernese costume contest this evening. I spent months working on my outfit. I want to meet Anne McCaffrey! I can change my shape. I'll fit in, I swear!"

"Holly, I don't know what I can tell you," Pat said. "We're doing everything we can. I just think that it would be best if you stayed here and used your power to keep this area safe. John and Brenda will stay here. I'll let you know when we have cleared the threat. In any case, you'll be able to leave when the hatchlings are able to fly. We just have to hold out until then."

The dragons inside the conclave center were not pleased to be forced to stay put. Pat didn't envy his guest liaison department heads the task of placating that group with their notoriously short tempers. Brenda gave him a wink of one jewel-bright eye, and he relaxed. She had some ideas.

"Can I count on your cooperation, just for a while?" Pat pleaded.

"For a while," the great golden dragon said, who had appointed himself the spokesman for the group. His name was Tang, and did not appreciate references to the astronaut breakfast drink. "Then we're going to take matters into our own hands, humans or not."

Pat cringed at the thought of what effect fifty full-sized dragons would have on the large population of the convention above—then wondered what effect those enthusiastic humans would have on the dragons, especially those from the isolated regions.

"I'll be at the banquet," he said. "You can notify me there. With any luck at all, we'll have this licked tonight."

"Do we have your promise on that?" a red dragon asked, so elderly her scales had faded to rusty orange.

"I'll do my best, Shelogh," Pat said. "I can't do better than that."

"I believe in you, Pat," Annette said from atop her six eggs. "Good luck."

"Thanks." Pat conjured his human appearance back in place, and was able to open the door with a scaleless hand by the time he reached it.

Underground, every hidden passageway heaved with tiny bronze-colored bodies. Long-forgotten streams, buried electrical conduit, pipes, sewers and walkways were filled with the marching ants. Here and there among them, a captain the size of a dog waded among her drones. Soldier generals were spread out along the route, but they were not needed to give directions. Every one of the marching fire ants had the voice of the Ant Queen echoing in their heads: find the dragons. Find them, no matter what it took.

When they reached the cluster of hotels in the middle of the city, they spread out into four armies, each containing many millions of ants. They swarmed up through the walls and ventilation ducts, squirming behind insulation and up through the plumbing, until they covered every wall in the four hotels. It was only a matter of time before the spells that were in place began to fade. Then the armies would invade, stinging every living creature to incapacity or death.

Was everything in place? Pat wondered, as he stepped into the ballroom where the DragonCon banquet was to be held. Forty round tables covered with white tablecloths and folding chairs were arranged before a stage where a quartet of musicians was tuning up. Large speakers stood at either end in front of small curtained areas that acted as 'off stage' used, among other reasons, to conceal the awards that were to be handed out that evening.

Regina, in a form-fitting evening dress of blue-green sequins that was not unlike her normal dragonish skin, came out from behind the stage-left curtain.

"Is everything here?" Pat asked.

"As you asked," she said. "How sure are you this is going to work?"

"I'm not," Pat admitted.

"Good," Regina said, grinning. "I might have thought you were crazy if you did. We're behind you a hundred percent."

Pat took a deep sniff, and his eyes watered. The sharp smell of formic acid was beginning to permeate the atmosphere. There must be thousands of the red insects infiltrating that one floor of the hotel. "I don't like letting the fire ants this close, but if we want to lure their queen out of hiding I don't think there's any choice."

"And get our magicians back," Regina said. "Everette and Bill are on their way."

Pat nodded. "I'd better see to our special guests." He straightened his tie. The room was beginning to fill.

He had sent a message to Shawna Lacey, inviting her to the banquet, as all the convention special guests were, but with a personal note informing her that a DragonCon award would be presented to her. The line that ensured that she would make it was letting her know that photographers from the local and national press would be there to record the moment for television and the papers. Whatever had disguised itself as the actress could not fail to show up for the honor, lest it raise suspicion. Pat thought it was most likely a soldier-general. The Queen was almost certainly hidden in some underground warren, controlling her forces from a distance. With the help of the few human magicians and the dragon mages in the conclave chamber, they ought to be able to lean on the soldier to give up her location. At least, he hoped so. The mood in the conclave was growing ugly. Instead of the usual détente and negotiations, everyone was getting cabin fever. Come Monday there might never again be a need for a DragonCon, conclave or convention.

"I'm very strong," Hisham explained to the elaborately-dressed woman on his right. "No, I am! I can stop a train with one hand." The woman looked blank. "I'm a conductor."

She laughed. "Heat or electricity?" she asked.

Everyone chuckled, including Ms. McCaffrey. Her table was in front of the stage at the end of the room nearest the door. Two chairs were reserved for Anne's son and granddaughter, who had not yet arrived. The rest were occupied by devoted fans from the Worlds of Anne McCaffrey program track, most of whom were clued in as to the potential danger lurking.

Koolness scanned the room. The music was very loud, which irritated his sensitive ears, but the lighting was low, an advantage for him. The others passed the salad and bread around. He could scarcely smell the salad dressing over the sharp stench. Wherever it was coming from, it was bad. The convention committee had taken Aranel aside and asked her to keep an eye out for Anne. The most trustworthy and talented among them had come along to the banquet, though it cut short the annual costume contest. Their usual mistress of ceremonies said she understood. She and her husband were keeping watch from the next table.

Shawna Lacey appeared in the doorway. She paused for a moment, as if posing for the photographers and videographers, then sashayed in. She looked stunning, her slim, curving figure in draped golden silk trousers and brocade jacket, tiny golden sandals and a tiara in her thick hair to match. Pat stood up to gesture her to his table.

All his senses seemed to go off at once. The smell hit him, causing his eyes to burn, and he heard a high-pitched whine in both ears that was not caused by the deafening music coming from the stage. It set his nerves jangling. He kept the smile on his face as she approached, more hesitantly now. He knew without a doubt that she was no soldier-general, but Hedaera herself, just as he was certain that she knew he was a dragon.

For the sake of the humans around him, he took her hand politely in his and escorted her to the chair opposite his at the table. He introduced his wife and daughter and their fellow guests.

For her part, the Ant Queen was gracious, as if she really was a notable Hollywood actress.

Impossible! the Queen thought furiously, jabbing a fork into her salad. She had to concentrate on chewing up and down instead of moving her jaws sideways. Dragons were not only hiding here, but they were fully integrated into the human conference as well. It came to her in a moment: dragons had created this convention to conceal their presence in this place.

The man across from her, the convention organizer, was not only a dragon, but a damned big one, from the scent of him. She was afraid, but at the same time she had a difficult time stopping herself from salivating. Dragon scent was everywhere. She felt the blissful anticipation of years of food stored away in her hive.

"The menu is pasta with sauce," the dragon was saying, "and baked chicken. I hope you'll like that."

She looked at him, her eyes intent. "I look forward to gnawing on the bones," she said.

Even though it was the size of a football stadium, the conclave chamber seemed to be shrinking around them. The dragon attendees couldn't concentrate on falk singing or any of the complicated games that Brenda proposed.

"I hear scratching," said Omoro, the African delegate. "Tiny feet, scratching. The sound is at the edge of my hearing. Millions of them. They are coming for us. For our children!" He looked anxiously at his mate, Mleda, a short-winged female with deep blue scales who was perched over two small eggs. "I wish we were safely back on Kilimanjaro."

"I hear them, too," Brenda said. "They don't know where we are. They're fishing for a response. They can't break through the concealment glamour. You just keep a positive attitude, and Pat will take care of everything."

"Can he destroy ten million ants?" Omoro asked anxiously.

"He's not working alone," John said. "He's got us. And we have all of you."

"This is not why I chose to come here," said the Asian dragon, clutching his head with his elegant paws. He raised his voice so that it echoed off the domed ceiling. "Make the sound stop! It is tearing at my ears!"

"We could," Brenda said, "but I'd rather hear it than not hear it. That way we know where they are."

"Keep it together, bach," said Corman, a Welsh red, one of the smallest of the attendees, hardly bigger than the wyvern from Scandinavia. "If you lose your wits, then the terrorists have won."

"Terrorists," the golden dragon said, scornfully. "I eat terrorists. And they are not very good, either."

"Then let's muster up good defense, here," John advised.

"My power is for protecting my children," one of the nesting females said. "I can hear them starting to move around."

"The rest of us, then," John said. "Let's give them a really warm welcome if they make it through the door." He grinned, and his sharp rows of teeth glinted. The others responded with fierce smiles.

But even while they started to stoke their inner fires, they could sense the overwhelming numbers of insects outside. They had passed the millions and were well into the billions. If the spells failed, some of them would undoubtedly be injured or die before they could escape to the open air. And the eggs, so close to hatching, were too fragile to move. The unhatched infants were vulnerable.

Everette Beach swiped a cobweb off his face as he followed the plant engineer into the depths of the Marriott basement. "You sure about the storage cupboard down here?"

"Oh, yeah," the skinny African-American man said. "Doesn't get used much. It's too out of the way. I almost forgot we had it, until you said it was a concrete box. How'd you know about it, if you don't know where it is?"

"Uh, well, one of our people put something in it for safekeeping, and he had to go home. Now we have to get it out."

"No problem. You gonna need help carrying it?"

"No," Bill Mann said. "It'll be easy to move."

He and Everette exchanged glances. *We hope*, he thought.

The engineer tripped on something and looked at his feet. Rusty red specks were piled up like miniature snowdrifts. "Gross," he said. "Look at that. There must be thousands of those ants down here. Half of 'em are dead. The hotel sprays every week, but it looks like it ain't strong enough to kill all of 'em."

Bill looked down. Piles of ant bodies stretched out before them, leading into the concrete tunnel. They must be carrying food to the others. When the exterminator's poison took out some of them, others just took their place. Ugh.

Some of the live ones climbed up and bit their ankles. They swatted them away. Everette stopped suddenly.

"Did you hear that?"

"Scratching," Bill said. "Something *big*."

"Yeah." Everette turned to the engineer. "Mind if I change?"

The man looked around. "Here? I mean, it's private and all, but if you got to change your clothes, you shoulda . . . "

"Thanks," Everette said. Gritting his teeth against the pain of the ant bites, he stretched out along the tunnel. It was so narrow he had to keep his wings close against his side to keep from bumping his elbows. He snaked his long, pale tan neck out through the tunnel to the next turning.

As he guessed, a couple of ant soldiers stood against a door. The scratching noise was the two ants talking to one another, antenna to antenna. They looked up in surprise as he dashed toward them.

"Hi, guys," he said. "Nice day for a fire, huh?"

"A what?"

Everette dragged all the power he had into his lungs, and breathed outward. A wash of flames licked down the concrete tunnel, filling the end with a burst of crackling light. To his pleasure, the fire also destroyed most of the tiny ants as well. He restored his human disguise, and hurried to the door.

"Hey, anyone in there?" he called.

"Everette?" James's voice came from the other side. "Get us out of here!"

Everette shook the handle. It was unlocked, but bespelled shut. It was going to take a little work to get it open.

Bill stumped into view, his dark-green head scales bumping the top of the corridor. He surveyed the slumped, fused bodies and shook his head.

"You could've left one of them for me."

"Sorry," Everette said, with a grin. "How are you at picking locks?"

"Stand back," Bill said. He took a deep breath.

"Not the Godzilla lightning!" Everette shouted. "James, get away from the door!"

Koolness glanced at the actress who joined Pat Henry at the table two away from theirs. Something about her looked wrong. Mr. Henry must have thought so, too, because he had a pretty strange look on his face. Most of that terrible smell was coming from the woman. If it was a new cologne, it would be one people would only buy because it was trendy. He and the others exchanged glances. Whatever was going to happen was imminent. He twitched his nose warily.

Pat stepped to the dais and signaled for quiet. The music stopped. "I'd like to thank everyone for coming to this year's DragonCon . . . "

The speech rolled off his tongue just as he'd rehearsed it. All around him he could sense movement, some from allies, and some from who knew? The room was full of ants of all sizes. All around the walls, marching platoons of worker ants blended in with the patterned carpet. The dog-sized captain ants occupied a variety of disguises, including a pair of badly-made dragon costumes with five stacked up inside each. He had had to change his plans on the fly, now that he had the Ant Queen within an arm's reach. She must have plotted to reach this point as well, and hoped that he would be able to counter her, at the same time defusing the threat against human and dragon alike.

Regina and the others were ready. He braced himself, and gave a big smile to the audience.

" . . . And I'd like to give a big hand to all our special guests who have graced DragonCon. I'd like to start with a lady who started coming here long before Hollywood discovered her amazing talents, and now is celebrated for her work on the silver screen. I refer, of course, to this lady," he gestured with an open hand, "Shawna Lacey!" Regina appeared at his elbow with a plaque. "Ms. Lacey, will you please come on up and accept this award?"

For a moment, the Ant Queen hesitated. She sensed some kind of trick. The dragon wished her to join him on the stage. Why should she cooperate? He was dangerous. The other dragon beside him was also dangerous. She had killed a soldier-general single-handed.

Then she realized that everyone in the big room was looking at her. They expected this actress to go up without hesitation. Was her army in place?

Yes, came the word through the antennae disguised in her head-dress. She might be surrounded by dragons, but her forces were advancing, ready to leap on and disable the magicians the dragons still had, all of whom were in this room. Once they were disposed of, the spells would break down and she could invade the nesting space with no trouble. How convenient. She would have a very good view of the excitement. She rose to wild applause and climbed the stairs. Pat took her hand and bowed over it.

The Ant Queen smiled and waved. Through her antennae, she sent out the signal to her forces. The two columns of captains concealed in dragon costumes rose up and moved toward Anne McCaffrey. A host of them crept underneath the tables toward the others.

The two bad costumes came to flank Anne.

"Excuse me, Ms. McCaffrey," one of them said in a high-pitched voice. "Can we have your autograph?"

Anne turned to look at them, and her jaw set firmly. She reached for her purse, and one of the costumed creatures slapped her hand down with one of its own. The hand seemed to be the wrong shape.

"Now, how am I supposed to sign a book if I can't reach my pen?" Anne asked calmly, even though Koolness could hear her heart start to pound.

On the stage, Mr. Henry couldn't move to help but Koolness could. He leaped out of his chair. In the twitch of a tail, he shed his human appearance and leaped over the table at the two costumed goons. The Pern fans didn't seem too surprised to see a full-sized, long-tailed cougar in their midst, but the guests at other tables were shoving back their chairs in alarm.

Koolness hit the goons high and rolled over them onto the ground. To his surprise each body broke apart into five pieces, each about the size of a cocker spaniel. They brandished mandibles and pincers at him. He snarled. They scuttled to go around him, still intent on Anne. Koolness batted the first one back and sunk his teeth into the neck of the next. The sharp taste made his sensitive nose buzz in protest, but he clenched his jaws until he heard a crack. He dropped the body and made for the next one.

Hisham shoved back his chair and seized one of them around its four limbs. The mandibles tried to bite him. He pulled his head away from it. Aranel tied up the jaws with a cloth napkin. Hisham tightened his grip until he heard the carapace snap. He dropped it and seized another which had reached Anne's chair and was attempting to climb. The other Pern fans joined in, kicking the huge ants away from their favorite author. Aranel lifted a chair and brought it down, smashing one of the ants to death. The audience laughed, thinking it was all part of the entertainment.

"Call them off," Pat said to the Ant Queen. He held her arm tightly.

"They are following the orders I gave them," the Queen said, with satisfaction. She tossed her head. "They only obey me. When the magicians are dead, my army will know where the rest of you are hiding."

"You won't be able to," Pat assured her.

"You fool, you can't stop me," she said. "I—we—outnumber you a billion to one!" With a laugh, she shed the likeness of Shawna Lacey. Her thorax and abdomen began to swell, leaving her waist impossibly slender.

The moment she began to transform, Pat threw an arm around her and hurried her behind the curtain.

The beautiful face disappeared into a bulging-eyed head with serrated jaws that clashed sideways. She snapped for Pat's throat.

No one except James Bond ever had a successful fight to the death in a tuxedo. Reluctantly, hoping the curtain concealed him adequately, Pat expanded into his dragon shape. As his wingtips appeared above the top of the riser, he heard an explosion. He peeked out of the curtain, and saw the audience applauding wildly.

The Ant Queen took advantage of his inattention and sank her jaws into his arm.

"Ah!" Hedaera cried. "Delicious!"

Pat smacked her away. Nothing human remained of her now. She laughed wildly. She snapped at him again and again, forcing him backwards out of the shelter of the curtain until they were in the center of the stage. She gloated.

"I'm so glad you invited me to this banquet, and banquet it really will be. I have enough of a force here to take over the entire crowd. It would be my pleasure."

"You can't conquer a whole room full of human beings," Pat said.

"Yes, I can," she said. She flicked an antenna. To Pat's horror, the carpet seemed to move. People began to jump out of their seats and bat at their ankles as thousands of ants swarmed them. A few people shrieked and dozens of them swore.

"They obey me," she said.

Soldier-generals, the largest of the ant breed, dropped their own disguises and went for the other dragons in the room. Regina slipped behind the curtain and emerged in her natural form just in time to meet a hulking ant. She roared at it. It shrilled back.

Pat set his jaw. Then the only way to stop the attack was to stop the one giving orders. Mouth open, he went for her neck.

Her movements were astonishingly swift. She turned her head to the side and bit his throat instead. Pat recoiled, hissing at the pain. The poison began to work at once. The tissue started to swell. If he didn't get rid of the toxin soon, he'd be strangled by his own neck muscles.

He took a mighty leap and landed on the other side. With his tail, he knocked all four feet out from under the queen. She landed on her back with a boom! Pat flitted upward and came down on her midsection. He dug his talons into the thorax and abdomen and pushed outward, hoping to break the slender section that joined them. The queen wailed. The soldiers and captains nearest to them abandoned their opponents and scuttled toward Pat. Hundreds of tiny ants crawled up under his scales, stinging his tender flesh.

No time for subtlety. Pat summoned up a measure of power and filled his lungs. Hoping no one was going to get heroic and try to help him, he breathed out.

The flames crackled as they struck the oncoming ants. Some of the giants simply melted. The others flattened themselves on the floor and dragged human diners down to use as shields. Pat recoiled. He refused to endanger any of his guests.

The fierce itch of myriad small bites muddled his brain. The queen used her immense strength to topple him to the stage. He fell on his back. She tore at his unprotected stomach with her pincers. Pat was mortified. It *tickled*. He kicked all four legs in the air, hoping to connect with her head, and knowing he looked like a Labrador retriever getting a belly rub.

The human guests ran for the doors, but they were blocked by more of the queen's forces. The ants herded them back to the center of the ballroom.

Pat filled his lungs with fire. He bathed the queen's thorax with flame, hoping he could make her explode by boiling the liquid inside her armor. She trembled as the fire hit her. Pat struck again and again, satisfied at the crackle of the splintering carapace. The queen's body grew brighter and brighter, then faded. Pat redoubled his efforts, drawing all the power he could. It had no effect that he could see, except that the Ant Queen grew larger and larger until her head brushed the ceiling. She laughed down at him.

"Thanks for the power!" she cried. "It saves me drawing upon my army." She thrust out her arms, and all the chandeliers went out. In the feeble yellow illumination of the emergency lights she glowed. She reached for Regina, who was pinned against the wall by a couple of soldiers, and lifted her up toward her clashing jaws.

Pat leaped for the queen and wrapped himself around the arm. Regina dropped free.

"Thanks, boss," she said. "What can we do?"

"Power," Pat said. "Give her all the power she wants."

"Cooperation!" the Ant Queen crowed. "That's what I like to hear. Give me all of it!"

"What . . . ?" Regina asked. She followed Pat's eyes. "Why not? We're already going to lose our security deposit for this year."

Together the dragons focused their fire breath on the Ant Queen. She threw her head back to bathe in it, as if it was no more than a shower bath. As many of the committee who could help, did. The queen grew and grew, until her mandibles touched the row of carbon arc lights set up to illuminate the stage.

The queen tossed her head as the first carbon arc exploded. She tried to move away, but she was already too large to get off the stage. Her mandibles pierced the lenses of more of the heavy lights. She thrashed and turned, and got tangled up in the framework and the yards upon yards of cable attached to it. Pat flitted over the heads of the crowd toward the lighting control board and knocked all the levers up to full.

Power she wanted, and power she got. The Ant Queen burst into flames as the full force of the electrical grid of the hotel hit her. Pat heard her cries over the zapping of circuits. Pat flew back just in case he had to finish her off. There was no need. He used the last of his power to blow under his scales and chase all the small fire ants away. The terrible itching stopped. He felt almost as if he could collapse in relief. He cleared his throat.

Brenda looked up. "The scratching! It stopped!"

The other dragons, in a ring facing outward around the nesting boxes, listened closely.

"The ants are gone," John said.

The tension drained from the conclave chamber as though a plug had been pulled. Power the others had drawn into themselves to breathe fire to defend their young to the death returned to the great pool of energy within every dragon.

"Thank Fafnir," a Scandinavian visitor exclaimed, pulling a huge guitar from under his wing. "Well! Would anyone like to join in a falk sing, then?"

"Certainly," said the Asian dragon. "Does anyone know 'Genghis Khan Knew My Uncle?' "

"No," said the Welsh red, "but if you hum a few bars, we'll fake it."

With the queen dead and unable to think for them, the rest of the ants stopped what they were doing and began to mill around aimlessly. It took little time for security, both human and dragon, to round them up and get them out of the ballroom, then start to herd the guests back to their tables. Pat slipped behind the curtain and resumed his human shape. The pants and shirt of his formal attire were all right, but the jacket, with its center seam ripped out and sleeves burst from the cuff upward, was probably a write-off. He put it back on and walked out to cheers from the audience, who sat down more peacefully than he would have believed. Fans, he thought gratefully, were the most resilient people on the planet.

"I hope you all enjoyed that little entertainment," Pat said, straightening his torn jacket. "That was, uh, special effects from an upcoming movie produced by, uh, our guests, and starring . . . "

"Me!"

Shawna Lacey marched into the room, followed by the rest of the magicians. Bill and Everette, bringing up the rear, gave Pat a thumb's-up. The head of childcare came running up to the Fulbrights with their little girl, who didn't seem at all upset that Mommy and Daddy had been missing for more than a day. Anneli Madden looked as calm and cool as if she had spent the time in the library.

The actress sashayed onto the stage to loud acclaim. No one mentioned the fact that she had been wearing gold lame and was now clad in creased black silk pants and a scanty midriff top. She gave Pat a cool, smug smile.

"I believe you have something for me?"

Regina ran for the plaque. Pat took it from her and presented it as the crowd cheered. Shawna gave him an air kiss, during which she whispered, "I'd like to talk to you later about some serious compensation." She gave him a sweet smile that presaged a long talk, possibly involving lawyers.

Pat saw her off the stage and turned to the magicians, who looked tired but pleased, and the fans around Anne's table.

"I'd like to thank all our bit players for helping out with our presentation. I don't remember exactly where cats fit in on Pern," Pat said, as Koolness sat on the bodies of the ants, trying to figure out how he was going to explain his transformation to his fellow fans who hadn't known, especially Anne McCaffrey, but when he looked up at her the twinkle in her eyes suggested she had known all along. "But let's give him a big hand!"

"Mixing my worlds," Anne declared. "A Hrruban, helping to fight wild whers! He didn't beat up a dragon, because Hrrubans are very civilized, and so are dragons. Very well done!" She began clapping, encouraging everyone else to do the same. Koolness stood up and slurped Anne's hand. He noticed that she was writing under the table with her special pen. He met her eyes and she gave him a wink. "Everyone's just going to forget about the ant bites. Take a bow."

"As you wish, my lady," he said, and did.

A hearty voice from the audience burst out above the wild applause that filled the room.

"This is the *best* convention *ever!*"

Pat smiled. "Glad you think so," he said.

Crack!

Right on schedule, early Monday morning, the dragon eggs in the conclave center began to crack open. Annette was the first to welcome her youngsters. All six were males, and every one bleated with hunger the moment their mouths were free. She bent to feed them a meal of whole plucked chickens. The other nesting mothers stood aside with pride as their offspring burst their shells and were welcomed into the worldwide dragon community.

At the side of the room, well out of the way of flying shell fragments, Anne McCaffrey sat in a place of honor beside Pat and his committee, beaming her pleasure. She clapped as each egg hatched, and crowed over the different baby dragons. The dragon chicks mewled for more food, and regarded their parents with huge, adoring eyes. They took their first tottering steps, tripped on their own feet, and waved their little wings that were drying faster than a butterfly out of the cocoon.

"I got it right!" she said, with delight. "It's like an Impression without the riders. Thank you, dear Pat, for such a marvelous opportunity."

"It was the least we could do for you," Pat said. "You and your helpers. Without them this room wouldn't have remained safe."

The humans and others behind her looked abashed but pleased.

To Anne's everlasting delight, one of the hatchlings, an opalescent chick with a blunt nose and softly rounded scales on the ridge of its head, tottered over and put its nose in her hand. She petted it and murmured softly. The chick crooned.

"It knows its godmother," Pat said.

"This was the best conclave we've ever had, in spite of everything," Regina said.

Pat smiled, showing all of his teeth. "If you think this was good, wait until next year."

"Next year!" Regina exclaimed. "We haven't even started cleaning up from *this* one yet!"

Pat laughed. "We have to think ahead. How do we top this?"

All that day, the dragons departed for their distant homes. Some crept back into the dealers' room to be packed up among the depleted supply of baubles and books. A few changed themselves into human form and walked out of the hotel. The Florida-bound dragons flattened themselves once again and became one with Janny Wurts's art, but on a single canvas, as one of her big pieces had sold at auction.

"It is too crowded," the opalescent female complained. "We had more room in the conclave chamber in spite of all the commotion."

"Ah, yes," the blue dragon said, reminiscently. "Those hatchlings will never forget the grand battle fought almost on their very birthday!"

Don and Janny looked at each other.

"Sounds like it would make a terrific painting," said Don.

"Maybe a book," added Janny. "Tell us all about it."